THE COLOUR OF SHADOWS

PHYLLIDA SHRIMPTON

HOT KEY BOOKS

First published in Great Britain in 2019 by
HOT KEY BOOKS
80–81 Wimpole St, London W1G 9RE
www.hotkeybooks.com

A CIP catalogue record for this book is available from the British Library.

ISBN: 9781471407611
also available as an ebook

1

This book is typeset using Atomik ePublisher
Printed and bound in Great Britain by Clays Ltd, Elcograf S.p.A.

Hot Key Books is an imprint of Bonnier Books UK
www.bonnierbooks.co.uk

For Christina

Saffron

It was an eventful week. Some might describe it as a journey, but as far as I'm concerned it was way more than that. This was an odyssey! It was seven days of revelations, realisations and unexpected events that spun me round, shook me up and spewed me out at the end.

It was a week where each day was like the turn of a kaleidoscope. Same life, wildly different order.

This is how it went.

Monday:
Secrets and Lies

Saffron

He called it a white lie.

I called it a black lie.

In fact, I called it a mega enormous, ten-year-long kind of black lie.

I found it in the attic. His lie, that is. Hidden inside an old leather briefcase, waiting patiently for the years to somehow erase it from ever having existed.

I wasn't looking for it, and *he*, my dad, sure didn't want or expect me to find it, but find it I did . . . behind all the things in the attic, hugging its secret tightly with fat buckled straps, covered in dust – pretending to be forgotten.

I was looking for old photographs for an A-level project. The kind that have sepia ancestors staring across time with their pale, fixed eyes, as if a secret madness had been exposed by the flash of a Victorian camera.

I'd never been in the attic before. It had always been forbidden, something to do with slipping between the rafters and crashing through the ceiling to the room below. But at seventeen I figured I was capable of working my way across the rafters without ending up in casualty. And as Dad was at work, and *she*, Melanie, my father's second wife, was collecting their . . . *child* from school, I went on the hunt, safe in the knowledge that no one would know.

The dirty grey of ancient spider-webs hung threateningly close to my hair, while the yellow glow of a single overhead bulb, dangling by a wire, made everything look like it belonged in a parallel time, lacking the colour that belonged to real life. The air was still, heavy with the ingredients for a good jump-scare movie, and a kind of irrational disquiet threaded its way up my back as I peered through the murky space, trying to decide where to start looking.

Camping equipment and Christmas decorations waited silently next to old suitcases, and countless boxes of varying sizes were pushed into the gloomy shadows of the eaves. But right at the back of everything, crushed and old, was a briefcase.

So I looked inside.

And there . . . where I least expected to find them, in the yellow glow of that parallel time, stained with paint and crayon . . . were the contents of my own heart.

I rang him.

'I don't care that you're at work!' I screamed at my father, in a voice that didn't sound like it was mine. 'I'm in the attic . . .' I paused to let the impact of where I was hit him before dropping my tone to pure ominous aggression. '. . . Tell me about the briefcase!'

The inadequate words that eventually followed his guilty silence totally messed with my head and everything I thought I knew. The dim attic air closed in on me, squeezing me too tight, and although I made it back down the step-ladder,

I might as well have crashed through the rafters with the weight of what I'd just taken on board.

I ran from the house, gasping at the cold morning air until my lungs hurt and my throat burned, my sight muddled by an old memory that played on a loop behind my eyelids.

A memory so beautiful, it hurt.

Bright sunshine in a blue sky and cloudy cold breath.

Me – seven years old, kicking my way through crispy leaves, searching for conkers. Archie, in his pram, staring widely at autumn clouds, and Daniel lifting armfuls of reds and yellows into the air.

Our mother, crouching down, at eye level with me, holding a huge, prickly green casing in her hand. Her wide, red mouth smiling as I pull the casing edges apart, to discover the conker equivalent of Aladdin's cave. Shiny quadruplets in their spongy white bed.

Her red lips telling me there will always be treasures to find in the world if I look hard enough, while my younger self spins slowly round, my eyes scanning every tree and bush for the treasures she is talking about. Then she curls both our hands carefully around our prize, like its new, protective jacket before kissing my fingers with those red, red lips.

I stopped running when I reached the wall just inside the park at the end of our street, unable to link this beautiful memory with the awfulness of what I had just discovered in the attic. I leant against the wall until I could breathe without my lungs sucking air in so violently it burned. Stupidly, I looked for the lipstick traces of my mother's kiss on my fingers, as if it was an invisible tattoo the years had not yet deleted.

Learning to find life's treasures at the age of seven would have been great if I hadn't been slapped so often since by the big, cruel hand of surprise. I knew for sure now that the world was a damn sight crappier than the Disney ideal I had once believed it to be.

And like the vanishing Cheshire cat in *Alice in Wonderland*, my mother's smile was all that hung in the air from those fairy-tale years, ten years after she too had disappeared.

The fact that my mother had simply 'gone' when I was seven, caused a kind of sonic boom to hit my family. She had walked to the shop to get some milk, and had never come back. My father had paced the floor that day, a tone to his voice I couldn't understand and I didn't like how it made me feel . . . all jagged inside. My youngest brother, Archie, then just a baby, screamed from being ignored and my three-year-old brother, Daniel, pulled at my clothes for something to eat. I found myself catapulted over the cavernous gap between child and grown-up, the responsible older sibling in a family that had just gone terribly wrong.

Cold lumps of butter and cheese triangles were squashed with the flats of my dirty hands between slices of white bread, as I built some kind of meal for them. I'd lifted Archie into his high chair, and cut his food into pieces he could pick up with his chubby little fingers as I'd seen Mum do, and, as I wasn't allowed to use the kettle, I made Dad a soupy mixture of tea and milk, using hot water from the tap, tea which had stayed untouched, unappreciated.

Gran had arrived the next day in her new shiny white car,

skidding into the gravel on our drive. She'd emerged wearing her silver fox-fur hat and her most expensive expression, which she switched briefly for what I now know was a, 'what the hell are we going to do?' look for the benefit of my dad. Gran, however, would have phrased it differently, rolling words like *frightfully* and *ghastly* around the plums in her mouth. Then she smiled brightly at the three of us kids, reaching her leather-gloved hands towards us as she ushered us into the house.

The arrival of Gran with her overnight case brought a sensation of anxiety. I walked into rooms where the atmosphere was full of uncomfortable edges and angles, where secret conversations hushed and mouths spewed bullshit before twisting into fake smiles. Obviously, at the age of seven, I didn't realise it was bullshit then.

The worst thing about being a kid is when the adults try to keep stuff from you, so you go around only knowing half the story, trusting them that everything will be OK. And now, even at the age of seventeen, thanks to that briefcase, it would appear that I *still* only knew half the story, and everything wasn't OK.

Had my dad known . . . right from that very first day? Had he manipulated my world and that of my brothers' for some selfish reason? For some *Melanie*-shaped reason? Had he any idea how much I had wanted, *needed*, my mum over and over again, every birthday, Christmas, school play and particularly Mother's Days, which had always been so excruciating for me. Whenever I was down, Dad had insisted on pushing Melanie forward into a mother's role. I'd even been forced to give Melanie a Mother's Day card, because, in his words, 'she is a brilliant mother to you'.

The crowd of angry thoughts jostled inside my head, so much so that I could hardly bear the chaos of them. My hands shook with the intensity of trying to cut my nails into my own skin – to win the battle of physical over emotional pain.

The pain was crescent shaped.

Fingernails hardened by Black Grape Ultimate Shine nail polish dug deeply into the palms of my hands as I forced them further into my skin. I slid down to the ground, pressing my knees into my face, trying to squash myself into a smallness that would make me disappear entirely.

Stay in control, Saffy. Focus on the pain.

Something kicked my foot.

The stuff going on in my head left centre stage and moved impatiently to the wings, just as I glimpsed a pair of old brown leather boots with frayed laces. The boots kicked me again. Not hard, more like a gentle nudge. Enough to tell me that I should be looking up at the rest of the person they belonged to.

'Go away,' I mumbled through my knees but the boots turned the same way as mine, as the rest of the person slid down the wall next to me. 'You're not invited,' I said, noticing the smears of mascara and tears left behind on my vintage fades.

'Sleeve?' The bottle-green cuff of a shapeless knitted jumper thrust its way towards the mottled blotch of my face. I knew that voice, of course.

'Tom?' His name came out through strands of my ginger hair, which were now stuck to my damp cheeks and across my lips.

'Looking good,' he said, and I cautiously checked for

the dimples that pull at his cheeks when he thinks he's being funny. They were there. I allowed myself the tiniest of smiles back.

Tom

I recognised the hair.

You couldn't really miss that colour, or the amount of it, like a box of crazy springs leaping in all directions.

She was running towards the park, and she was looking pretty mad. As usual.

Being the good friend that I am, I ducked behind a tree before she could spot me. I saw her lean against a wall, then slide to the ground like a sack of the proverbial. There was always stuff going on with Saffron and this time was obviously no exception. The fact that she was now sitting in a puddle meant that today's 'stuff' was substantial enough for her not to notice that she was wetting the arse of her designer jeans.

She was probably crying as well, judging by how tightly she was hunched over. I wanted to leave her to it. I wanted to stroll on by as if I hadn't seen her because Saffron Hayes no longer needed me in her life any more than I needed her in mine.

To get involved would be stupid. I knew for sure it wasn't a good idea. I wasn't going to do it.

The next thing I knew, I was sitting next to her on the ground getting the arse of my not-designers damp too.

Saffron

I plucked at the hair stuck to my damp face in a vague attempt to look less deranged. Then I twisted it round and pulled it over one shoulder. *Looking good?* A sarcastic laugh came out of my mouth and embarrassingly caused a bubble of saliva to pop from my lips.

Even the presence of Tom couldn't calm me like it used to, so we sat, side by side in a puddle, saying nothing, my face failing to return to its normal complexion – basically, white, with a million speckled pigmentation flaws that nature adds as an extra insult to gingers. When Tom eventually stood up I expected him to leave because he never stayed long any more. He just kind of came and went these days, like a spring tide, and as I probably looked a horrifying mixture of dribble and snot and mad hair and make-up, I couldn't blame him for wanting to make a fast exit.

This time however, his fingers reached down for mine, pulling me easily to my feet. 'Hot chocolate? You can tell me all about . . . whatever it is, when our butts aren't numb and damp. I don't know about you but I don't fancy spending any more time sitting where every dog in the neighbourhood comes to take a piss.' His eyes scanned the area around us.

He let go of my hand and I brushed the seat of my jeans down trying not to think about the dog piss thing. 'We used to call this place dog-shit park, remember?' he said, a lazy grin spreading across his face. 'And do you remember the time I rescued you from this exact spot?'

'How could I forget?' I muttered, noticing how his eyes followed my fumbling fingers as I repeatedly tried to tuck a springy curl of hair behind my ear.

I had been just eight when Tom, a whole two years older, had appeared as he frequently did out of nowhere and found me. I'd been in the park, bunking off after-school care, trying to pretend I was like the other kids – the ones whose mums picked them up from school – when I snatched a packet of sweets off another girl.

'That kid called me the "nasty girl with the ginger hair"... just before she set her Rottweiler on me.' A pathetic laugh forced its way out – thankfully no bubble of saliva this time.

'Her Rottweiler?' Tom spluttered. 'You mean her mother? Nicking stuff from small children isn't the way to win friends and influence people, you know.'

'I hated what they had,' I muttered, still hating what they had. 'That girl had a *real* mum who sat on the bench handing out nice things for her to eat every day after school.' I knew I sounded petulant, like a spoilt child, when I said it out loud, but right now there was too much bedlam inside my head to care.

'But then you just stood rooted to the spot ... when the *Rottweiler* came at you!' Tom laughed, encouraging another small smile from me. It *was* funny when you thought about it.

Especially as the girl's mother had marched towards me, high ponytail swinging, muscles bulging and teeth clenched, until Tom had appeared out of nowhere, grabbed my school bag and my hand, his blond curls and my red ones bouncing around our heads as we ran out of the park. Not exactly a white knight in shining armour but a streetwise kid with chocolate-button eyes and a dirty school uniform.

That was the day Saffron Hayes was reborn. Less of a butterfly though, more of . . . a bluebottle fly. I became the kid who, from that point, couldn't give a red-haired shit about anything. *Apart from Tom*. Being the girl who supposedly didn't care about anything was hard work but Tom always managed to find his way into my fortress. Being best friends with him had been crazy fun, like jumping into a kids' book and living a different life.

We hadn't gone to the same school, but we used to meet all the time whenever I went out, unplanned . . . like he was Peter Pan, appearing out of nowhere and belonging to no one. He wasn't like the other boys from my school, all name calling and shoving. Tom was different. Funny, easy going and totally wild, which made it even more exciting to know him.

Whenever we met in the park we'd sit perched at the top of the climbing frame and make it a castle, a ship or a mountain, or we'd look for squirrels and woodpeckers with make-believe binoculars, or climb trees and drop acorns at passing strangers, swing on the rope tyre hanging from the old oak, or wade in the river looking for fish. On rainy days he would come to mine and we'd invent things to do round the house. Like the piranha game where to touch the ground would mean dying

15

the death of a thousand teeth. Or we would play hide and seek, or build a den, or we'd make a ski slope on the stairs using sheets of cardboard. Tom's imagination was endless and when he took me into his world with him, nothing else mattered.

Now as we head out through the park's huge iron gates I look back over my shoulder as if I might see us, as children, running hell for leather away from the girl and her angry mother. 'When we ate her sweets, you told me they tasted better because they were free . . . Do you remember?' I said, looking sideways at him. '. . . Then I told you my mum was dead?'

I'd just come out with it that day. No fanfare. Punching the air with my words. Tom hadn't flinched. He simply squeezed my hand and breathed one word . . . '*Shit!*' No pretence, no feel-good words, just a squeeze and a single profanity, and I had loved him for it. Then we had stood in silence by the river taking turns at throwing stones at an empty floating Coke can.

Disappointingly I could now probably count on my Black Grape teenage fingers and toes how many hours in total we'd spent together since puberty stole the last shreds of our childhood. We never 'hung out' any longer, just occasionally bumped into each other, and our encounters never lasted long these days, because Tom, for reasons he never gave, always had to leave.

This time, instead of dragging me along the path away from the park, yelling and laughing, we walked casually towards town in search of a cafe. The sun offered a generous warmth despite it being October, turning me pink and hot, and as I wiped my hands on my jeans again, this time to remove the sweat that glistened in the creases of my hands, I was in no doubt as to why Tom had let go so quickly when he pulled me to my feet. No one likes a sweaty palm.

I studied him from the corner of my eye, my heart now a tiny bird fluttering in the cage of my chest. Tom was noticeably older, taller and broader now, although the blond curls that once leapt about on top of his head were now pulled round the back into a man-bun tied by a blue scrunchie. Gone was the dirty school uniform and instead were beige cargo shorts, ancient brown leather boots with their frayed laces and a collarless shirt under the shapeless bottle-green knitted jumper. He was a bit – well, actually *a lot* – Bohemian, and it suited him, made him more . . . *edgy*.

'You've grown again,' I said, noticing how his dark eyes now looked down at me from his impressive height.

'You haven't,' he said, grinning.

'Harsh. I'm five foot two . . . *almost* two!' I said.

'That's almost like a real person,' he said, our eyes catching, forcing me to look away. Unfortunately for me, with Tom, my insides kept flipping and I had to make them be still because that would be *liking* him and I didn't want to *like* him . . . not in that way . . . not when he wasn't interested in me. We had been best friends once and now we were just casual friends, and that was all, and part of me was glad now, because it was hard to ignore that Tom had grown into someone who was fit and I had . . . well, I had . . . *not*.

'You have a habit of appearing when I'm not exactly at my best,' I said, as if I looked much different when I was at my best.

He put a finger to his chin as if casting his memory across his

17

mental diary. 'Last time I saw you was outside your college . . .'
His dimples appeared again.

'Mmm . . . Art,' I confirmed, deflating just a little bit more.

'Art,' he echoed. 'Covered in paint.'

On that particular occasion, I'd lost hold of the water pot and pallet I was carrying to the sink and I stupidly attempted to clutch them towards me instead of letting them drop on the floor, resulting in a modern-art explosion all down my front. I was surprised Tom didn't run for the hills every time he saw me. 'Shouldn't you be at school now?' he asked.

I answered with a frown. 'Yes! But *something* has come up.'

Tom

So, despite giving myself a stiff talking to about leaving Saffron well alone and making a quick exit, my hand involuntarily hauled her off the pavement while my mouth offered her a hot chocolate and a free therapy session. And now, here we are, walking to the cafe on a parallel path with memory lane while waiting for the big reveal of whatever has come crashing into her life this time.

'So, what's the "something" that's come up?'

'I'll tell you over the hot chocolate,' she answered, the frown on her forehead squeezing several large freckles together.

'The suspense is killing me,' I said, before trying a different tack. 'How's your dad? Does he still think I wait on street corners to contaminate you with my urchin-ness?' Saffron said nothing. She used to leap to his defence when I spoke like that. 'He doesn't think you're low life, Tom,' she'd say, or, 'Of course he knows you've got a home to go to,' or, 'He's forgiven you for teaching me how to swear. It's all in your own mind, stop belittling yourself all the time.' But I was never convinced. When I used to walk up the gated drive to their house, past the long black saloon car to press the bell, which chimed inside their massive house, which always smelled of polish, made me feel kind of shabby. 'You can tell him I've progressed. I no longer live out of bins and drink puddle water,' I said, waiting for a reaction, *any* reaction, but then I glanced over at her and realised I had absolutely just picked the wrong kind of small talk.

The hands balled into fists and the chin jutted out; her voice had an edge to it. Even more freckles disappeared into the furrows on her brow. 'My . . . father . . . is . . .' She'd pursed her lips as if sorting through a pile of foul-tasting words in her mouth, unable to find the right level of bad. 'My *father* . . . is a lying ARSEHOLE.'

I'd obviously walked right into the middle of another Saffron-shaped minefield and there was no treading carefully and no going back. 'Care to elaborate why?' I asked.

I didn't know a lot about Saffron's dad, other than that he was posh and when his new wife Melanie came on the scene, and Charlotte was born, they would all go to the park en masse, looking like the perfect family in a perfect world. Saffron's dad treated her like the most precious china doll, like all his children were precious china dolls. And then there was me. A scruff from the council flats, who stuck to Saffron like crap to a blanket.

'Your dad's a bit over protective, but hardly an arsehole,' I said. 'He has always given you everything you ever wanted.'

Saffron's voice went up a few levels. 'Apart from the one thing I actually wanted!'

'Which is?' I asked. Saffron didn't answer. 'Maybe he thinks he knows what is good for you and what isn't,' I said, fishing for the right thing to say.

She looked up at me, a gathering of tears on the rims of her eyes. 'Maybe he has been trying to control my life. He even said you were like a wild animal, always on the street like you didn't have a home to go to. Do you remember?'

'Yeah. But that was hardly a crime – I wanted to be like a wild animal.' I remembered exactly when she told me this. We were playing at the top of the climbing frame, being pirates on our ship the *Black Adventurer*, heading into battle with the *Golden Fortune*, a big galleon laden with jewels – otherwise known as the slide. I'd been clinging to a pole, yelling at the top of my voice that I was going to shoot the captain dead if they didn't surrender. Saffron had spun upside down on the bar below me, her mad curly hair hanging in plaits towards the ground, her hands pretending to hold a telescope. I jumped down a level until I was hanging next to her, my legs, like hers, hooked over the bars, where we swung backwards and forwards.

'We're like two bats . . . or two monkeys,' I said, putting my hands in my armpits and screeching.

'My dad says you're like a wild animal,' she said as we viewed the upside-down world and her upside-down father.

I stopped swinging and looked at her, our cheeks red and fat from gravity. 'If I was a wild animal, I wouldn't be a monkey and I wouldn't stay in this crummy town.'

'What would you be?' she asked, stopping swinging too.

I climbed back up to the top level of the climbing frame and stood precariously balanced, no hands, on the very top

21

bar. 'If I were a wild animal, I'd be a bird and I'd fly away,' I'd said, my arms outstretched, my face tilted to the sky, my hopes stretching way out beyond the horizon.

'What bird would you be?' she asked.

I didn't have to think too hard. I moved my arms in the slow, lazy beat of my favourite bird. 'I'd be a heron so I could leave the town far behind and fly across the country, over fields and along rivers.'

'Would you take me with you . . . if you ever flew away?' She was still hanging, looking up at me and holding the curly ends of her two long, fat plaits in her hands, waving them like wings. I wished with all the might my heart possessed that I really could fly away – away from dog-shit park, up and over all the houses and the blocks of flats, to a place where I felt like I could breathe. But my wings were just arms, and her wings were just copper curls, tamed and contorted into submission, her cream satin hair-ribbons reminding me that Saffron Hayes belonged to a different world from mine. I wanted to tell her that she didn't need to fly away but if she could, then yes, I would take her with me.

Instead, I'd looked down at her and said, 'I can see right up your nose from here.'

The memory of Saffy's upside-down face evaporated as she turned to me now, older and angry, her hair tumbling untethered down her back, her legs moving fast to keep up with my stride. 'He's the worst father ever!' she scowled.

'He's not, Saffron. He's like a father who gives a shit, that's all.'

'You are so wrong about him, Tom. The most wrong anyone

has ever been. You know nothing . . . yet! Come on. If we don't find a cafe soon, I'm going to have to vomit this crap all over the street and then I don't get that hot chocolate you promised.'

Saffron

Why could nothing in my life go smoothly? Not even walking next to Tom. I'd been mid-sentence, telling him we needed to find a cafe soon, when he suddenly yanked at my arm, pulling me away from a lamp-post that I was only inches away from walking into, and then he laughed so hard he had to bend double.

'Come on, Saffron, where's your sense of humour? You would have laughed about that once upon a time,' he complained as I stood waiting for him to finish. 'I'm sorry, but you're still so slapstick it's hilarious.'

'My mind was elsewhere, all right?' I snapped. 'In fact, it was down there.' Down a narrow alleyway next to the offending lamp-post was another memory – a seven-year-old me, weighed down by a heavy zebra rucksack containing all the things a detective might need to find a missing mother: a bag of crisps, some lemonade, a tiger face-mask, a photograph of my mother, some money from the change pot in the hall, and some chocolate.

'I stopped looking,' I said softly.

Tom straightened up, trying to compose his face into normal.

'You certainly did. I didn't know whether to save you from getting a black eye or get my phone out and put it on YouTube.'

'I don't mean I stopped looking where I was going! I mean I stopped looking for my mum. That's where I first went hunting for her all those years ago! That's where my dad found me and that's when he told me my mum had died,' I said, pointing at the narrow alley and the market area at the end of it.

'I know, I remember! That's where I first met you . . . wild red hair, the photo, the zebra rucksack, the all-essential tiger mask,' Tom said, walking back to where I was standing and following my gaze as if he could see the memory of it too.

'I was *seven*, Tom!' I shot him a look, challenging him not to joke again, challenging myself not to cry again. *Mum in the doorway with her purse and her winter coat telling us she was going to the shop. Bright red lipstick. Bright red smile. Gone.*

'I went looking for her because I thought she'd got lost and no one could find her.'

'And instead you found me . . . and Maggie,' Tom said.

Crazy Maggie was one of the town's many homeless, but probably the most noticeable of them all. You could often hear her yelling at people before you saw her and if you couldn't hear her first, you could definitely smell her – a pungent aroma created an invisible aura around her. If you could see smells, Maggie's would be . . . *sludgy green*. Kind of staining the air wherever she goes.

'She's still the same,' I said.

'Only smellier . . . *drunker*,' Tom said.

'I thought she was just a pile of material on the pavement. A mound of rags on top of flattened cardboard, like stuff left over from the market or something for the skip . . . until I saw her feet sticking out. Her old black shoes and all those socks! I lifted the blankets, and there she was, wearing that dress with huge orange flowers and that old woolly hat with hundreds of badges.'

'She's still on her summer hat at the moment. The enormous straw one with plastic strawberries hanging off the brim . . . elastic round her chin to hold it on. Do you think the elastic catches in her beard?'

I shuddered. 'Ew, don't, Tom . . . it makes me want to gag!'

The stink that had exuded from Maggie's blankets when I first lifted them up to see what or who was underneath, had caught in my throat. I'd never smelt or seen anything like it. Her face was a mass of dirty folds of skin with three moles like the points of a triangle on one of her cheeks, her lips were fat and cracked at the corners and her eyes were shut, lost somewhere behind the purple and crusty folds. And, of course, there was the beard.

The seven-year-old detective that I was that day had resolutely pulled my mother's beautiful photograph from the zebra rucksack and held it in front of this strange person. I'd prodded her slumbering body to ask if she'd seen my mum, until eventually one eye opened and rolled slowly round until it was looking at me. It surprised me so much that I fell backwards. She lifted her head up so her other eye could join the first in its mission to focus on what had woken her up. The whites of her eyes were yellow and covered in red veins, but despite everything, the irises were an unexpected blue, like bravely thriving forget-me-nots in a war-torn bomb site.

'I need a drink,' she'd mumbled, her voice deep and throaty like my grandpa's had been after a lifetime of smoking. I picked myself up and rummaged in my zebra bag to pull out my can of lemonade, which I handed to her. She wheezed out a dry laugh. 'I mean a *real* drink, lovey.'

'She wants booze,' a voice called over. A kid with dark brown eyes ran over to me and snatched my can of lemonade. Tom, as he introduced himself to me, pulled the ring of my can and sipped noisily, letting out a strangled burp before handing the can back. I wiped at the can top with the sleeve of my jumper and took a sip myself.

'What's booze?' I asked him, watching the mess of curls around his face jiggle as he threw back his head and laughed at me.

'What's booze?' he asked, mimicking the way I spoke. 'It's alcohol, shit for brains!' I didn't think I liked being called 'shit for brains' but Tom was smiling at me and cheerful dimples had appeared on each cheek. 'Here, Maggie.' Tom picked up a bottle that was leaning against her trolley and handed it to her. 'There's a bit left in this one.'

Maggie grinned, exposing a row of stained and broken tombstone teeth, then drank straight from the bottle as if she was so thirsty she was going to die without it. Some ran down her chin, which she wiped with the back of her hand before rocking backwards and forwards, holding the bottle like a doll.

'Is she all right?' I asked Tom while still staring at this strange person.

'She's homeless. She lives like this – don't you, Maggie?' he replied while she rocked her bottle doll and nodded in answer. The concept of someone not having a home, or a television, or a bed, shocked me.

'No house? What does she eat?' I asked him as if I was peering at an animal in the zoo.

'She begs . . . or nicks,' Tom answered.

'She can hear and she can be spoken to directly,' Maggie piped up, her voice all phlegmy.

'So have you seen my mum, then?' I asked again, thrusting the photograph nearer this homeless person called Maggie, watching as she squinted at what I was showing her.

'She's got your hair,' Maggie said, focussing with difficulty on the photo where my mother stood ankle-deep in the sea, clutching at the hem of a patterned maxi dress, smiling at the camera, her long, wild, waist-length hair blowing in the breeze.

'Oh, she has! Her hair is mental too,' Tom cried, snatching the photo to get a closer look. They both laughed, and another crackle of phlegm sounded in Maggie's throat.

I felt the pink, which always came when people laughed at my hair, warm my cheeks, while the winter sun shone through Tom's curls, lighting him up like a renaissance cherub. So unfair that other people have beautiful hair.

'Oh blimey . . . gotta go,' Tom suddenly said, shoving the photo back at me, turning on his heels and starting to run. Then he looked back briefly before shouting, 'See you around, Annie.'

'It's SAFFRON!' I called back as he disappeared around a corner.

Then I realised why he'd left in such a hurry. I should have felt bad that my father was so upset at finding me a mile from the house in a rough part of town, but at the time I just felt . . .

28

rudely interrupted in my mission, being suddenly lifted off my feet into his arms as he shouted my name, pulling my head roughly towards him, while crying into my hair and thanking God.

'But I'm looking for Mummy,' I insisted as Maggie looked up at us both and held out her hand.

'Spare any money?' she asked. I slipped from his hold when we got to the car, and reaching into my rucksack I ran back to give her my chocolate, my crisps and my money. The forget-me-not eyes followed us as once more Dad dragged me back to the car and drove away. 'Don't you ever do that again, EVER,' he shouted at me. 'The streets aren't safe for little children . . . Don't go near people like her, do you hear?'

I shrugged and turned away from the alley, but the memory of that day followed me, unwilling to let me go. I knew, once inside the cafe, that I was going to have to tell Tom why absolutely everything that had happened since then, had been a lie.

A lie in a briefcase.

Tom opened the door and let me through first, the busy cafe sounds causing him to speak louder. 'Find a table. I'll get the drinks.'

I found a table. Squashed near a large window, clouded with condensation, giving a misty view of the busy street we'd just left. Tom stood at the counter ordering our drinks, no longer the skinny streetwise kid who called me 'shit for brains', but a nineteen-year-old boy who called me Saffron in a way that came out of his mouth like a beautiful sigh, whispering a delicious secret. Everyone else called me Saffy, or Saff, but the way he said my name was the only time I ever liked it. I studied him from the safety of the table, envious that he was still so easy with himself, always so carefree.

My *lucky* spring-tide friend.

I watched him walk back through the clouds of savoury and sweet aromas, the tip of his tongue sticking out, two huge mugs crowned with hats of white whipped cream balancing on the tray he was carrying. My nails dug into the palms of my hands again, and like that long-ago day in the park, I just blurted it out, as he placed the tray carefully on the table, before his backside even touched his chair . . .

'My mum *isn't* dead,' I said.

Tom

Saffron sat opposite me in the warm, coffee-scented air of the cafe and hit me with her 'my mum isn't dead' line.

The thick rope she had twisted her hair into was springing a leak. Red strands were escaping and heading in various directions about her head while she stared hard at me as if I was supposed to find a miraculously suitable reply to a line like that.

How does a mum being first dead then alive even happen? This latest Saffron crisis was major, so much bigger than one mug of hot chocolate.

From the first time I met Saffron all those years ago, it was like meeting the real-life little orphan Annie just after she'd put her finger in a live plug socket. And every time I bumped into her after that, it was like I'd stepped into a scene from a badly written drama series in which I ended up playing some kind of hero role.

But that, I would come to realise, was Saffron.

A wild, red, chaotic, shit magnet.

Saffron

The cafe, unimpressed by my life-changing announcement, continued to buzz with all things foody. The coffee machine burped its contents into a glass jug, the oven beeped its timer, and china chinked against china. A woman negotiated her way past us with a drink. A couple sat silently facing each other, both sets of eyes looking down at their phones, fingers tapping at the screens. A small child pushed a chocolate brownie into his face, smearing it across his nose and cheeks.

The world had not stopped.

Tom's dark eyebrows remained horizontal and totally unsurprised, his brown eyes calm. He pulled out a handful of change from his jeans pocket and counted it. 'Eight pounds, thirty-six pence,' he announced, then placed it on the table between us as he sat back down.

Not a flicker more.

'Didn't you hear what I said?' I asked, leaning forward.

But then, in his Tom kind of way, he stretched both his hands out towards me, pushing his thumbs past my fingers into the sweaty curl of my palms and glancing at the money on the table, simply said, 'I guess this one is going to take longer than a couple of hot chocolates.'

In my devastated world, right then, Tom's thumbs felt like they were all that I had to hold on to – and as he pulled away, I imagined, gripping tighter, an embarrassing tug of war where I wouldn't let him go.

I knew that Tom would not be staying for long. As always, he would catch me, carry me along with him for a glorious moment, then leave me with nothing but the hope he might return. Yet despite the fact that I knew this, and despite my current totally-bent-out-of-shape situation, and the very real fact that I looked like blotchy, sweaty, crap, I was so glad he was here with me. For now.

'So . . . your mum *was* dead and now she's *not*. Right?' Tom looked steadily at me.

I nodded. 'I know that sounds totally ridiculous. Like thinking my mum has been dead all this time was just a silly mistake.'

'Well it's not your *average* family fuck-up,' he answered.

I felt the sting of tears again and knew I was quite possibly going to fall apart in a public place, right here, right now. Tom took a sip of his drink but as he lowered his mug there was a thick line of cream that hung off his top lip, like an old man's moustache. I drew a surreptitious line across my own top lip with my index finger, indicating that he might want to do something about his face. He looked steadily at me and took another sip, this time dipping his nose into the cream as well.

Confused, I frowned at him, unable to believe he could act the clown when every part of me was hurting.

'What?' he asked, straight-faced.

That *thing* Tom had, was going on – soft eyes, lovely face, full dairy goatee. Another unwilling smile eventually pulled at my mouth.

'I know what you're doing,' I said, licking at a salty tear on my lips. 'You have no idea how . . . how majorly *distraught* I am.'

'It worked, didn't it?' Tom wiped his smile into a paper napkin and repeated his question. 'So, your mum was dead and now she's alive?'

'Exactly! That first day . . . when my dad had to come looking for me?' Tom nodded slowly. 'Well, he told me later that Mum had been found by the police. That she wasn't well . . . she was in hospital, and was *apparently* so ill she couldn't be visited.'

'O-K. But why "apparently"?' Tom frowned.

'Because it was a lie!' I replied, my voice getting higher, my teeth grinding together. Taking the long spoon, I stirred my drink angrily through the pile of cream on my mug, watching it disappear until I was confident I could take little sips without the same facial fiasco Tom had used.

'He lied about it all for *ten whole years!*'

Tom sighed. 'Can you start from the beginning because whatever it is, I'm getting ever so confused.'

So eyeing the eight pounds and thirty-six pence worth of time still left on the table, I told him about the moment my father chose to deceive me.

'He told me a bedtime story that same night he found me on the street with you and Maggie.' I mimicked my father's sympathetic voice: 'Mum has been found, but she isn't well. She's in hospital and we're doing everything we can to get her home soon but we and your brothers can't visit her there because she's too sick.' I could still remember how the walls of my room had closed around me as he sat on my bed and told me the evasive words I tried to hold on to and make sense of. Instead of looking directly at him, I'd concentrated on his shadow, which had draped across my bed and along my floor as his voice spoke of 'rest' and 'treatment' and 'time'. Then I watched how it slipped darkly out of the room behind him when he finally closed my bedroom door. Alone, I'd studied my own 'other me', cast against the wall from the glow of my bedside light. I wondered if this was where all the bad things that happened to us went. Caught in a puddle of dark around us, never, ever, leaving us alone.

'He told us to make get-well cards, Archie and Daniel and me . . . Can you *believe* that? Christmas cards, birthday cards, letters, pictures . . . endless flowers, coloured handprints, hearts . . . smiley faces . . .'

'Cake?'

Tom scraped his chair back, and scooped his money off the surface of the table into his hands. I looked up at him, then back to where his eyes were pointing and there, in my hands, was the long spoon, now severely bent in the middle. 'You tried to murder the spoon, Saffron – somewhere between Christmas cards and smiley faces. We don't have enough money to pay for the cutlery, so I thought we should get cake instead. Yes?'

I looked up at him, my voice barely a whisper. 'He even helped us write the envelopes and stick down the stamps.'

'Cinnamon swirl, then,' Tom answered and made his way back to the counter.

My phone screen lit up, pulling me out of my stupor. Several missed calls and texts from my father were lined up in banners across the screen.

Dad: Come home, Saffy, I need to explain x

'Yes, you do, Father. Like you should have done years ago,' I snapped.

Dad: Saffy please answer the phone. We need to talk x

'We sure do,' I snapped again.

Melanie: Please contact your dad x

'And you can butt out,' I said, swiping quickly to delete her from my screen. 'They can both send a million messages for all I care,' I said out loud, '. . . on their way to the graduation ceremony for gifted and talented liars!' The child with the chocolate-cake face looked at me and I stuck my tongue out at him, making him cry.

'Mature,' uttered Tom, as he placed a pot of tea, a jug of boiling water, a donut and a cinnamon swirl on the table. 'I got us some tea. It lasts longer.'

I launched straight back in. '. . . And then . . . I was fed bullshit for *an entire year.*'

'O-K . . .' He stretched out the word again, as if waiting to hear exactly how bullshitty the following year had been. 'I'll be Mother.' He put the tea cups side by side and dribbled milk into each. Lifting the pot, he poured out steaming amber liquid before plopping in two cubes of sugar and stirring. Then he suddenly smiled. 'Sorry . . . I've just realised what I said, about being Mother.' He pushed my cup towards me, still smiling, but hurriedly supressed it when he caught sight of my face.

The thing about me and Tom is that we always found everything funny. The more inappropriate, the funnier it was. But not today. Nothing was funny today. 'You wouldn't find it quite so funny if you didn't know where *your* mother was,' I said.

Tom's face changed into an unreadable expression. 'You're right. I know where my mother is. I'll behave. Promise.'

'Anyway,' I continued. 'My father spent a whole year updating us . . . about her poor health! What the doctors were doing to try to help her but how she loved receiving our cards.' The tone of my voice reached a rapid angry crescendo, forcing me to take a burning sip of very sweet tea to prevent the scream of frustration that was dying to get out. 'She was never ill, Tom . . . not even a tiny bit!'

'So why did he say she was?' Tom asked, appearing interested at last.

'Because he's a coward! And I know why he told me she'd died. You remember? The day of the Rottweiler, that was the day after he'd told me she'd lost her battle with her health. Now I know he only told me that because he *had* to.' I put my hands over my stomach, as if nursing the foetus of hate itself.

'Why did he *have* to?' Tom asked.

'I'd had a nightmare. It happened a lot in the beginning. I would climb into bed with Dad . . . so I could lie down in the space where my mum used to be. It helped, you know? To begin with I could still find the scent of her on the pillow . . .'

I breathed in deeply, eyes shut, my nose searching vainly for the forgotten scent of her. '. . . Until one night there was no trace of her left. Simply washed away with apples and blossom . . .'

Tom gently tapped the side of his cup with his spoon, to snap me out of my trance. 'Come back to me, Saffron!' he called. I came back to him, shuffling in my seat at the awful memory.

'So, the night before the Rottweiler day, I'd had this really bad nightmare.' The memory of that awful night was so clear. I'd woken in the night, and I'd run, barefoot and frightened, to the space beside my dad. And there, beneath the covers, Mum was there! Beside him . . . like she always used to be.

She had come back to us.

I touched her warm skin, like she'd never left, and all the seconds and hours and days of missing my mother simply rushed away and became *right* again. And then . . . just at the moment where my world had so wonderfully turned the right way up, the covers were snatched away in a frenzy of wheeling limbs. Lit up by a badly timed full moon through the window, huge and unexpected, were a pair of breasts. Naked and protruding. Pale hair tumbling across them.

Different hair. Different skin. Different scent.

Dad leading me back to bed.

'I had climbed in my father's bed next to . . . *her*. She was in my mum's place!' I said to Tom, the moment of horror still leaving a taste of bitter awfulness on my tongue. 'And she wasn't wearing anything . . . what-so-ever!' I shivered like a wet dog.

'Awkward . . .' Tom whistled.

'And that's how I found out my mother was . . . "dead"!' I said, giving the word unnecessary air quotes. 'Dad dished out another lovely "chat" just like he did the night after she disappeared. Sitting on my bed, telling me she had died and how he didn't know how to break it to us.' I remembered being unable to look him in the eyes, instead watching his dark shadow again, his voice telling me about the woman in his bed . . . trying to explain why her naked body had stolen my mother's space. 'I had to listen to it all – how my mother had gone to heaven, how he hadn't known how to tell us all, how he was going to introduce Melanie when the time was right and blah blah blah . . . How Goddam shite was that? My father is a coward who can't tell the truth!'

'So you think they . . . ?' Tom began.

'When our bedtime stories were over, he'd spent his nights shagging another woman? Yes! That's exactly what I think!'

The mother of the boy with the chocolate-cake face craned her head round and frowned at me. I gave her my frowniest frown back. I'd never told anyone about that night. Instead I had mourned as only a child can. In images and with feelings instead of words.

Sadness.

Her smiling mouth.

Her wild, curly hair.

39

Her vivid green eyes.

Loss.

Fear.

Anger.

And that naked *person* in the space where my mother should be? That was the hate, now firmly nestled inside me.

'Well, I suppose that's one way to let you know he'd met someone else. But all I can say is, thank God you didn't catch them in the act of . . . you know . . . actually *bumping uglies,*' Tom replied.

'Don't become a therapist,' I told him, pushing away the absolutely repulsive vision he'd just created.

'Sorry.' He tried to look suitably admonished. 'But I guess that's how you met –?'

'Smell-an-ie,' I interrupted, using the childish name I'd christened the replacement for the mother-shaped hole in our lives.

'Yeah, Melanie,' he said, and the sound of her name fell too prettily from his lips.

'Mummy's gone so I've got you a new one. Yayyy!' I said, mimicking the voice of my father. 'Hurrah for me! And from that point onwards *she* slipped into our lives like snot off a spoon and no one seemed to mind that she was a poor imitation of a mother. A patronising waste of space who was simply after a meal ticket from my dad and a chance to live in our big house.'

'So where was your mum all that time?'

Tom lifted the lid of the teapot, poured in some hot water from the matching jug and stirred the leaves around. Randomly,

I liked the fact that in this cafe, the china was the old fashioned kind, with little gold embellishments or painted flowers. I loved how cutely out of place he looked holding such delicate china in his big hands.

'God knows!' I picked up my phone and swiped away the next batch of texts and calls from Dad.

'He seems pretty keen to get hold of you,' Tom said, nodding towards my phone.

'He can wait!' I answered, shoving the phone face-down on the table as it buzzed with another call.

'So, now I know how you found out that your mum was dead, but how did you find out that she wasn't?' he asked.

Again, it was hard to ignore how ridiculous that sounded. 'This morning – the cards.'

'What cards?' he asked.

'In the *briefcase* – I found all the get-well cards we made for Mum when she was in hospital . . . or not in hospital, as it happens. I was looking in the attic for some photographs and I came across it. *He* never sent any of our cards to her . . . because *she* was never sick. When I confronted him, he had to admit it. Basically, my father has been covering for the fact that he pushed my mother out so that he could replace her with something younger.'

'Did he actually say that?' Tom asked, his eyes widening.

'Well no, he didn't say it in so many words but that's what he did. He lied about her being sick and then he lied about her being dead. But he gets a new younger wife out of the deal.' I sat back in my chair, arms folded, and waited for his reaction. For once Tom didn't seem to have anything to add

41

to the conversation, funny or otherwise. The donut on his plate had a huge bite taken from it, spilling its raspberry guts. He licked at lips that were covered in sugar, before sipping his tea and staring at me, a slight frown hovering over his warm eyes.

'What did he say when you confronted him?' Tom asked.

'*I'm sorry!* That's all he said. I'm sorry.' I felt my lips quiver all on their own again at the total, one hundred percent, inadequacy of my father's reaction.

'Profound,' Tom said, placing his cup carefully down on its saucer before picking up the remainder of his donut. 'Did you ask him what happened?' The donut disappeared into his mouth, leaking jam onto his bottom lip.

'Of course I did. He admitted he'd lied and said he would come home from work as soon as he could get free, and explain everything.'

'Then why don't you go home and let him explain everything?' Tom asked, pressing his finger into the sugar on his plate and licking it.

'Because I'm here. Telling you about it,' I said. 'This is monumental, Tom. Huge! I have been denied my *mother* for most of my life, and you're acting as if it's no big deal to go home and have a little chat about it.'

'I'm not . . . and you need to breathe,' he instructed. I breathed out slowly but imagined thousands of tiny black flies spilling out of me, then being sucked back inside as I breathed in.

I had been so utterly naive. I had *believed* everything my father had ever told me. When he said Archie, Daniel and I couldn't go to the hospital. When he said we couldn't go to the funeral because it would be too emotional for us. When he said there was no memorial plaque because he had scattered her ashes into the wind. Which we hadn't been allowed to do either. I had been so stupid!

'So what now?' Tom asked, draining his tea into his mouth and swallowing with a loud gulp.

I stared at him for a while, maximising the whites of my eyes so that he didn't miss my total amazement that he should even have to ask. 'I need to find my mother. *Obviously!*' Images of that last day returned again. Winter coat. Red lipstick. Red smile . . . Gone. 'I need to find out why she didn't come back or why he wouldn't let her back. I bet *she* was already on the scene.'

I dipped my voice again before the entire cafe stopped their conversations to listen to mine, but a man on the other side of us continued to stare at me over the top of his glasses. 'Does trunky want a bun?' I snapped at him.

'Trunky?' Tom repeated, a fascinated grin appearing across his face. Then he checked the time on his mobile phone and I knew my spring-time friend would be leaving again.

'You gotta go?' I mumbled, handing him a napkin for his mouth.

He clicked his phone off and slid it to the side of the table. 'Yeah, soon,' he answered.

'Is there someone who's going to worry about you being late?' I asked, while something dark and green chewed at the lining of my guts.

Don't answer that, please don't answer.

He answered.

'Angela? Yeah, probably. I should be getting back. What about your boyfriend worrying about you?' he asked.

A finger of embarrassment poked at me and I swallowed. A couple of months ago I had been going out with someone bland and weedy for the shortest time and it made me shiver that I ever thought it was a good idea. Tom had seen us together. 'You know, the guy with his jeans hanging really low . . . little fella . . . kind of skinny,' he said.

I was just going to have to style it out. 'What, him? *God!* No! He was someone from school . . . He wanted me to show him where . . . where the Dr Martens shop was in town.'

'So you thought you'd hold his hand in case he got lost?'

I looked across at Tom. There was only one person I wanted to hold hands with and he was about to go and meet his girlfriend. 'I'm with . . . Mike, he's . . . a body builder.' Where did *that* come from? A *body builder*? And I don't even know a Mike. I could at least have come out with a cool name like Ash or Ben and had them going to university to study marine biology or sports science or something. Red crept up my neck and reached my cheeks before I could pick up my almost empty cup to hide behind it.

'Body builder?' Tom echoed, nodding appreciatively. I moved my head rapidly up and down, using my most convincing expression, then hurriedly pushed my chair back and excused myself.

'I need to go . . .' I muttered, hurriedly escaping from the chair and heading for the loos. Inside the stall I held my head in my hands. *He knows I was lying about having a boyfriend.* What is wrong with me? Why can't I be like a normal person?

I thought about the way Tom always said my name, and wondered if he said his girlfriend's name with the same warm tones that he spoke mine. 'An-gel-a,' I said out loud. It's a musical name. Fun and sexy. I hated it! He's back there at the table, checking his phone and worrying about her while all I have is a pretend boyfriend, a resurrected mother and a lying father. But why should I care about An-gel-a? It wasn't as if I'd lost Tom or anything, because I never had him in the first place.

'*An-gel-a,*' I said her name louder. '*An-gel-a.*' I sounded out each syllable, twisting them into something ugly in the air, then I flushed the chain and opened the door to reveal a woman waiting her turn, trying to look like it was perfectly reasonable for someone to be strangling a name in the confines of a toilet.

When I washed my hands in the sink and looked in the mirror, I saw what Tom had been looking at for the last couple of hours. Coils of hair had escaped everywhere around my tear-streaked face and all my make-up had slipped, revealing my white face, stained with ginger freckles. Some of the freckles joined to make splotches. Like rust gathering more rust.

My pale eyes stared back at me above the dingy shadow of mascara-smudged skin. No green eyes for me. My mother had kept them all to herself. Mine were the colour of farm slurry. *God, Saff. You look like Princess Fiona after sunset!* Yep, an ogre. That is exactly what Tom saw. No wonder he never stayed around. I washed my face with soap from the dispenser, rubbing at the black under my eyes and drying off with a paper hand towel. Then I smoothed my eyebrows,

45

pinched my cheeks and licked my lips . . . like that was going to help.

As I hurried back to our table Tom was texting on his phone to someone in his real life . . . probably Angela. He could have any girl he wanted. Any An-gel-a or someone else with a beautiful name. A name that meant something wonderful. Not Saffron. Saffron meant *orange*. A perfect name for a misfit kid with an orange head.

Tom cleared his throat, like an apology.

'I've got to go, Saffron.' He slid his phone into his back pocket and pushed back his chair, while panic began to fizz in my chest. Tom and his thumbs, the only solid things I had in my life, were leaving. 'Go home, Saffron,' he ordered, picking up my untouched pastry and leading the way out. 'Talk to your dad. There *will* be a reason that he told you all that stuff. Trust me.'

I followed him out like a petulant child. 'Yeah, there was a reason he told me that stuff! He's a liar and a cheat, who swapped my mother for a blonde, size-eight, fortune-hunting bitch!'

'Why don't you say what you *really* feel?' he replied, as we stood on the street corner ready to go our separate ways. Tom took a bite of my cinnamon swirl and offered it to me. I took a bite too, but only because he had, then he looked down at me and I felt the loneliness of his imminent departure. 'Give him a chance to tell you.' He smiled through raisins and pastry. 'Promise?'

I shrugged and swallowed my own mouthful. 'Promise.' My agreement catapulted me into the moment I would have to tackle my father and the truth about what happened all those years ago. Then I watched him leave, back to his own life.

Back to his Angela.

Tom

So, the oh-so-perfect Hayes family held a secret! A secret that was damaging. A secret that could not be made sweeter by Daddy's money, the designer clothes, the fast car and the huge house.

Jogging away from Saffron felt a bit like abandoning a fragile ornament that needed to be held together to prevent it from breaking into several pieces.

I felt as if I should be her bubble-wrap in the light of this latest update, but this was a mess her father needed to man up about. I didn't want to get sucked into the Hayes mud bath and there wasn't anything more I could offer her at that moment. Even so, the hot chocolate and the eight pounds and thirty-six pence had lasted an hour and a half, which was a whole lot more time than I planned when I first saw her running towards the park crying her eyes out.

I couldn't change the past for Saffron and I couldn't save her from the pain of the present. And I certainly couldn't help her in the future. I jogged my way home, via the old-fashioned flower shop on the corner of Bridge Street, where I spent money I no longer had to spare on a few pink carnations and white gypsophila, which the florist tied together in a yellow raffia bow.

Saffron

All those years without my mum. All the precious time I'd spent missing her. Missing her being there for the important stuff. Even for the not-so-important stuff. All those whispered conversations in the night when I'd talked to her as if she was looking down at me from her place in the clouds, answering me silently as only a dead mother can.

I thought she could hear me. I thought, when I listened carefully enough, I could hear her whispering back. We had *whole conversations*, for God's sake.

I felt so incredibly cheated in every way!

My phone vibrated again and I stared as DAD lit up the screen. I wanted him to know just how horrible it felt being kept in the dark, just how awful it was not knowing where someone you loved was. Again, I ignored his call.

The tiny shops of the narrow street became bigger and newer as I headed away from the cafe. Normally shopping for me was an essential part of my lifestyle. Almost a need. Exciting shopping fests that always reaped rewards. Bags with fancy names containing new clothes and new make-up, hanging satisfyingly heavily in my hands, plus a belly full of sushi and a frappuccino to sustain my shopping stamina. My allowance paid for much of my stuff, but if I needed anything more I could always persuade Dad to hand over some money using a joke pouty lip, or a puppy-dog stare. I would show him something online and tell him how much I needed it in my life and yay! I would have the money. It wasn't like I wasn't grateful or anything but he was *very* generous.

Was it guilt money? Had he been making up for something? Paying for my contentment with retail therapy?

The clothes in the windows were now simply shapes behind glass to me. Instead, I scanned the people around me. My mother could be anywhere. Every person with red hair in the crowd would get a double take.

It was an unbearable thought, but would I even recognise her any more? Would her hair be short . . . or grey . . . ? The red I was scanning the streets for, no longer vibrant, no longer part of the person in my memory? Or worse . . . would she not be able to recognise *me*?

We moved house shortly after I rumbled my father over his moonlight adventures. *She* said the house wasn't big enough for any additions to the family. *She* had wanted a bigger, shinier house. *She* didn't seem to care that our old house held memories that were infused within the brickwork, that moving house would pull us out of our roots, stripping us bare of our past.

Where had my mother been all this time? Had she been working all the hours of the day to get a place big enough to house us all, to challenge the courts and win custody of us, only to find we'd all moved away and she couldn't compete against the chartered surveyor and his five-bedroom house? Maybe, like me, she was now scanning the streets, looking for her children. Searching for long-gone baby faces now formed into the dips and hollows of the adults we were becoming.

Having crashed blindly into several people, walked into a lamp-post for real this time and been sworn at by a guy on his bicycle, I turned towards home. My strategy was still vague, my head crammed with unanswered questions. Hopefully my father had been stewing long enough now, perhaps I could let him explain himself, preferably without the unexploded bomb inside me going off. I had a temper to match my hair but, remembering Tom's advice, this time I needed to hold myself together, at least long enough to hear everything he had to say, in hopes he'd answer the questions banging in my head.

Coming out of town, I found myself behind Maggie, who was talking to an imaginary person by her side. Her stench reached my nose even from a reasonable distance. Her shapeless body swung from side to side as she moved, her hands gripped firmly round her old shopping trolley full of God knows what.

She was wearing a different dress, probably pretty once, blue with red polka dots, and as Tom said, she was still wearing her summer hat. If she hadn't been decorated with old food and dirt and other unthinkable things, she would have looked the part in a TV drama, like a vicar's wife or something.

I remembered the first time I had met her and how she had looked at me with her forget-me-not eyes and how she'd continued to play on my seven-year-old mind. Despite the fact I was missing my mother, the idea that someone had to sleep on a pavement and not under a roof, tormented me for weeks afterwards. When it rained or when it was cold I would imagine Maggie out there without a house like mine, or a house at all!

So when we were making the totally pointless get-well cards for my mother, I had also made one for Maggie. I wanted her to have a house so badly I drew one for her on blue card with cut-out windows edged in yellow paint for curtains. I gave her house a red front door and carried it in my school bag for weeks.

The day I finally saw her again, I tore my hand out of Dad's and went up to her, thrusting my picture towards her nose. 'I've made you a house, Maggie,' I told her proudly, as Dad caught up with me. Disappointingly she shoved my picture in her pocket without even looking at it.

'See!' Dad said. 'She's crazy. Keep away, Saffy.' Dad's anger bounced off the top of my red curls and swirled away down the street, leaving me alone with my hurt.

Silly crazy lady hadn't even cared about my gift.

She definitely *is* way off her rocker, I said to myself as I caught up with her, her one-sided conversation reaching my ears. She even waited for her imaginary friend to reply.

The plastic strawberries swung from the brim of her hat and her shopping trolley was full of rubbish. I was amazed at the amount of crap she pushed around with her and wondered what was going on in her head that could make her think this life was in any way normal. Supermarket shopping bags, full of . . . whatever they were full of, were packed inside, one on top of the other. Bottles, pictures and children's toys were strapped to the wires of the trolley. The sides were lined with folded cardboard and blankets and an old umbrella poked upwards from one corner. There was a large red mug tied near the handle, containing a knife, fork and spoon. An old-fashioned tape player hung off the front, visible inside a clear plastic bag, while some sort of wheeled shopping basket was strapped to the top of everything by elastic bungies. All in all the trolley was almost double the size it should be because of all the rubbish that Maggie had tied to it.

I crossed the road as the waft of her sludge-green odour was burning the hairs off my nostrils just as my phone buzzed and DAD flashed across the screen again. His profile photo was taken just this summer of me and him wearing snorkels and masks in the Algarve. We'd spent hours face-down in the cool, rocky water, pointing and thumbs-upping each other, while the others did something less interesting on the beach. I still had the huge shell he'd found and given to me, its pearlescence still cupping the rhythmic whoosh of the sea.

'What?' I said sharply into the phone, finally relenting and answering him, if only to stop him bugging me.

'Thank God! Come home, Saffy, I've been going out of my mind!' Dad's voice sounded desperate. Guilty.

'Well, if it's even a little bit of what I feel then I'm glad,' I hissed back. 'I've been trying to put my head on straight so that I can deal with this, all right?'

'And have you? . . . Because . . . because I've got stuff to tell you.'

The subtle drop in volume made his voice sound soft and somehow even more desperate than before. I was glad. I wanted him to feel bad. The pain of this whole revelation was killing me and it was all I could do to snarl, 'Too right you've got stuff to tell me,' into the phone before switching it off without saying goodbye and shoving it back in my pocket.

Someone shouted something at Maggie, laughed then flicked a fag butt in her direction, which started a sequence of 'bugger off's and a semaphore of arms at the guy who threw it. I turned away from her messed-up madness and made my way down a side street towards home. I had my own crazy problems to worry about.

By the time I finally let myself in, the street lamps were creating a bright haze against a dark sky. The two hall lights spilled twin circles of yellow onto the terracotta floor tiles where I slipped off my boots. Various coats and bags hung on the hooks, leaving nowhere for mine so I lifted the small navy blue coat trimmed with white fur round the hood and dropped it on the floor, placing my own jacket on the hook. It was mean and it was petty but it helped ease my hurt.

The coat belonged to Charlotte, the product of my dad's and Smell-an-ie's affair.

The house was littered with Charlotte's childish paraphernalia. Little horses and cuddly toys and her obsessive love of fire engines. Brightly coloured clothes and pyjamas designed like a fire-fighter's uniform. She was seven now. The same age I'd been when my world fell apart. *Her* world, though, was safe and cosseted and spoilt.

Right then, if it were possible, I wanted to melt her down into a burning pile of black ash, leaving nothing but the bow in her hair to show she ever existed. She was the living, breathing outcome of something that had nothing whatsoever to do with my mum. She was the cuckoo's egg in our nest.

'I've been so worried.' My father's voice came from the doorway to the lounge, so close it made me jump. He waved his phone at me, as if his worry was inside it, looking so dishevelled and weary and *old* that for a teeny tiny moment I felt sorry for him. Then she appeared, acting as if she had a right to be by his side, a right to be part of our lives.

'Poor you,' I challenged.

'Me too, Saff,' Melanie offered. The way she spoke was too . . . musical, her Welsh accent a vocal cheese grater on my nerves.

I flinched and, for once, stared her directly in the face, her blue eyes framed by pale hair, looking down at me. 'You weren't worried about *me*. If you were, you wouldn't have come here in the first place and ruined my whole life!'

'That's not reasonable!' shouted Dad to the back of my head as I span round and went up the stairs two at a time. Flinging open my wardrobe doors, I pulled out black leggings and an oversized grey jumper, but Dad pushed the door open and filled the frame of it with his bulk. 'That was not reasonable,' he repeated.

'Er . . . I'm changing? Get out of my room!' I felt newly empowered. As if I had given myself permission to unleash my anger and my father should let me whip him with it, because he had done something vile and so wrong.

I tugged off my clothes and dropped them on the floor, the seat of my jeans dirty from the damp pavement and the make-up smudged knees, pulled on my cosy gear plus a pair of fluffy green and white bed socks before flopping on the bed.

My room was pristine. This morning I'd left the bed unmade and my college books scattered across the floor. Now, apart from the day's clothes I'd just stepped out of, it was tidy again, the little en-suite to my room all shiny and perfect. It was all too perfect. Too not me. *She* always came in and straightened everything as part of her clean-freak routine. I hated her coming into my room. Into my space. Touching my things.

The soft springs had creaked against my weight, alerting Dad to come in. Making his way across the paradise-blue of my bedroom carpet, he sat down beside me on the bed, reaching out to place his hand on mine. I moved sharply, out of his reach. His touch would burn. It would hurt and my barriers would come down.

'Don't come *near* me. Whatever you've got to say, you can say it from over there.' I pointed to the small cream leather sofa in the corner of my room where he obediently retreated, showing me the palms of his hands in surrender. When he was seated, I looked down at him from my higher position on the bed, my force field strengthening, making me feel in control. I was the judge and he the villain. 'So Mum has been alive all these years and we – me, Archie and Daniel – never knew. How – could – you – do – this – to – us?' I pronounced each word for maximum effect, then waited for a very long time while he stared back at me, unblinking, before sighing loudly, tipping his head back as if searching the ceiling for his answer. His fingers found each other and twisted themselves into impossible knots. 'It's all been a bit of a mess, Saffy . . . I don't really know where to start.'

'I'll help you. Where is she?'

'I don't know where she is.' His gaze dropped down from the ceiling and landed on my own. 'It's the truth, I don't know where she is now.'

'So what happened then? You said in your texts that you needed to explain. So start explaining.'

'I do . . . and I will . . . It's just not easy.'

'Try!' I snapped.

'Things are OK, aren't they, Saffy? You know, as they are?' His fingers unravelled themselves momentarily, offering themselves towards me, begging me to believe him. 'Your mum and I split up but you kids stayed with me . . . it happens all the time.'

I rolled my eyes heavenwards with extreme annoyance that he could play this thing down. 'That's not an explanation. That's an evasion. Even if you'd simply split up, there is such a thing as custody sharing, you know. She was a mother with three children . . . our mother! You must have stopped her from seeing us.'

Dad studied me for another long moment, until his hazel eyes behind brown-framed glasses began flitting around the objects in my room as if the answer might be resting on one of them. He shifted his position, and re-crossed his legs. 'Monday' printed on the sole of his sock waved at me as his foot fidgeted in mid-air. 'You have to understand . . . it wasn't an easy time. Your mother, she . . .'

He struggled over what to say, his fingers constantly restless. He was about to blame her! I could feel it in the air. My strategy to listen calmly was fading rapidly. 'I thought you were going to offer some amazing revelation when you texted me in the cafe, but you're just going to blame her, aren't you?'

'Yes. No. I don't know . . .' He sighed, taking off his glasses and rubbing a hand backwards and forwards across his forehead before running it over his hair, as if trying to erase whatever was going on behind his skull. 'Your mother was . . . difficult. Unpredictable. She would always be too much . . . or . . . not enough.'

His words petered out, floating in broken pieces between us as if I was the one who was supposed to put them together and make sense of them. 'What's that supposed to even mean? She had, like, a personality, then?' I said.

He swapped his legs over until Monday of the other foot waved at me, a tiny flesh-coloured hole peeping out above the M. 'Yes, she had a personality,' he repeated, illogically smiling to himself at some distant memory. I waited, confused as to what he could be remembering, but he wasn't forthcoming.

'I don't get it! Why can't you just come out with it? Why did you split up and why didn't you do the sharing thing?'

'I'm *trying* to explain . . . She was hard to live with.'

'She was harder to live without.' I stared steadily back at him. Daring him to challenge that!

'I know.' He sighed.

A silence fell between us as we both searched our memories of the dim and distant past.

'You were always arguing with her,' I said. The distant sound of long-ago raised voices filled my ears. Fleeting memories of me as a small child listening, unwillingly, to the harsh words that frequently filtered through closed doors in our house. Now, all these years later, my little girl's heart beat rapidly inside my older teenage heart, at this regurgitated recollection.

'Yes, we both argued . . . a lot! Too much. We tried to keep it from you but in the end it was impossible. She would do things . . . go shopping, spend loads of money buying stuff we didn't need . . . or she would book trips, theatre outings, or full blown exotic holidays –'

'She sounds . . . *awful*!' I interrupted sarcastically. This must be the Disney childhood I remembered. Until I was seven, I had a mother who provided all the wonderful things her children's hearts could desire and I had a father who found all that . . . *difficult*.

'You don't understand, Saff.' Dad sighed, and his hands went back to rubbing his forehead and stroking his own hair. 'She spent money we didn't have back then. Always spending . . . always looking for the next thing.'

'No, I don't think I do understand. But let's face it, it just doesn't make sense that a mother who spent too much money showering her family with lovely things should disappear, does it? It doesn't explain why we haven't seen her for ten years. Not unless she's been murdered and set in concrete under the patio – shoved over for a younger *bit on the side*.' I nudged my head spitefully towards the younger bit on the side who was slinking into my room with two drinks and a plate of tortillas, as if we were having a casual party here. 'Proper dinner is downstairs when you're ready,' she said.

Dad wearily thanked her. I said nothing.

'Did you know *her* before you buried Mum under the patio?' I asked, jerking my head in *her* direction.

He answered 'No' far too quickly, causing Melanie to halt in the doorway on her way out.

'Teddy? We *did* know each other.' She glanced warningly at my dad, whose name was Edward, or Eddie at a push, but definitely not *Teddy*. Her pet name for him irritated me beyond endurance, scratching its way Welshly down my ear canal, vibrating against my ear drum each time she spoke it. He looked back at her as if they shared a secret. 'We weren't *together*, Saffy, not in the biblical sense . . . We just *knew* each other. Like friends,' she said.

'Yes, I meant I didn't know Melanie in *that* way. The way you're thinking,' Dad responded, an uncomfortable, higher tone to his voice. Defensive. But it wasn't lost on me. Another lie. I hadn't got that wrong; he had definitely tried to make me believe he hadn't known her in *any* way whatsoever before Mum left.

'You're *still* lying, aren't you?' I asked, unable to believe it. Grabbing a pillow, I buried my face roughly into it, forcing an angry *ggrrnnnn* through the cotton.

Then on top of everything, the brat pushed her way in, flinging herself onto my bed, wrapping her arms, octopus-like, around me. 'Oh, you're back, Saffy! We were sooo *worried*,' she lisped into my sloppy grey jumper, making me flinch as her tentacles touched me.

'Not now,' I whined, stiffening against her small body. This child wounded me. She wounded me somewhere inside my chest where the me as a little child still lived. This child, however, unlike me, was a whole person. Unbroken. She was pretty and petite with shiny blonde hair that hung with enviable straightness down her back, flowing gently like silk when she moved.

The first time I saw her, she was all red and squashy looking, a wet sheen to her newly born skin and hair. We all had to buckle ourselves into our brand new multi-seater car, having recently sold the five-seater saloon we always used to have, pulling off the drive of our new, bigger house. Then we'd trooped into the hospital ward to view the new person that was responsible for so many changes in our lives. My father scooped the bundle into his arms while I tried to ignore the inflated and rosy-cheeked person responsible for pushing her into the world. It was like they'd joined an overnight secret society, the three of them. I would never forget the look he gave the baby as he cradled her in his arms. It was a look that wrenched something very special out of me.

As she grew from a squashy baby into doll-like child, it was as if her skin had been airbrushed with peaches and cream. Her eyes turned to vivid blue like her mother's and there was not a single freckle in sight. But, for me, this child was honeysuckle. A sweet and beautiful vine that crept around my heart, squeezing me until I was suffocated by something beautiful yet completely destructive . . . a lung-crushing weed with a deceptively fragrant flower.

She was many jarring things: new toys and parties, drawings taped to the fridge, the height chart marked on the door frame, the baby-faced imposter in my father's arms. Basically she was the real-life representation of the unthinkable activity that happened in that space in the bed where my mother should have been.

'Well, *that* was a beautiful moment,' I said sarcastically, when she was finally peeled off me and lifted off my bed.

'Tell the *whole* truth, Teddy,' Melanie said, her arms circled protectively around her child while her equally blue eyes remained determinedly on my father. It was as if they were the *real* family and I was nothing more than a bolt-on addition who didn't blend in with the architecture of the family unit.

But I was here first!

Suddenly the imposters were crowding my space, crowding my head and it was *my* bedroom they were crowding into and I couldn't stand it. 'OUT!' I ordered them both, tightly hugging the pillow that now contained my anguished groans. 'This is between me and my dad.' As they backed out like scalded dogs, I leapt off the bed and slammed the door behind them.

'They are not the enemy, Saff,' Dad said. But his defence of his new family irritated me almost as much as they did.

'They are not my family either,' I returned. 'Your *wife* is not my mother.'

'Her name is Melanie.' Dad sighed at my refusal to say her name. 'She had nothing to do with your mum leaving.'

'You think?' I spluttered angrily across the room. 'And before Mum left . . . when you knew *her* but apparently not in *that* way, you must have *wanted* to know her in *that* way otherwise we wouldn't be this cosy little family unit we are now, would we?' I wouldn't let him go. I was like a hunting dog chasing a fox. 'She said to tell me the *whole* truth.' I held my hand out as if the truth was now a tangible thing he could pass across the paradise-blue carpet.

He replaced his glasses and spread his fingers out on each knee, studying them intently. 'As I was trying to say . . .' He paused as if the truth was stuck in his throat, then he breathed out with a rush of air as if suddenly dislodging it. 'She wasn't well.'

I snatched my hand back, refusing to take this offering. 'Well, apparently she wasn't *unwell* either! She was so *not unwell* you took all our "get-not-unwell" cards and hid them in a briefcase!' My frustration at this ridiculous conversation was making me tired. There was another interminable pause while we stared at each other.

'I mean, normal like . . . up here,' he eventually said, pointing to his head.

My jaw suddenly hung loose. My father's face faded out and was replaced by the memory of my mother showing me the four conkers while Daniel played in the autumn leaves and Archie sat plump and happy and healthy in his pram. This was a beautiful memory. She was a beautiful person. She had been a good mother. *How could he say such a thing?*

I could feel myself closing down. I definitely wasn't waving the white flag but my brain was pulling up the drawbridge to keep the enemy out until it could function again. My father had no revelation to offer me. He was simply blaming all their arguments on my mother and stockpiling his excuses for shipping . . . that *bitch* in, in her place.

'You're trying to tell me she was mentally ill?' I asked, challenging him to do just that.

'No, nothing like that . . . oh I don't know what I mean . . . just that . . .' His voice faltered to nothing.

'I can't deal with this right now. All I want is the answer to two simple questions. Why she left and why you lied, and you can't seem to tell me either of them. You need to get out.' I pulled the duvet over my head, hiding in my fortress of feathers, suddenly knowing that there was only one thing for it. I had to find my mother so she could tell me herself.

The room felt silent, until at last I heard him stand up, move towards my bed, where he patted my shoulder through the duvet.

'I'm sorry, Saff. We'll try again later,' he said as he closed the door behind him.

Tuesday:
Disappointments and Obstinacy

Saffron

The waking sounds of a new day filtered through the house. These sounds, once so familiar, now felt like they belonged to someone else's life. Showers, toilets, toast, kettle. Archie yelling at anyone listening for his school jumper. The newly deepened voice of Daniel telling Charlotte to get out of his bedroom.

My brothers. My turncoat brothers. They had moved on. They had accepted. They had forgotten.

Archie had accepted Melanie from the very beginning, because, well, he was a baby and didn't know any better, but although I tried to forgive him for it, I desperately wanted him to know, and *frequently* told him, that she was not, and never would be, his proper mother. Daniel, although suspicious of her at first, had given in far too quickly, getting too easily bored with me constantly showing him photos of our *proper* mother, to remind him that Melanie was an imposter!

I was the only one who could see *her* for what she was and as it turned out I had been right. I *would not* be a traitor to our mother. Especially now that I knew that our mother wasn't even dead!

I was surprised to find I'd slept all the way through the

evening and the night without stirring, but my eyes felt bruised and puffy from crying so much yesterday. The plate with the uneaten tortillas had disappeared, along with the two glasses of juice that *she* had delivered the evening before.

The image of Dad tapping the side of his head last night, indicating that Mum hadn't been right in the head, would not leave. I remembered how Tom and I had first talked about Maggie as we threw stones at the Coke can in the river. 'What makes someone get nutty like that?' I'd giggled.

'She's a bit gone in the head,' he said and pointed at his brain, crossing his eyes and whistling. 'She's known as Crazy Maggie.'

'What made her crazy though?' I frowned.

'Booze,' he answered. 'The streets . . . life.'

My mother had not been affected by booze, homelessness or 'life'. My mother had a red smile that told me to look for treasures. I began to erupt again with a lava-hot rage that threatened to spill out of me. I would never forgive my father for making out there was something wrong with her and for denying us the chance to grow up with her in our lives.

If I couldn't rely on my father to tell me everything, then maybe my mother could. 'Do you know any relatives on Mum's side?' I demanded, walking into the kitchen where Dad was assembling a bacon sandwich. He had his back to me but instantly turned his head, smiling with inappropriate cheerfulness, considering the seriousness of his crime.

'Good morning,' he answered, making his way to the kitchen table with his breakfast and a mug of tea, 'and no, I don't. She didn't have any family that she kept in touch with.'

I wasn't in the mood for general chat, but I needed answers

quickly if I was going to find my mother. 'So, what *do* you know about Mum before she was Mum then?'

'Actually, not a lot.' He lowered himself into a kitchen chair and reached for the tomato sauce, lifting up the corners of the bread and squeezing a generous amount on top of the bacon, while I thrust my 'I'm still incredibly angry with you' expression in his direction.

'Well, you must know something. You don't just marry someone without knowing who they are.' Seeing as I'd missed dinner last night, I had a sudden intense and unwelcome desire for a bacon sandwich too, but to sit and eat at the table with my dad felt like a sociable move, a friendly gesture. There was nothing sociable or friendly about how I felt towards him at that moment. Instead, I poured some fresh orange juice into a glass and remained standing while I sipped at its coolness. 'AWAY!' I shouted as Archie wandered in, wearing a gecko onesie and rubbing his eyes. It was almost comical how his eyes went totally round and he actually walked backwards through the door, like a film in rewind. 'Well?' I turned back to Dad, looking down at him again, as if I had become the adult, and he the squirming child.

'There was no need for that,' Dad said, nodding his head to where Archie had exited.

I ignored him. 'Didn't she have anyone at your wedding? . . . Parents? . . . Friends? There must have been someone.'

'We were the only ones who came to our wedding.' He sighed again. 'We married in Gretna Green.' I frowned at him, not knowing where this Green place was. 'It's a place in Scotland that does quick, cheap weddings,' he clarified.

'Romantic,' I replied, the sarcasm barely disguised.

'Actually, it was,' he said, and I could see a ripple of something resembling a happy recollection play across his face again. 'It was your mum's idea. A mad, fun, fast wedding, cheap as chips and no guests. My parents were devastated and our friends were amazed when, out of the blue, we sent everyone a photo of us standing by the Gretna Green sign.' I tried to imagine their wedding day, where the two of them stood like a couple of Billys next to a sign. It sounded like a huge anticlimax as far as weddings go. I pulled a chair away from the table and sank down on it.

'She was amazing, exciting and totally wonderful. And I didn't care about what I didn't know, I only knew that I loved her.' He looked up at me with that ripple still playing on his face like little hints of love and whimsical wishes. I was confused by the way he dipped back into the past in a way that looked as though he missed it. '. . . And, um, well it was all a bit swift for another reason . . .' he added, as if this gem of information was nothing more than a P.S. at the end of a letter.

A silence fell between us, like midnight snow heavy with the gathered pollution of a rotten thought. Dad took another bite of his sandwich, intently studying the remains of it in his hands as if it had just become more interesting than the huge thing he'd just released into the room. 'I was an accident, wasn't I?' I asked eventually. I hadn't been a planned and longed-for baby, I'd been a horrible shock . . . a split condom.

'We wanted you, we just weren't *expecting* you. Your mum . . . well, she was forgetful with the Pill . . .'

'Oh . . . my . . . God! Once more, you're blaming her? Like she was the only one responsible for safe sex!'

He groaned, put the remains of his sandwich down and pushed the plate away. 'I was young. I thought it would be . . . you know . . . OK. But trust me, Saffy, once we got used to the idea we were delighted.' He reached his hand towards me, hoping that I would reach out too, but I let his empty hand hang in the air. That kind of thing belonged to yesterday. That kind of thing belonged to a time before we became strangers.

'And once you were *delighted* you didn't think to get to know the rest of her family so they could be *delighted* too?'

'I told you, there didn't seem to be any. Your mother didn't keep in touch with her family. Her parents had died, her brother, David, had moved somewhere in the arse end of the world and there wasn't anyone else apparently. We had a small wedding reception later, just with Gran and some friends.'

Gran? I wondered if she was another traitor in the mix. 'Does Gran know? About the last ten years? That Mum wasn't ill, dying or dead? Has she been lying too?' Another horrible silence crept into the kitchen, releasing its scummy pollution into the air.

'She knew . . .' he said, quietly.

My intestines were tying themselves into knots again, the air around me becoming thick as if I was breathing it in lumps. 'So if Mum had no other family, why would she leave the only family she did have? It doesn't make sense!'

'It . . . it just went wrong. Look, we'll have another go at this tonight. I've got a meeting at work now that I just can't get out of . . . believe me, I would if I could.' We both looked at the wall where a large wooden vintage teapot sprouted twelve wooden vintage cupcakes in a circle around it. A little spoon and a big fork told us it was ten past eight.

'Really? You can't phone in and tell them you've torn your family into shreds and perhaps you should stay home to repair it? Am I – *we* – not more important than some meeting?' My life was breaking off in bits, and he wasn't going to risk upsetting someone else's day to stay at home and do something about it! I followed him round as he put his plate in the dishwasher and looked for his shoes, chipping angrily away at him.

'You only told us Mum had died because you were sleeping with *her*, didn't you?' I pointed to the ceiling where Melanie was upstairs.

'Can we not do this right now?' he said, reaching for his suit jacket, a pained expression on his face.

I carried on chipping. 'That day I found you in bed with her . . . you told us Mum was dead so you wouldn't look bad about having another woman in your bed. Didn't you?'

'I didn't know what else to tell you. We'll talk about it later . . . I *promise*.' He picked up his car keys and headed out of the front door with me following close by his side. 'Bye, love,' he called and it took me a second to realise he wasn't saying this to me, he was calling out past me to Smellanie. *She* was his love, I was just his love child . . . or, more accurately, I was just his mistake. I followed him into the drive and right up to the car, still wearing my leggings and sloppy jumper from the night before, my socks gathering the damp and dirt from the pavement into their fluffiness.

'It *was* her, wasn't it?' I persisted. 'You wanted a clear path for her!'

He looked agitated. I was clearly catching him between doing the right thing by talking to me and his wish to go to work for whoever was at the meeting that was more important than I was.

'Why did you have to tell us Mum was dead?' I repeated. I was almost shouting so the whole street could hear me.

'Because I wished she was!' he hissed, climbing into his car and clunking the door shut. His words plopped out of the sky like seagull crap on my head and my jaw unhinged as if the muscles in my face had also rotted away. *He wished she was dead!!!*

The electric window slid open, and my father looked up at me as he reached for the seat belt, a dark red tinge diffusing its way up from his neck to his jaw. 'If you're going to keep asking questions when I haven't got time to answer them, it's going to go horribly wrong.' He turned the key in the ignition, revving hard at the engine.

'You had ten years to find the time, Dad. *Ten years!* Was that not long enough for you?'

His hands curled over the rim of his steering wheel and squeezed until his knuckles peaked and whitened. 'But right now *really* isn't the time for it, Saffy.'

'You were *never* going to tell me that my mother was alive if I hadn't found that briefcase, were you? How could you keep something that MASSIVE from us? Well, I'm going to go and find her and there's nothing you can do about it.'

'Yeah, well good luck with *that!*' He revved the engine again and pushed the button to raise the window back up.

'I will find her and when I do, you can wave goodbye to me.

And you'll lose the boys too . . . They'll hate you for this . . .
WE WILL ALL HATE YOU FOR THIS!' I was almost posting
my words through the gap in the window. Shoving them into
his car – hoping they hurt as they hit him. Then he was gone,
the twin exhausts blasting him down the street.

The bag – a huge black hold-all filled with everything a girl
might need for a new, improved, grown-up detective mission –
bulged at the zip. No zebra rucksack or tiger mask for me this
time. Pants, socks, jeans, warm jumper, tops, shoes, college
books, perfume, deodorant, shower gel, shampoo, hand sanitizer,
comb, hair-bands, drink and snacks. My phone, bank card and
the old photograph of my mother standing ankle-deep in
the sea, were shoved in the end section, all waiting for an
appropriate moment to leave and find my mother.
    'Daniel?' I put on a white T-shirt and faded denim shorts,
then pulled my over-knee-length black socks over my black
tights, fastened the buckles on my chunky boots and placed
my leather jacket on top of the hold-all. Then I waited for my
brother with his snail-like reactions to drag himself into
my bedroom. 'DANIEL?' I called for like the hundredth
time, still not entirely sure how to tell him about Mum, but
I needed to offload this now. In the early days, Daniel would
cry pitifully, his arms clinging around my neck while I told
him our mummy would be home soon. Archie had been too
young, but Daniel and I had been in this together.
    Still, when he eventually walked into my room, with the
familiar stupid expression of a thirteen-year-old, his face
morphing between the child he was and the man he was going

to be, I found myself fiddling with the frayed hem of my shorts, reaching blindly around for the right way to put it to him. I'd had nearly twenty-four hours to get used to the heart-splitting hurt this whole thing had wreaked on me and I was about to do the same to him.

'S'up?'

His eyes looked down at me, rather than up, and I wasn't sure when that had happened – the growing up thing – but I let myself believe it kind of brought us to a similar level of understanding. Like his height made him older than he was.

I shut the door behind him and lowered my voice so that Archie wouldn't overhear. Until Melanie came on the scene, I had been everything to my brothers, big sister and surrogate mother combined. I'd cuddled them, wiped their noses and dried their tears. 'I found something out yesterday . . .'

'Yeah?'

He was hardly articulate these days. As if all the words he ever learnt had become condensed into sounds of one syllable. 'Um . . . I . . . found all our cards to Mum . . . in a briefcase . . . in the attic!'

As I waited for enlightenment to do something interesting to the unresponsive face in front of me, I noticed how soft brown hair had drawn delicate lines on his top lip and along the shape of his jaw. The penny, though, was taking a while to drop through all the dense matter in his brain. My brother was currently being what I could only describe as . . . a dumb-arse thickster! 'Don't you *get* it, Dan? She *never* got them.'

'I don't know what you're talking about. What cards?'

Was he for real? Was I the only one who remembered? The

tremors from yesterday stirred up again, spreading from the inside out, threatening to shoot sparks from my fingertips. 'The get-well cards. When our mum was ill, before Dad told us she'd died . . . we made get-well cards for her . . . all of us, round the table . . . only, she never got them because she was never ill.'

Daniel gave an almost imperceptible nod of the head. 'Oh, if you say so.'

I could hardly believe what I was witnessing. 'If I say so? Surely you know what I'm telling you?'

He gave a careless shrug, while I stared at him with bewilderment and disbelief at his general apathy. 'Yes, I get it. I'm just not bothered by it,' he replied.

'You're not *bothered*? How come you're not going ape-shit like I did?' My heart was quickening and I was trying to whisper, for Archie's sake, but it wasn't happening, my voice coming out in raspy squeaks.

Daniel rammed his hands into his pockets as if he couldn't give a monkey's and shrugged again. 'Because I don't really give a fuck.'

'You don't give a *fuck*? Our mum is alive and that's all you've got to say?' Honestly, his school headmaster could have appeared, complete with all the teachers from his school, totally stark naked, doing a street dance, right in front of me, and I would not have been more surprised.

'I don't remember her.' He shuffled his feet along my paradise-blue carpet, making waves in the deep blue threads.

'So! All this time when we could have had our own mother and you don't give a flying *fuck*!'

'I didn't say it was a flying one. Just a regular one.' He

smirked. 'I like Melanie. I like things the way they are. And you're always wading in and ruining things for all of us.'

Now, that hurt! The already bruised and raw place inside me had just been kicked by my once-upon-a-time little brother. He was accusing me of ruining this artificial family because he couldn't remember his real one. I'd tried so hard to keep the memory of Mum alive for him, for both of them, but I'd failed. I suddenly wanted to jab my fingers through his non-expressive face and pull it off his skull. 'But what about her – our real mum – now you know she's alive?'

'What about her?' he said, barely rippling an eyebrow. 'It's not exactly something to be proud of is it . . . your mum bogging off without a trace?'

My fury at his betrayal was barely contained. 'She didn't *bog* off! You're acting like she's some kind of dirty secret! How could you be a traitor to your family like this?' I sank on the bed in total defeat.

'*This* is my family . . .' he said, pulling his hands out of his pockets and sweeping them around to indicate the people in our house. 'Except . . . you never have anything much to do with us any more.'

If I dug deep enough I'd know he was right. Instead, I fired back at him: 'Dad knew Melanie before Mum left, so he must have been having an affair. That means he is the one with the dirty secret . . . He must have made Mum leave.'

Daniel shoved his hands back in his pockets. 'No one *has* to disappear because their husbands are shagging someone else. If that was the case, most of the kids at school would be without mothers. In fact, Jaydon's dad was shagging another woman while his mum was also shagging another woman. Now he's got three mums! He should win an award for bringing the most mums to parents' evening!' He smirked again to himself at the thought. 'And Scarlet's dad –'

'Yes, I *get it*, Daniel. People shag around! But this is *our* mum. She wouldn't just have gone like that. Don't you remember all the fun stuff she did?'

He almost laughed. 'No. I told you, I don't remember her. I was three years old!'

'Well, I do. So that can only mean one thing. I'm telling you, Dad *must* have done something awful.'

'What? Threatened her with underfloor heating or a holiday in the Caribbean?' he scoffed. Now it was his turn to get angry red splotches, the only give-away that he did, despite his cool exterior, give a shit. 'Honestly, Saff, you need to move on too.'

I stood up and pointed to my hold-all. 'I'm not moving on, Dan. I'm moving out! I've had enough of living in a house with secrets and lies.'

'Where would you go?' he asked, as if I was being totally ridiculous.

'I'm going to stay at Tom's for now and if you say a word about where I am, I'll show them *that* video. In fact, I'll show everyone *that* video – it will go viral.' I rubbed my eyes to impersonate him pretending to cry. Not long ago, he and his friend had burnt their school initials on the cricket field of a rival school as part of a dare. The whole event caused a massive eruption. The local newspaper was involved, community police were involved, kids at both schools were interviewed. No one ever knew it was them . . . apart from him, the kid who helped him, and stupidly videoed it . . . and me, because I happened to borrow his tablet the next day and found it. When I threatened to tell everyone he cried like a baby. But now, unfortunately for him, my little brother is permanently one small keypad click away from the biggest telling-off of his entire life.

Daniel did an about turn, opened my door and started to walk out, then stopped suddenly in the doorway, speaking disturbingly quietly. '*You* used to be like a mum to me and Archie . . . then Melanie came and you stopped caring.'

The door slammed behind him.

My voice turned into a whisper as I watched my powder-blue dressing gown swing from its hook on the door. 'You didn't need me any more.'

'Are you home early today?' *She* put her head round my door as I applied a second coat of mascara on my lashes.

'Do you mind knocking?' I asked, no question intended.

'Oh, sorry,' she said, and, *jeez*, she actually knocked on the door, right then, with it already open, and her already in my room. 'Are you?' she asked again, her expression looking all sympathetic at me as if she had nothing to do with this whole nightmare. I put the mascara wand back and screwed it in place, neither looking at her nor answering. She was never quite sure when I was home, my sixth-form being more like a college – a blissful release from the rules and regulations of regular school. No uniform and a varying timetable . . . perfect for an unpoliced daytime existence. Melanie continued regardless. 'Well, anyway, if you are there's leftover lasagne in the kitchen, if you want it. I made it myself, it's got bacon in it – gives it an extra dimension.'

Do you want a medal?

'Well, actually it's in the fridge, in the kitchen. It's warm today, don't you think? But I heard we're in for change in weather . . . a proper storm followed by a cold blast.'

Yeah! Somebody died and made you the weather expert.

I dismissed her from my room with a strangled sound, which she probably misinterpreted as a thank-you . . . if she were really fishing for it. She always was.

When the house had finally decanted itself of traitors, I rang school to tell them I was ill, put on a hoodie and stuffed my grey beanie in my jacket pocket – just in case she was right about the weather – slipped my leather jacket on over everything and reached for my bag. Jeez, this thing was heavy! I considered taking something out but there was nothing I could do without. All of it was totally necessary. So, lumping it awkwardly over my shoulder, I made my way down the stairs and across to the front door. Hanging from a coat hook was one of Melanie's handbags, a beige and pink leather Prada, with a fat wad of money poking temptingly out of a straining matching wallet. The idea of it made my heart race. It would be very useful as a contribution for food at whoever's house I ended up staying in. Scooping up change left lying around the house was one thing; this was real money . . . But she'd lived off my father's money for years – did it really count as theft? My fingers reached for it anyway and counted. *Two hundred and fifty pounds!* What was it for . . . Botox? A new diamond-encrusted tutu for the brat?

She was a cuckoo and she had pushed me out of the nest, so I took it to help cushion the fall.

* * *

I let my feet take me wherever they wanted to go, until I found myself sitting on a bench by the river. The hold-all had been burning a groove into my shoulder, forcing me to take to wrapping both arms tightly around its middle in a clumsy embrace and really wishing I hadn't packed so much. I dumped the hold-all on the ground and rested my arms, aware that the day had an unusual atmosphere to it, like I was sitting in an old painting. An October sun was forcing a spill of yellow through a tiny gap in the moody sky that dropped splashes of gold on the river in front of me. It was a little bit of beautiful in a life that had just turned completely ugly.

Then someone dropped a bag of dog poo into an overstuffed bin next to the bench I was sitting on and the beautiful painting peeled away revealing reality – I was on a park bench in the middle of town because I didn't have anywhere else to go . . . yet.

Me: I've left home. Can I stay at yours?

I didn't know if Tom lived alone now, still with his mum or even with Angela. It wasn't something I'd thought to ask. That was a bit odd now I thought about it. I'd known him for ten years but all I knew was he'd said he used to live with his mum on the estate on the edge of town before he moved to one of the big blocks of council flats. I didn't even know exactly which one. We never bothered discussing stuff like that when we were kids, too busy being pirates or warriors, and now we were grown up, we didn't have that kind of friendship.

I had been the one to ruin it. A stupid moment when I hoped we had something more than we did. I was thirteen and Tom was fifteen and we'd been sitting by the duck pond, cross-legged on the grass, throwing bits of bread and talking until the bread had long gone, the sun sinking low in the sky and goose bumps appearing all over our arms. Summer had lightened Tom's hair and his skin was glowing like a field of ripe barley and a new kind of feeling had begun to find its way into the pit of my stomach whenever he was around. My thirteen-year-old heart loved him, it was simple. He'd stood up, stretching out his long limbs, brushing little pieces of grass off his shorts and off the golden hair on his shins, then he reached a hand out to help me up. I took it and I held on, staring into his eyes and hoping desperately he found small, orange-haired girls, who'd carefully applied a load of freckle hiding make-up, attractive.

Clearly he didn't. In one swift cringe-worthy moment I lunged at him for a full movie-style kiss and he, in shock, recoiled. I had ruined everything. The moment Tom released my hand and gently pushed me away was the moment the shiny effervescence of our childhood friendship floated away. Yes, we met sometimes and, yes, we laughed and talked and, yes, I still adored him, but Tom had kept his distance from that moment on. He had made it very clear we were just friends and no amount of wishing was going to change that.

My phone remained painfully silent, meaning he was probably in work, so heaving the somehow even heavier hold-all over my shoulder, I headed into town. 'No hurry,' I said sarcastically to the blank screen of my phone, but just as I said that his reply flashed at me.

Tom: I'm coming. Where are you now?

Me: South Street. Library side

Tom: 10 mins

Yes! Tom would come to my rescue after all, because in a real crisis, he always did.

Tom

I had just enough time.

I could get on my bike, find Saffron and still get back before John was ready to begin assembling the bespoke kitchen units we'd just finished making for a client.

'Really sorry, John. Can I take an extended break? I've got something I need to sort out. I'll be back before you know it. Promise.'

John grumbled, then pushed the sleeves of his overalls up to look at his watch. 'Be back at eleven,' he said generously. 'You're useless anyway.'

'If I'm useless, how come you tell everyone I'm your best apprentice yet?' I called over to him as I got on my bike.

'You're my only apprentice yet,' he grumbled.

'Then how come you give your only-apprentice-yet more than the minimum wage?' I grinned at him as I cycled past.

'Because I'm a bloody old fool!' he shouted as I rounded the corner.

'I've left home.' That's what she texted.

How does she do it? Here I am again, cycling as fast as my

legs will let me, trying to catch yet another hand grenade heading towards Saffron Hayes, and lob it over the nearest wall before it explodes.

The lights turned red but I dodged through them anyway just as a guy in his car honked the horn and gave me his special one-fingered wave. 'Effin bikes. You're not exempt from the sodding Highway Code, you know.' I gave him the same charming smile I'd just given John, impressing him so much he employed all five fingers to give me another kind of special wave.

I was out of breath by the time I saw that hair bouncing over the top of a very large black hold-all slung across her back.

Saffron

I stared at Tom in disbelief. 'Did you come all this way just to say *no*?'

Tom had skidded to a halt right in front of me, almost causing me to walk into him. His cheeks were flushed from the exertion of cycling, and his hands, gripping the handles of his bike, were covered in paint.

'You can't stay at mine, I'm sorry. I've only snuck a few minutes off work to convince you that you need to go back home. You can't sort this by running away.' He eyed the bulging hold-all I'd dropped on the ground between us and, for whatever reason, didn't look apologetic. Why would he think it was that simple for me to turn around and go home? He couldn't possibly miss the fact that I was serious enough about running away to pack an awful lot of stuff.

'I'm not running away. I'm running *to*. I need to find my mother and I kind of hoped you'd come all this way to help me, to take me to your house, or at least give me a key or something?' I looked up at him with a 'pretty please' smile. 'Isn't that why you're here . . . to help me?'

'I am helping you, Saffron, by telling you that this isn't the solution. Go home before the storm comes and it literally rains on your parade.'

An uncomfortable space gathered between us as we stared each other out. I was doing my best to look unaffected by the way he made me feel, which was hard because every time I saw him it felt like a banner popped out of the top of my head saying 'You're gorgeous, why don't you like me?'

'Just for a few nights?' I pleaded, hearing the desperation in my voice. I knew I was pushing it, the banner on my head and the bag at my feet . . . I'm surprised he was even being so polite. Then dismounting his bike he bent down and picked my hold-all off the ground.

'Jeeezus, Saffron, what have you got in here? This lot could break a donkey's back!'

'Er . . . *duh*. I've left home! It took me long enough as it was to work out which things I could bear to leave behind, the LV or the D&G, so many choices. Come on, Tom, please, it shouldn't be for long, just until I find someone else to put me up. Or until I find my mum, of course.'

Tom held the hold-all out towards me. 'I . . . she's not . . .' He stammered. The cheeky face he always wore slipped to the pavement and for once he couldn't get his words out. It was becoming obvious that Angela wasn't going to like it if I stayed, but in true Saffron Hayes style I persisted.

'Your spare room? . . . Sofa? . . . Utility room . . . bath, even? I'll keep out of your way. I'll be positively invisible. Angela would hardly know I was there. Promise.' I followed the sway of his head as his refusal became obvious, my frustration mingling with panic and disappointment in equal measures.

'I'm sorry, Saffron, it's just not possible. What about a friend?'

'I'm sorry, Tom, it's just not possible,' I echoed moodily. 'I thought you were my friend?' I'd only been at my school a month, I hardly knew anyone else well enough to suddenly move in. Asking them would seem a bit weird.

'I'm not the right kind of friend,' he said, lowering my hold-all back onto the ground and breaking my heart at the same time. 'Don't you have a best friend or something?'

I wanted to say, 'You are my best friend' but instead I said, 'I had a best friend once. I mashed a purple birthday cake into her face!' It was shortly after finding Melanie naked in my dad's bed, when the new, 're-born' Saffron Hayes had been invited to what was about to become an iconic birthday tea party, according to literally everyone in my school. My soon-to-be *ex*-best-friend's mother had stroked her daughter's hair just after she placed nine beautiful handmade and candle-lit cupcakes onto the table. Nine perfect silver and purple domes, each with intricate fondant stars and moons. To my own motherless self, the look they gave each other was, quite frankly, nauseating.

'You mashed cake into your friend's face at her birthday party? Other gifts were available, you know.' For a moment we looked at each other, then we both suddenly giggled like we always used to. 'Perhaps next time I have eight pounds and thirty-six pence we should avoid the cafes!' But then the moment was over . . . Tom wasn't going to relent. 'Ask a different friend . . . one who isn't afraid of being attacked by food?'

I shook my head, shaking all amusement away.

'Your boyfriend? The body builder?'

'He's . . .' I searched for elusive words to describe my boyfriendless situation. My mind was a total blank.

'He's busy training for the World Body-Building Championships?'

My frustration flared. He was now blatantly mocking me. He knew I didn't have a boyfriend. Tom was possibly my last chance at finding somewhere to stay the night without paying through the nose for a hotel and he knew it. 'Take your ridiculously heavy bag and go home, Saffron. You're being daft.' If Tom had anything else to say, I didn't hear it. I was furious, and the angry red rushing across my face was threatening to become a seriously huge, all-body takeover. I heaved up my 'ridiculously heavy' bag, which was actually *unbelievably* ridiculously heavy, and walked away down the street before I punched him.

Tom

Well, that didn't go well! Perhaps calling her 'daft' wasn't the best idea.

I cycled after her for a bit, feeling bad and shouting at her to stop but she was determined – stomping ahead so fast it made the spirals of her hair leap violently, threatening to take out the eyes of any passers-by. There was no point in pursuing her further, plus I couldn't let John down by being late back for work. I glanced at the time on my phone. Just enough left to get back to John by eleven if I got a pedal on.

However many times I told myself that Saffron didn't belong in my life and I didn't belong in hers, she just kept showing up. That in itself was OK, but bringing all her problems with her was a different matter – as if I was the only person who could help her. But this time she wanted to move in and bring half her house with her! I'd managed for four years to keep my distance . . . ever since that incident at the duck pond when one minute we were laughing about a stupid joke she told me and the next she was looming in for a kiss. What do you call an overweight cat that swallows a duck, she'd said. A duck-filled fatty pus! It was stupid really but it made us both laugh so much, most of the ducks had swum off by the time we'd finished.

I had stood up and reached for her hand to pull her up. 'You nutter, Saffron. No one makes me laugh like you do,' I'd said, and then she went for it, lips puckered and heading in my direction. But we weren't children any more. I was building a wall between us, unsure whether I was keeping her out or me in. The moment I let go of her hand, I knew I'd just let go of the friendship we'd had since she was seven and I was nine.

There was nothing else for it, she had to go back to her own home – and if I knew one thing about Saffron, it was that she loved her home comforts too much. It wouldn't be long before she gave up the idea of running away, went home, and searched for her mother while languishing in the kind of luxury she'd always been accustomed to.

Saffron

I absolutely wasn't going to lose face and go home, however 'daft' Tom thought I was. Anyway, what was daft about trying to find a mother who'd been hidden from you for an entire decade? It was perfectly rational to want to find her. What daughter wouldn't?

My friendship group, such as it was, all had reasons for saying it wasn't possible for me to stay mid-week, which left me holding my phone, staring at it as if it too was somehow responsible for letting me down. A couple of them said I could come at the weekend, probably thinking I was weird for asking in the first place, but that was no good to me tonight. My only other option would have been Gran . . . but she was a traitor too.

It would seem that the main problem with leaving home at seventeen is that you're not yet eighteen.

'I have money and I have a bank card,' I complained to the receptionist at the first hotel I came to, although in reality I only had the cash I'd stolen and whatever was left on my bank card, which probably wasn't much.

'Like I said, you need a credit card if you wish to book

accommodation in this hotel,' she repeated through pink glossy lips and a well-practised smile. I crouched down below the counter to rummage in the side pocket of the hold-all.

'I've got *real* money,' I insisted, re-emerging above the counter to show her a fistful of money.

'You still need a credit card. It's our policy,' she repeated, and I noticed how she managed to remain irritatingly in control of her carefully made-up face, while mine was turning beetroot with frustration.

Whenever I'd stayed in a hotel before, Dad had booked it. He would stand at the counter, sorting out everything, while Daniel and I would mooch around the foyer, investigating the restaurant menu or checking out which direction the spa was in. Archie would always take it one step further, as Archie always did, charging through the corridors making engine noises. If he was really lucky, there'd be a revolving door where he could make faces and rude gestures at us through the gaps as he went round and round. He once mooned right up against a glass-fronted lift as it went up and down through several floors of a hotel foyer, making me and Daniel laugh hysterically while Dad rolled his eyes and mouthed 'Get down here NOW,' pointing angrily to the ground by his shoes.

An elderly couple walked in behind me, wheeling their identical tartan cases along the recently polished floor, coming to a squeaky stop behind me. Archie would love this floor. He'd be taking running dives, counting how many tiles he managed to slide across on his stomach before coming to a halt. 'Most minors get their parents to put the room on their card,' the receptionist said, breaking into my thoughts.

'I'm seventeen! Hardly a minor,' I snapped. 'I could go to work, take driving lessons . . . learn to *fly*, all without my parents' permission, but I can't book a room for the night in a hotel!'

She leant towards me, the pink lips stiffening into a rigid smile as she murmured quietly through her teeth, 'Listen, love, without a credit card you could be walking off with the trouser press and the entire contents of the minibar, having shoved the towels into that bag of yours. It's not happening, OK?'

I pushed my fistful of money back into the hold-all and heaved it back onto my shoulder, almost making the mistake of asking her where on earth she thought I could put a trouser press. Thankfully I suddenly realised what I was about to say and managed in the nick of time not to give her the material. The pink lips loosened as she swiftly addressed the people behind me. 'How may I help you?'

There was no glass-fronted lift or swimming pool in this hotel, or even a revolving door, which meant that Archie would only give it three stars at best, and that was only for the slidy floor. On my way out, however, I noticed a board advertising the price of rooms and realised that I couldn't have afforded it anyway. Could have been embarrassing.

Hours later, I'd discovered that every hotel and guest house in the town were going to give me the same line – I needed photo ID, a credit card, or my parents' help.

I needed Daniel to bring me my ID but he wasn't answering his phone. It didn't help that instead of recording 'Hi, this is Daniel Hayes, please leave a message after the beep' or anything remotely normal on his answerphone, my brother had simply recorded 'Yeah,' which made it sound like it was really him answering. I'd started talking to him several times before the recording 'beep' interrupted me. 'Where the hell are you?' I yelled at his name on the screen of my phone. 'ANSWER YOUR PHONE!'

Outside yet another hotel I dropped the hold-all on the ground again and rested my head against a wall. The hazy sun was now totally lost behind a sky that was marbling with purples and greys, and the muggy heat of the day was intensifying. School would have tipped out by now so Daniel could be anywhere – hanging out with his mates, all spots and testosterone. I imagined his phone ringing from a discarded bag or blazer, chucked on the ground while he and his mates hung out in the park or round at someone's house. What was wrong with him? Virtually every teenager on the planet had their phones glued to their sides, apart from Daniel, who hardly ever looked at his or had the sound turned on or the battery charged. He was totally crap as brothers with a phone go.

My own phone, however, started vibrating with more calls and bleeping with voicemail alerts and texts from Dad. The stolen money and half the stuff missing from my room had obviously alerted them to the fact that I'd gone, which felt wholly satisfying and frighteningly real both at the same time.

Dad: Where are you? Call me x

Me: I'm fine. Staying with a friend. I'll call later

I wasn't going to call later but it's not very cool to leave home then fail before the first night because your father had got in his car and driven round the streets looking for you. I stretched my back out and made to move on again. Tom was right, I'd packed enough to break a donkey's back let alone my own. The palms of my hands were sweaty again and sore from holding the handles and storm flies were now crawling on my skin. All I wanted to do was sit down and rest for a bit, but time was ticking on and the evening was now ominously close. Another text appeared on my phone from Dad.

> Dad: I didn't mean to get angry this morning.
> I handled it badly. I'm sorry x

> Me: I'm not coming home until you tell me
> what happened

At seventeen it was completely legal to leave home without his permission so really there wasn't much he could do about it, except blame himself! For a long time I watched the dots on my screen appear and disappear, yet no text arrived. It told me everything. My father was incapable of telling me exactly what happened.

Tom

'Oy! I said put the kettle on. You're in breach of health and safety regs – a man could die of dehydration over here before you'd bleedin' notice. Your turn to buy the biscuits as penalty for ignoring managerial instructions.' John lobbed a box of tea at me and it hit me on the ear.

I picked up the box and placed it next to the kettle, which I filled and flicked on. 'Sorry, boss. Bit preoccupied,' I said, heading out to get some biscuits from the garage shop next door. Watching Saffron stomp off down the street with her hair bouncing along behind her had kind of got to me for the rest of the day. The bag she was carrying was almost as big as her and I could tell it was way too heavy for her to carry for long. I wanted to carry it for her. I wanted to take her safely home and promise to help. I wanted to, and I probably should have done . . . but I didn't.

'I pay you too much,' John said, reaching for his mug and the biscuits I'd just bought. 'Double choc 'n' nut cookies? Fancy!' John took six at once and dunked them into his mug, two at a time. 'Shit and piss!' he hissed as one of the biscuits broke in half before it reached his mouth and disappeared back into the tea. He quickly shoved two dusty fingers into his mug and scooped the sludge into his mouth. 'Where's your head been all day? Your mind's not been on the job since you went walkabout this morning. It's got to be a girl. It's always a girl.'

'I could tell you but then I'd have to kill you,' I joked, not sure I wanted to elaborate on the whole Saffron thing I had going on.

'Kill me then,' John said, reaching for another biscuit. 'Only, put me out of my misery and tell me what the fuck is making you as useless as a knitted condom or I'll tell you all about the time I sacked my apprentice and got a proper person in to do the job.'

I told him then . . . about Saffron, and Angela, and everything in between.

Saffron

My feet were killing me and so were my shoulders and I was badly regretting packing my college books, the make-up mirror, loads of toiletries *and* the extra two pairs of shoes on top of everything else. It was dawning on me that I had absolutely no idea what to do if Daniel didn't get back to me soon, as going home to get my ID myself was not something I was prepared to consider.

The air had turned a weird yellow, and the sky had gathered more gloom, bruising the clouds with an impending storm. 'That's all I need!' I said, my face tipped upwards, at which point, in a super ungainly slapstick kind of way, I tripped on the kerb and found myself sprawled like an upturned turtle on the pavement, the weight of my hold-all pinning me down.

I think I was saying 'Ahhgggrnnnng' when the face of a concerned man appeared, looking down at me as the first drop of rain landed on my cheek. 'You OK?' he asked, reaching out his hand and unravelling me from the hold-all. 'Your bag is pretty heavy,' he said.

No shit, Sherlock!

'Yeah, ridiculously heavy, I know,' I sighed, using Tom's words, as the guy pulled me to my feet.

'Going anywhere nice?' he asked, holding the bag while I brushed myself down and examined the hole I'd just made in my tights.

'Just on my way to visit a friend,' I lied.

'Cigarette?' He offered me a packet with one of the cigarettes extended but took it for himself when I declined. 'University?' he asked, nodding his head in the direction of the university buildings, while flicking at a lighter and squinting as he released a plume of smoke between us. More raindrops landed on his shoulders and my hair.

'School. Sixth-form college,' I answered, wishing I was at university so I had options to stay with people who didn't have to ask their mums and dads!

When another drop of rain hit me on the side of my nose, followed by several on the pavement, I knew that the sky was going to burst open very soon. I didn't want to be caught in it when it did.

'Watch where you're going now,' the guy said, sucking deeply on his cigarette again, smoke mushrooming from each nostril and throwing a glance down at my clumsy chunky booted feet before walking away.

A listless woman wearing the orange shirt and blue waistcoat uniform of the American diner I was sitting in offered me a menu before asking me what I wanted to drink. I expect if I had to work there and wear that awful outfit I would be lacking in any enthusiasm too. Her badge said she was called Annabel, a pretty name that didn't belong to the expressionless face in front of me. She held her notepad and pen in her hands while staring out of the window at the world outside and the lazy fat rain that was plopping onto the pavement.

'Burger, chips and a Coke please,' I asked.

'And bacon and cheese on the burger, please.' I loved my food and ever since smelling the bacon sandwich Dad had cooked that morning, I was famished. The roll of Melanie's money in my bag was proving to be useless so I might as well enjoy eating some of it. Even the Youth Hostel wouldn't let me in without ID, according to the website. How can cash not be 'secure payment'?

When the meal arrived I posted chips into my mouth with my fingers, while wondering where the hell I was going to go when I left the cafe. 'Answer your phone you little shit,' I hissed yet again, as another of Daniel's 'Yeah's came out through my phone. What was he doing? He *must* be home by now. His stomach always got the better of him, he was such a hog. I ordered apple pie and ice cream to follow my burger and chips, and as I ate it, I uploaded my mother's photograph to all my social media sites, asking everyone I was 'friends' with to 'please share' on my behalf.

Searching for her name, Caroline Hayes, only brought a disappointing array of photos from women who bore no resemblance to my mum even after trying to mentally add at least ten years to her face. I didn't know when the photo I had was taken – it could have been longer than ten years ago for all I knew. It's not like there were many to choose from in our house – presumably because Dad had tried to hide all evidence of her to stop us asking too many questions. She would be forty now. What did forty-year-old mums look like? Grey? Fat? After a disappointing hour I tried typing her maiden name, 'Caroline MacIntyre', and did the same thing all over again.

What if she didn't even use media sites? Not all old people did. In fact, one boy in my A level art class said his mum didn't even have a smart phone! How did that woman even *live* without one? But surely *someone* who knew my mother would see my post and that someone would let her know I was looking for her. I had her hair so I knew exactly how hard it would be for her to totally disappear into a crowd.

Until this morning, I'd never really questioned why we didn't know any family on my mother's side, and her brother, David MacIntyre, had such a common name that the world was full of them, as I was quickly finding out.

A load of filling from my burger had at some point cascaded down my front, leaving a trail of relish and plastic cheese on my white T-shirt, with a huge slice of onion sticking to it like a badge. Taking a handful of folded paper serviettes, I tried to wipe it away, but merely spread it around, pressing greasy red stains into the fabric in several places. 'This is the worst week of my whole life!' I moaned under my breath. 'If you'd answered your phone, Daniel, I could have my ID and be heading for a B & B, a hot shower and some clean clothes by now!'

The first feelings of real worry were beginning to prickle their way up my back. What if I didn't find anywhere to stay? Would I go back home? Visions suddenly crowded my head: the briefcase, the unsent get-well cards, Melanie's nakedness in my mother's bed, the years and years of imagined conversations with the ghost of my mother, Dad telling us she was dead because he wished she was. We had been children, we had no choice in what he *wished*. We had believed it because he made it that way. The hatred I felt for both of them surged until I was bursting and I knew without a doubt that I was not going home even if me and my hold-all had to stay out all night.

By my third Coke, my phone was giving off tiny *tings* to alert me to people reacting to my posts. My heart joined in with its own caffeine-enhanced reaction for each of the first fifteen *tings* in case it was her – only for me to find it was just people pressing 'like' or 'shared' or making sympathetic comments like 'I hope you find your mum soon', or unhelpful ones like 'I thought only dads did the running off'.

By the 135th *ting* I was getting fed up with all the people who thought it was OK to chuck their opinion out there for all the world to see. In amongst the supportive stuff were stupid comments including how she must have reasons for not keeping in touch and I should forget about her, or she must have been murdered, or possibly kept as a sex slave. One person suggested she was having an identity crisis and supported their argument with a photo of a ginger-bearded hill-billy, while many postings claimed to have seen her in several different locations around the world. She'd been on the number seven bus in Wolverhampton, was an air steward on a plane bound for Russia, served in a pastry shop in America and was possibly someone's dentist in Ireland. She was everywhere . . . and yet she was nowhere.

While I sat there, Dad rang my phone again and I left it until voicemail came on. I still wasn't going to give him the satisfaction of answering it.

'*Saffy, I know you're with your friend Tom so I hope you're OK. I keep trying to find the words to tell you how it was and what happened all those years ago, yet somehow the right words just evade me. I need to tell you everything but I don't know where to start.*'

There was a pause, then an intake of breath and I found myself fidgeting with the ever-increasing hole in my tights as I waited for the rest of the message. '*Your memories of when your mum was here? I know how you remember her . . . slim, pretty with sun-kissed skin and freckles. Amazing auburn hair that fell in whirls to the small of her back and very green eyes that shone like they were lit up inside. She was like autumn on a warm, sunny day. You look very much like her and you have all her best bits, if only you knew it. And . . . and she was always doing something mad like dancing in the rain or running barefoot in the grass. She loved parties and garden picnics or last-minute holidays to far-flung places.*'

As he talked, I found old memories sliding into my mind like faded photographs dropping out of a virtual family album. I tried to grab each one and hold on to it as it came hazily to the forefront. A barbecue where people just kept arriving, games organised on the lawn, music and children and food and drink. Holidays at the end of very long flights, coconut trees and temples, heat and sunburn and jetlag. A mountain, a festival, a camping trip. And arguments, slamming doors and long unhappy silences.

'*She was . . .*' He stopped mid-sentence, followed by a long pause.

'She was what?' I asked the message, my heart quickening.

106

My mother was . . . awesome? Exciting? Not as young as Melanie?

'*She was . . . irresponsible,*' he sighed eventually, '*and I . . . I . . . and I didn't think she was looking after you properly. I believed I could do a better job . . . with Melanie.*'

The message ended there, the answerphone unable to squeeze any more of his bullshit into its recording time. He had taken it upon himself to be both judge and jury back then. He had decided that her flamboyant behaviour was irresponsible because she wasn't a stereotypical mother. Well, perhaps Daniel and Archie and I had wanted a non-conformist mother. Had he thought of that?

I dragged the huge bag into the minuscule toilets and heaved it onto the hook behind the door. There was no way I was going to put my bag down and I wasn't going to open the zip to get a clean top out and risk everything inside falling onto the dirty floor either. I used the toilet, attempted to wash the stain on my top, checked the corners of my mouth for food, then zipped up my leather jacket and manhandled my bag out of the cubical. Everything I tried to do with this bag was such an effort.

Glancing outside where the steady rain was now covering the ground with a dark, damp sheen, I pulled out two crisp twenty-pound notes to pay. 'Was everything OK for you today?' asked Annabel, putting the notes into the till.

'It was the best meal I've had in a long time because my stepmother paid for it,' I said, pocketing the change. It had been the only thing OK with my day. Stepping onto the street, the rain gathered in size and speed almost instantly, like it had just been waiting for me, but the brilliant idea that popped into my head in that second made me wonder why I hadn't thought of it before. I reached for my phone.

Me: Can I use your credit card for a hotel?

My text was captured inside shiny droplets that landed on the screen, magnifying the letters in perfect watery domes. Even if Tom couldn't put me up at his house, he could help me get somewhere to stay. He could do that much at least. A huge sense of relief came over me at the thought of being out of the rain and cosied up in a hotel room very soon.

Tom: I don't own a credit card

And that was the end of that brilliant idea. I would not be staying anywhere tonight.

Tom

So Saffron wanted my credit card! I didn't even have a credit card. Every penny that came into my pocket was out of it again in days. Hours, sometimes. The eight pounds and thirty-six pence I'd spread over the table in the cafe had been all the spare money I had until the end of the week, except for the two-pound coin I'd found in my overalls to buy biscuits at work. Even the florist had to put Angela's flowers on account.

'Is everything all right?' Angela asked, muting the TV. 'Only, your fork hasn't made it to your mouth.'

I shoved the fork of bolognese in and talked through it. 'Oh, it's just someone who assumes that money is an easy game.'

Angela frowned at my cryptic comment. 'It would be an easier game if we actually had some, but something tells me it's more than that.'

When I didn't reply Angela shook her head and un-paused the show. The sound of it filled the already-full room. We lived in a tiny two-bedroom flat, which had a spare bed. The door to that room was open and I could see the clean floral duvet from where I was sitting. I could have told Saffron she could stay in it. I could have rung her there and then and told her to come round but I didn't. Instead I scraped the last of my meal off my plate and onto my fork and tried to imagine what Saffron would think if she could see me and Angela right now. Our dinner was on our laps because there wasn't enough space in our flat for a table, let alone for a dining room to put a table in. And, invisible amongst everything, was my own secret sadness that this way of living was no way of living at all.

If I was a wild animal, I would be a bird and I'd fly away.

Saffron

The clouds finally completely dumped everything they had to give just as I was crossing Jubilee Gardens, the central green in the middle of town. The yellow air from earlier had turned almost purple as the rain threw itself down, making the ground come alive with bouncing pearls of water. A sudden crack of thunder overhead forced me to run as best I could with my hold-all to the edge of the green for the nearest shelter, which happened to be the pay point of a car park.

A small patch of concrete under the Perspex canopy of the pay point was still dry, so I gratefully placed my hold-all down, trying to avoid the worst of the greying discs of discarded chewing gum glued to the ground. Sitting down on my bag and hoping not to crush my carefully packed stuff, I pulled my over-the-knee socks up as high as they would go, vainly trying to cover the hole now steadily spreading across my thigh. My leather jacket was reasonably waterproof, but my beanie was soaking and so was my hair, which had rain slipping off the spirals and dribbling onto my shorts and tights. Shivering, I felt more than a little sorry for myself as the storm, oblivious, continued to batter against the Perspex, and the open sides did little to keep the rain from blowing in.

A man in heavy walking boots appeared, wearing dark grey trousers and a black outdoor jacket with the hood pulled over his head to protect him from the weather. He looked homeless and I felt a twist of unease pull at me. I was not at all comfortable with being in such a small place with someone like him. He carried a huge dirty rucksack and a cardboard sign asking for donations for a room for the night, plus a red cap containing some loose change, which he placed on the ground next to the sign. Then he removed a large black plastic bin bag from his pocket, which he proceeded to spread on the ground before sitting on it and placing the cap on it. He was obviously a lot more prepared than I was. He nodded over at me and I turned my gaze rapidly away to study the chewing-gum discs on the ground.

'You'll get your stuff damp,' he called over the noise of the rain. His voice had an indistinct northern accent, and as he pushed his hood off his head, I could see from his face that he was young, probably early twenties, and he had shoulder-length brown hair that hadn't seen shampoo for several days, possibly even weeks.

'Yeah, well, I don't have a plastic bag,' I answered, believing, right then, that a plastic bag would have been a luxury item. He was right, the rain was forming rivulets on the ground, which were trickling my way along the dips, but I eyed him nervously, putting a protective hand on the zip pocket of my hold-all that still contained the cash I'd stolen. He could probably overpower me within seconds, or rob me, scattering used syringes in his wake, or *anything*. I prepared to leap up and run if necessary, but I could hardly see as far as the cars in the car park for the sheets of grey rain cascading down. Even with a leather jacket on I would be soaked through within seconds.

The guy then fished in his other pocket and pulled out another bin bag, which he handed to me. 'Go on,' he said, waving the bag in my direction.

'Expecting guests?' I asked, trying to sound confident, but taking the bag all the same.

He laughed. 'Got to be prepared,' he said, as he brought out a packet of cheese and onion crisps, which he ate slowly, picking them out of the bag with dirty fingers, before unscrewing the lid from a bottle of summer berry juice and sipping at it. In the meantime I spread out the bag he gave me, checking carefully that it was clean, before placing my hold-all on top of it and sitting back down. I got out my phone, checking impatiently to see if any relevant messages were through yet from either Daniel or someone who knew my mum, but there was nothing new – only another voicemail from Dad, which could wait.

'This is normally my area,' the guy shouted, looking at me with dull eyes that vaguely resembled a dead fish. 'Chuggy has it when I'm not here, but he's somewhere else now . . . but you could try it when neither of us are here.' He shifted his position until he was cross-legged and moved the cap full of change in front of him.

'Oh . . . God! . . . I'm not *begging*,' I answered, eyeing the cap, horrified that he would think such a thing. 'I'm just keeping dry.' I pointed towards the rain as if he might not understand this very temporary dilemma.

A woman suddenly ran up to the pay machine, hurriedly

shoving her parking ticket in the slot of the machine. She carefully ignored us both, looking in every direction except the ground – at the unexpected people near her black patent-leather heels. She held on to a navy umbrella in one hand with its pattern of red Scottie dogs, while digging in her pockets for change with the other. Then she rooted in her handbag before again looking frantically around her, every which way but down.

The guy raised his dead-fish eyes, trying to meet her gaze, but she wasn't having any of it; she would not look down. Couldn't he see she obviously didn't have enough change to pay for her ticket, let alone give to him? I felt like standing up and announcing, *I'm not like him. I'm not begging. My father's a liar but he's also a chartered surveyor. I'm respectable.* Thankfully I thought it, rather than did it, because just then, the guy spoke to her. 'How much do you need?' he asked, in his flat-vowelled kind of way, loud enough for her to hear through the noise of the rain. This took both me and the woman by surprise, her blue eyes and my farm-slurry eyes darting between the hat with the change in it and the guy holding it out to her. He had to repeat what he said twice, before she could bring herself to acknowledge him properly. Reading the cardboard sign asking for money, she was clearly uncomfortable with the idea that a homeless person was, in fact, appearing to offer *her* money.

'Go on,' the guy said, placing his fingers over the loose change. 'What d'you want?'

The woman flushed pink from the obvious embarrassment of having to take money from a *homeless person*, while I nearly laughed out loud at the irony of it. Here was someone who had a car, an umbrella and a pair of very new and shiny shoes, being given charity by someone who had next to nothing except the change in his hat. Eventually, she managed to answer him. 'Well . . . I need another twenty pence.' She squirmed.

The guy fished out a twenty-pence piece and handed it up to her with his long, dirty fingers. She took it, with her own beautifully manicured nails flashing a diamond ring, and dropped the coins into the pay slot. The ticket whirred and spat itself back out, cleared of its fee. She took it, still flushing to the roots of her recently washed hair. 'Thank you,' she said, smiling genuinely at him, before she left, as if he had now earnt the right to be a real human being.

'Isn't it supposed to be the other way round?' I asked him. 'You know . . . they give *you* money?'

'Yeah. Ideally, but I had twenty pence and she needed twenty pence. Normally people have change left over for parking so if I'm lucky they give some to me – that's why I've made this my area – but occasionally it works the other way round.'

I re-read his sign saying twenty pounds would get him shelter for the night and my hopes lifted. 'Can anyone go there?' I asked, pointing at the battered bit of cardboard, believing this could be the perfect solution to my bed for the night.

'It's a night shelter . . . for the homeless. There are rules . . . and you've got to be over eighteen to stay in this one.' He unscrewed the cap of his berry fruits and took another sip.

Here we go again! 'What if you're seventeen?' I persisted.

'Depends . . .'

'Depends on what?' I asked.

'If you're vulnerable. If you're a runaway or not. If you've had to get out of a bad situation, abuse or something, then

115

there's support for that. If you've just left home just because you fancy it, then you're on your own.'

'I haven't run away from home just because I *fancied* it,' I answered heavily, unwilling to explain how I wasn't convinced the council or Social Services or whoever they were would understand if I said I'd run away from my five-bedroom, three-bathroom house, with conservatory and double garage, situated on the desirable west side of town, because my chartered surveyor father, who gave me a generous allowance, had been lying to me. My guess was that my situation probably wouldn't class as 'at risk' other than at risk of sounding a bit pathetic.

I was failing miserably at running away, but I was one-hundred percent NOT going to go home and my previous hint of panic was now properly licking at my guts. What was I going to do? 'So seventeen year olds can't run away?' I sighed.

'Only if they're eighteen,' he answered and managed to smile at his own little joke, revealing fairly decent teeth for a homeless guy. 'They *can* run away, and do. In some cities the streets are full of them . . . and younger . . . much younger, quite often. If they don't want to go in to foster care or whatever the council organises for them, they end up sleeping rough or find squats, friends . . . pimps.'

I imagined a squat with mashed-out people, off their brains on stained mattresses peppered with old needles. The thought made me shiver, as did the idea of a gold-chained pimp 'helping' me find somewhere to stay for the night. I might not have been totally successful at leaving home, but I wasn't naive – there was no way I was going to end up in any kind of dodgy situation.

Even so, I was currently at a complete and utter loss about where to stay.

A fat-bellied man in a uniform appeared out of nowhere, his hair and shoulders glistening with rain, and told us to move on. 'Come on, William, and you, miss, you know you can't be here.' I watched 'William' immediately and obediently get up, pick up his sign and reach for his hat with the change as if he was on automatic pilot; as if, for him, being moved on was part of a completely normal routine. But it wasn't part of *my* routine. *He thinks I'm one of them* . . .

'I'm only doing my job, guys.' He sounded apologetic, while making sweeping movements with his hands as if he were sweeping rubbish away.

I was incensed. 'I'm just waiting for it to stop raining, and *he* just gave a woman some money to get out of the car park . . . to *help* her!' I said, looking up at him, past his belly and into his apologetic eyes, refusing to get up obediently as William had done.

'It intimidates people,' the security guard answered. 'The women don't like it when they've got their purses out and the homeless are hanging about,' he finished, trying to mime-sweep us away then, instead, stood with both arms pointing at the exit, as if we wouldn't know how to negotiate our way out of the two-metre-square area without his help.

'I'm not homeless! And I'm not doing any harm.' I was indignant that he would even think to put me in the same category as William. I wasn't going to move. He couldn't make me and he couldn't touch me, or I'd scream – loudly! I was prepared to stay there, glued to the pavement like the old gum that was down there.

'It isn't worth it,' William mumbled. 'He'll have you moved anyway.' He hoiked his rucksack onto his back, pulled his hood over his unwashed hair again, and began to leave.

'He's right, I will,' said the fat-bellied man, one hand on his hip and the other holding a walkie-talkie. I could hardly believe I was being moved on, but if I didn't get up right now this guy was going to have me forcibly removed and that would probably involve name taking and parent contact, which I wasn't about to let happen. I regretfully lifted my hold-all back onto my sore shoulders and stood up. I was being treated like William. Like I was an inconvenience on the street to be avoided . . . like dog crap on the pavement.

We made our way through the car park, me and William, as if we knew each other, as if we were part of the same kind of life. As if my Vans and Valentinos made no difference any more. 'Are you going to that shelter?' I asked him, raising my voice as a roll of thunder sounded overhead, pointing to the wording on his sign again.

'Nah,' he answered. But he didn't look disappointed as such, more like his dead-fish eyes had accepted his fate long ago.

As we walked with our heads down, the rain carried on chucking its way out of a spectacular sky, inking the clouds with navy and grey and purple, which flashed with sheet lightning only seconds after each deep rumble of thunder. It all would have been great viewed from the panoramic window of a penthouse suite, but in tiny shorts and ripped tights . . . not so much! 'Where are you heading then?' I asked William, wondering where someone like him would spend the night.

'The bridge down by the river. It isn't the Ritz, but it's dry. You can come if you like, might be safer than anywhere else if you're new.'

That wasn't quite what I was hoping to hear. 'The bridge? To sleep?' Could I stoop that low? Could I really sit under there all night until tomorrow . . . with a homeless person?

I would not go home. I *needed* my dad to feel the empty space I left. To feel even just a little bit of the whole rotten organ-ripping, heart-tearing agony that I had going on, and even then I didn't think he could appreciate just how bad I felt. I knew it was a stupid idea, but the red-haired girl who didn't give a shit, who had lived inside me for years, followed William to the bridge.

Saffron

The bridge had guests. My nose told me before my eyes did that Crazy Maggie had found her way there, and the storm had also brought a couple of others – a man and a woman had lit a fire on the opposite side of the river. Maggie was out cold, her chest heaving up and down under her layers of blanket and her straw hat balanced over her face. Once William and I arrived, it was all . . . positively cosy – almost a party!

The bridge was a concrete structure that spanned the river running through town. It was held up by fat concrete pillars that helped form a screen between the pedestrian path and this band of homeless people. I sat down nervously on my newly acquired plastic bag, pretended a confidence I didn't feel, and eyed up everyone's cardboard with a jealousy I didn't know it was possible to muster for something normally reserved for recycling day. The ground beneath me was dank and the air had a chill to it that only lurks in such unloved corners.

I was trying very hard not to be frightened. This was not where I'd planned to be when I walked out of the house this morning. When I'd packed my pyjamas and my stripy slipper socks, I'd imagined staying in Tom's house or, the very least, *someone's* house, their mum cooking dinner and offering me the spare bed. I wondered what Tom was doing. Was he curled up on the sofa watching television with Angela, or going out to the pub with his mates, or having a romantic meal somewhere?

Despite the fact that I was not happy being under the bridge, the people there didn't *feel* like a gathering of villains waiting to do me harm, more like a pathetic gathering of people who'd failed to keep within the boundaries of normal. William hadn't questioned why I was following him like a stray dog across town, he'd merely said, 'You'll be all right with the people who use this place, they're generally harmless.' *Generally* harmless? I replayed William's words in my head. Could that be translated as, they were *mostly* harmless but *occasionally* dangerous?

There was evidence of other people having spent the night here many times before, making me wonder if other homeless people could turn up at some point. A crumpled, discarded navy-blue sleeping bag was lying on the ground on top of a thin mattress, which was lying on top of more cardboard. Empty food cartons, an empty bottle and some cans littered the ground, and someone had once built an elaborate structure out of cardboard and plastic worthy of a Cuban shanty town. Tucked away between two bushes to the edge of the bridge was a green tent that you would hardly know was there unless you were looking for it.

It was still early, the light not yet completely sucked out of the day, but I was exhausted from tramping the streets with the weight of everything that was now thankfully off my back and on the ground, out of the rain. The bridge, being just a bridge, was cold and dingy and I longed for my bedroom so badly it hurt. The night stretched ahead of me and the stuff in my bag was no good to me here other than to lean against. The magnifying mirror, pore strips and frizz control serum was pointless when I couldn't wash or change . . . or even sit on a comfortable chair. No big blue cushions here, plump and soft against the oatmeal weave of our huge matching sofas. No rug on the floor or fifty-five inch TV on the wall, or bowl of freshly made popcorn on the coffee table. No Daniel and me watching our favourite series on television, him clicking his fingers to command Archie or the brat to bring us drinks. Thankfully there was no evidence of syringes. Even so, despite what William said, I felt like I was surrounded by total weirdos and because of that, the storm and the intermittent roar of overhead traffic, I was absolutely not going to sleep a single wink.

A rustle of fabric and plastic told me that Maggie had woken up. She made the revolting sound of phlegm being forced up her throat, then snorted through her nose before swallowing hard. Grunting and heaving she made her way to a sitting position, raising a hand in greeting to the people over the other side of the river.

'All right, Mag?' the woman called, just as a roll of thunder clattered its way overhead, followed almost immediately by the horizon flashing a white sheet of light behind buildings and trees. They waved their cans at her then the guy nodded towards the outside world. 'It's a goodun, ain't it?' he said, not waiting for an answer before waving his can in my direction. 'Who's yer friend?' he asked.

Not me. Not me. Don't notice me. I am not her friend.

The hiss of a can being opened was the only answer she gave as she held it up to him like some kind of alcoholic greeting. A homeless salute. Maggie's slurping and sucking on the can were at odds with the red strawberries pinned to her straw hat and the bracelet of pretty blue beads that hung off her wrist.

I pulled a bottle of orange fizz from my bag, which created a hiss of its own. I burped its artificial sweetness through my nose, which stung high up in my nostrils, and wished I had alcohol too. I could suddenly see why they did it. A dark and desperate form of escape. The flipside of fun. There were hours and hours to endure until tomorrow, an interminable age, an empty stretch of time, to wish away as fast as possible. I was just going to have to ride it out until I could have breakfast in a warm cafe somewhere before hunting down Daniel on his way to school. There was absolutely nothing to do under that bridge except wait and check the endless *tings* on my phone for news of my mother. And listen to another voicemail from Dad . . .

'Hi, Saffy. Hopefully you're being looked after and you're having a bit of space. I'm not very good at this, am I? I keep trying to explain and I keep getting it wrong. I suppose telling you Mum had died was a knee-jerk reaction to you finding us that night . . . I'm so sorry but you weren't supposed to stumble upon that. We'd been seeing each other for a while but I wasn't ready to tell you all. And I know I said this morning that I wished your mum was dead . . . and that was true, I did . . . do . . . Oh God . . . this is still sounding all wrong.'

There was another long pause before he began trying to absolve himself of sin again.

'I wanted you to love Melanie . . . I wanted us to start again as a family.'

A large swallow gurgled in his throat.

'Do you remember when you were little and I'd come home from a work trip and gather you kids into my arms? You would climb onto my shoulders, Daniel on my back and Archie would cling to my leg while I walked through the house? There is no feeling like it in the world, Saffy. My family was everything to me . . . is everything to me.'

There was another pause.

'Your mum was beautiful and fun . . . so much fun, but that's not enough in my book. It's like she would gather you up in everything that was exciting, throw you into the air, and forget to catch you all. She was like . . . she was like a world unto herself, Saff . . .'

The answerphone beeped again and I was left with silence, within which I just hated him more. She sounded wonderful. Who cared if she threw us into the air or was a world unto herself, whatever all that meant? What made Melanie better than that? I imagined him pacing the warm kitchen at home with his phone to his ear, fumbling for words that might make me forgive him. Maybe a coffee steaming on the side or a tumbler of whisky with ice. The boys would be in their bedrooms playing games and Charlotte would be asleep, cocooned in feathers and teddy bears. I wasn't part of all this any more. I had a responsibility now and that responsibility was to tell my mother I loved her and had never forgotten her.

A nobble of stone dug into my skull when I leant my head against the wall so I shuffled a bit to the side and piled my hair inside my damp grey beanie, using it as a built-in cushion.

I probably looked like a young kid with a massive head, but at least I was less noticeable with my hair tucked away – and it worked – the wall became soft behind my head, allowing me to close my eyes, willing myself to be anywhere other than where I was.

Behind my lids it was warm and the sun shone. I was back in the garden of our old house, the lawn stretching down to a high beech hedge with a summer house in the corner. The paddling pool was out and Daniel and I were chasing each other with cups of water, dipping them in the pool and throwing the contents, squealing and laughing. Daniel was only three and kept missing, but he loved the game all the same. Archie was on a rug laughing as the drops of water flew through the air and landed on him, his fat arms reaching out to catch them as we ran past. It was so hot. The blistering kind of brightness of rare summer days. We stopped our game and fell on the rug next to him, sipping at lemonade and giving Archie a taste. Then I pulled them both onto my lap and we hunted for shapes in the sky. Only one cloud in a vast expanse of blue rolled slowly above our heads, obligingly changing from an elephant to a cat to a sea-horse in front of our eyes. 'Look! See the ears, and the trunk . . . now the tail?' I said to Daniel while Archie clung his little hands round my neck, his hot body against my skin. We played this game until the last cottony animal floated over the horizon and Archie began to scream. Then Dad appeared, stepping into the garden at the end of a long day, an angry look on his face, his arms reaching for Archie whose red sunburnt cheeks were bright against the white linen of his work shirt.

'Soup kitchen,' Maggie suddenly said, jerking me away from

my sweet memory with its confusing end, and I watched how she heaved herself up and William followed.

'What's the soup kitchen?' I asked William, unwilling to engage in any nutty confrontation with the town's crazy.

'Dinner. It's Tuesday so it's over this way,' Maggie answered before William could speak, smacking her lips. She took a clear plastic hood from her pocket and pulled it over her hat, tying a knot under her chin. I stood up too, even though thanks to the burger, chips, apple pie and ice cream, I wasn't in the slightest bit hungry. Sticking with them felt safer than being left on my own.

'The soup kitchen is a mobile cafe that comes on a Tuesday to this part of town,' William explained. 'It's free for the vulnerable and homeless.' He tapped his own chest to indicate that he was one of the vulnerable and homeless.

'And what do you do all the other days?' I asked, wondering how they survived between soup kitchen Tuesdays.

'Volunteers sometimes collect leftover sandwiches and cakes and stuff from cafes at the end of the day and distribute them round by the library. We'd be a bit stuck without that, although some people give us money.'

The soup kitchen was a large white van and there was already a group of people hanging round it when we got there, their heads bent low to avoid the worst of the rain. The side doors of the van were open and inside was a table top holding two big pots containing something steaming. A lady wearing a green hijab, which circled her beautiful face, was inside the van, ladling soup into cups and handing them over to outstretched hands. Beside her, doing the same, was a young girl wearing several piercings, a blue beanie and a huge smile. Maggie, who'd ditched her trolley back at the bridge, was queuing for some hot food while William was standing by a man with a large sack of clothes.

So this was the town's homeless. The hidden people who came out from cracks in the ground to be fed by visible people who cared. It was a bizarre experience. Like an entire underworld I was never aware of, existing right here in the place where I live, like the city was seeping a festering secret that oozed out after dark. There were even kids who were possibly younger than me, like William said, trying to be independent of whoever they were running from, yet reaching out their hands for something to eat, like a scene from a modern-day *Oliver Twist*. Where were they sleeping tonight, I wondered?

It reminded me of a conversation I'd had with Tom that same day he'd rescued me from the girl and her mother in the park when I bunked off after-school care. Maggie had trundled past as we threw stones at the can in the river. 'She must be lonely,' I'd commented.

'Yessss!' replied Tom, congratulating himself on having successfully hit the can. 'She's not the only one, you know. There are other street people.'

'Street people? You mean there are more Maggies?' I'd asked naively.

He snorted as if I'd missed something very obvious. 'Hundreds of them. Thousands, even. Grown-ups *and* children . . . all over the country.'

I'd argued with him then, thinking him stupid and using his own special terminology. 'Children aren't homeless, *shit for brains* . . . they're too young! They can't not have a home. Even orphans have a home.' Then it was his turn to frown back at me, as if he thought I was the one that was stupid.

'There are places that are called "homes" but they're just houses with a telly in them. Some kids don't want that kind of home. If your dad treats you right then your house is a *proper* home . . . even if your mum isn't there any more . . . even if your dad's new girlfriend is going to be there instead.' He had placed his hand between my shoulder blades and nudged me along the path, back in the direction of my house. 'Go home, Saffron. It's getting late. He'll be worried about you, especially seeing as after-school care finished half an hour ago.' Tom pointed at the town clock, saying it was nearly six o'clock.

My feet had hardly touched the ground as I ran along the path towards my house, my lime-green school bag banging against my back all the way. It was much later than I thought and I knew I would be in a whole heap of trouble for not being where I was supposed to be, especially as the police were already at our house, their car parked outside, Dad pacing the front drive.

'Where the hell have you been?' he demanded through gritted teeth. Weirdly, because I was in *so* much trouble, my new didn't-give-a-red-haired-shit defiance suddenly inflated, my courage growing inside me, like the Incredible Hulk of inner strength.

'Out?' I replied, allowing my beating heart to thump hard against my chest, undetected and perfectly disguised by a new impervious me. Ten minutes later, when the police had gone, the lecture over, Dad sat with his head in his hands, looking tired. I wanted to tell him I was sorry for making him feel so bad. But my body wouldn't allow me to go near him, and my mouth wouldn't open to say those words. Those feelings were trapped in a whole other life that existed before he brought *her* to our house. Before he slept with *her*. Before he told me my mother was dead.

'I think this needs a punishment, Saffy,' he said wearily. I stared hard, daring him to try. *You can't hurt me any more.*

'I don't care what you do.' I glanced over at the woman I'd found in his bed the night before. The woman with the shiny hair, who was now sitting in one of our armchairs – thankfully fully clothed. They shared a look with each other, and she suddenly looked too comfortable in our house, like she was a part of it and a part of my father, like he had just grown a woman-shaped limb. 'Is *she* going to hang about?' I asked.

My dad had looked me carefully in the eye before nodding. 'Yes!' That single word, a poison dart through my heart. 'You will see Melanie more often. Remember our conversation last night?' As if I needed reminding. Her naked breasts were burnt on my memory for ever.

Later, when Dad removed my CD player as my punishment, threatening to remove more of my precious things if I carried on behaving the way I was, I wondered if this was what Tom had meant. Is this how kids ended up in a house with just a telly in it?

No, *this* is what he actually meant. These were the children whose houses are not homes. 'Where do they sleep?' I asked William, wondering if it might be better to team up with people nearer my own age.

'Like I said earlier, squats, night buses, other people's sofas, doorways. Some of them camp out in the bushes by the motorway. Some of them are in gangs and some of them stay in the middle of town. I read that there's over a hundred thousand teens living rough, everyone with a story. But I still think you're probably better off under the bridge for tonight. The main high street isn't a good place to be in the middle of the night if you want to keep out of everything. Drunks, drugs, fights . . . it's a different world, trust me. I've learnt the hard way.' I listened to William telling me about a life I knew nothing of as I studied the people in front of me standing around the soup kitchen, clinging to their groups . . . like a post-apocalyptic culture, ready to protect themselves from an alien society. William was probably right, the bridge would be safer, tucked away out of the main thoroughfare.

I suddenly felt as if I'd been walking around my whole life without looking down – without noticing that the path beneath my feet was transparent and another life existed beneath it.

Dotted around were other helpers, men handing out clean donated clothes and coats to people who were trying them on for size. They didn't look too bad, the clothes . . . if you were desperate I suppose, but the lovely stuff in my bag became unexpectedly lovelier. The labels, the make-up, the toiletries and shoes. They were mine. Bought for me, picked out by me and carried by me. The heaviness of my hold-all suddenly becoming a burden I was grateful to have.

In a couple of hours all this would be gone and the people who walked this way in the morning would never know it had been here.

An older lady had set up an area with a chair under a temporary cover. Maggie was sitting on it eating the food from the van. The lady was removing Maggie's shoes and her many layers of socks, peeling them away until she revealed the most revolting pair of feet I had ever seen . . . and the lady was actually smiling! Talking to her as if they were simply having a picnic on a summer's day. My stomach suddenly attempted to reject its contents until I could taste sick, yet she carried on, smiling and scraping layers of dead skin away from dead black toes poking out of discoloured feet. She wiped them gently and dressed them carefully. I was essentially watching a real-life horror movie with an angel in it.

I had to move away from Maggie and her feet if there was going to be any chance of me keeping my earlier food down. I stood in a doorway, watching the rest of the show. The rain had slowed to a drizzle and it caught the orange light of the street lamps, briefly becoming illuminated before disappearing into the carpet of dark beneath it. I'd lost sight of William who, after winning a warm jumper from the guy with the clothes, had disappeared, so I resorted to waiting for Maggie to finish her beauty spa. I was clinging to the relative safety of another woman even though she was the town's crazy. I was tired and cold and my beanie was struggling to hold on to all my hair, the wet wool heavy on my head, but I wanted to disappear in this crowd, to hide in the cracks with everyone else. I checked my phone yet again – *please be there* – but the list of reactions to my posts was exhausting and did not reveal my mother. *Where are you, Mum? Don't you know I need you?*

When Maggie was ready to head back to the bridge for the

night, I stepped out of my doorway shelter and followed her, the stink only partially dampened by the rain. Yesterday I was avoiding her and today I was seeking her out. 'Do your feet feel better?' I asked her, hoping to cover up for the fact that I needed her company more than she needed mine.

'Oooh, they do . . . really lovely. My toenails had become so thick, bits of them were flying through the air. Nearly suffered shrapnel damage!' She laughed out loud at her joke before starting herself off coughing, until eventually a silence fell between us as we walked side by side along the path by the river. She stopped intermittently to top up her alcohol levels, drinking from a small bottle that she kept in her pocket. Before long I knew she would be finding her invisible friend and talking garbage again, but suddenly she piped up. 'It's not so much about my feet,' she said, 'it's about Maisy's hands.'

'Who's Maisy?' I asked.

'Maisy. The woman who does my feet. It's about her hands.' We walked a few more metres while I wondered what to say back. I was pretty confident Maisy and her hands would be dipped in a vat of anti-bacterial gel right now.

'Right,' I muttered, lamely.

Maggie stopped for a brief moment, took a drink from the bottle and turned to me. Her eyes, in the shadows of the park lamp, looked both clear and deeply sad as if the clouds of crazy had parted briefly. 'It's touch, lovey. You know, from another human being. She's the only person who'll go near me. Touch is a rare thing when you're me.'

'This your first night?' William asked, when he eventually made

132

it back to the bridge, pulling cigarette papers from his rucksack and waving a colourful and shiny little package towards me.

'I don't know what that is,' I said, not answering his first question but referring to the package.

'Spice . . .' he answered, dropping a pile of what looked like herbs or leaves into the cigarette paper and rolling it up, then sucking repeatedly on it as if he was in a hurry to get high.

I was instantly furious. *'That's that legal high stuff, synthetic marijuana, isn't it?* So you beg from hard working people for *shelter,* then use their money to take drugs instead of spending it on getting a bed for the night?' William said nothing. 'How could you? People give that money in good faith and that stuff's not even real weed, it's, like, *really* bad!'

He looked at me briefly. 'Yep . . . it's your first night! Real weed is illegal . . . I take out a bag of weed to make my day a little better than it is, and I'm arrested. Simple as that!' He tapped his hand on the shiny packet. 'Drugs are like being lifted out of a rotten place . . . cradled like a baby.' He shut his eyes and exhaled slowly and I guessed I had been dismissed.

When a huge man with a black beard stepped up to me, I thought it was the end of the line. William said the people who used this bridge were *generally* all right, but this was a mountain of a man looming towards me. I curled my fingers round the handle of my bag and wished I had asked the other kids where they were sleeping. He stood, near my feet, looking down until my insides started to tremble. He was wearing faded jeans with turn-ups at the bottom that were wet from the rain, and a dark padded jacket, down the back of which hung his long dreadlocks. I gripped my hold-all, preparing to scream really, really loudly if he took one single step closer. 'Got a knife or something like that?' he asked.

'Yes,' I lied, tapping my passion-fruit lip balm in my pocket. 'A big one.' *Why did he ask me that?*

'Good,' he replied. 'You look new. You shouldn't be on the streets with nothing to keep you safe. And put your phone down your pants when you sleep or it'll get stolen.' His voice was warm, clashing with the miserable cold of the bridge, then he moved away, towards the green tent, and opened the fly. 'If you've got a home, it's better than this,' he said, just before he climbed inside. I breathed out a lungful of panic. I guess that was his way of offering me advice and it made me feel a tiny bit easier. The huge guy was one of the *generally* harmless and relatively normal, despite the fact that he lived in a tent in the bushes, but I didn't want to go back home like he said. I wanted a new home with my mum.

'You can't sleep on that all night,' Maggie muttered, pointing to the plastic bag I was sitting on. 'You're going to get yourself a whole bunch of piles.' Unexpectedly, she handed me a wad of cardboard, which I placed on top of the plastic bag and sat back down. It felt like a small bit of comfort to my very uncomfortable butt. But despite the fragile companionship of this weird community, I wasn't going to sleep on it all night like Maggie said, because I wasn't going to sleep at all.

Something landed near me with a delicate thud. Maggie had also thrown a blanket. A large square of red wool in a clear plastic bag lay perfectly folded in front of me. 'Cashmere. That'll keep you warm. You wait till the middle of the night when the temperature drops and you're freezing your tits off.' Maggie

134

huffed at me then. I didn't know what that huff meant but it caused another gurgle of old phlegm to rattle its way up her pipes and into her mouth. From deep in one of her pockets she produced a crumpled bit of paper and spat the massive globule into it, giving it a good old examination before screwing it up and pushing it back into her pocket. My gag reflex went again, pulling at my stomach and filling my mouth.

With the tips of my fingers I took out the blanket, which to my surprise was actually a clean and incredibly soft pashmina. Instead of the pervading hum of ammonia I might have expected, a faint whiff of laundry powder was clinging faithfully to its fibres. Maggie huffed again, finished the last drop in her bottle, then opened a can and drank from it. 'You're a first night virgin,' she added.

'Is it that obvious?' I muttered, my heart sinking at the idea I wasn't blending in as I hoped. A possible target for some weirdo on the prowl. 'First night and only night. I'm never, ever, going to spend another night on the street once my brother brings me my ID and I can get somewhere to stay . . . somewhere decent.'

'Lucky you. You can leave us nobodies in the dirt where we belong.' She gulped greedily at her can until it was empty. Maggie was obviously going to get out of her head as soon as possible, so she could join William who was now somewhere off the planet.

One moment looking for photographs, the next moment spending the night with the town's loony tunes.

It was only one night. *I could do this.*

My phone lit up with a text.

Dad: Night, love. I'm here if you need me x

I stared at the shallow words before deleting them for good. 'I've never had so many texts from you, Dad. You're obviously on one massive guilt trip!'

The rain continued for the rest of the evening and well into the night. The initial deluge had given in to a relentless steady downpour, accompanied by huge cracks of thunder. My head longed for something other than brickwork and the bulky hold-all to rest on and my body became racked with uncontrollable shivers. White plumes of breath were now billowing out of my mouth, the earlier stormy heat to the day now gone. It was *freezing*! My pillow on my own bed seemed like an unreachable cloud – a wondrous, unappreciated, gathering of duck fluff, and I missed that sack of feathers more than the best friend I didn't have. I stretched the pashmina over my legs, pulling it towards my stomach. It was so warm that I could feel the tense muscles in my body begin to relax.

Maggie talked to herself for some time, the people opposite continued to top up their fire with pieces of paper and card, and a glow of light shone through the material of the tent. Several people hurried by on their way home through the rain and a gang of teenagers went running past, their footsteps slapping in the puddles, their random shouting echoing around me. Each time someone came past I prayed they wouldn't notice me, hiding under my beanie with only pashmina and lip balm for self-defence.

Time dragged, each minute that went by was worse than the next. My senses were alert to every sound that didn't belong to the cracking and rumbling of traffic overhead, my eyes wide, constantly searching the shadows for anything that might come out of them. This was *terrifying*! My phone battery or data wouldn't last if I watched videos on it, so I rationed myself, only looking at the alert banners as they popped up across the screen from time to time, in case there was news of Mum.

I wished more than anything that Tom would appear like he had in the park earlier. Nudging me with his brown boots. Pulling me to my feet . . . taking me away from here.

I was shivering violently now. I'd pulled a grey sweatshirt over the top of my leather jacket and had a sock on each hand but if it hadn't been for the red pashmina I knew I wouldn't have coped with the cold. I desperately wanted my mum. My slim, pretty with sun-kissed skin and freckles mum, with her auburn hair that fell in whirls to the small of her back and her green eyes that shone like they were lit up inside. She was like autumn on a warm, sunny day, he'd said. I allowed my mind to recreate her, as if she were actually standing right in front of me, forming her from my photograph and the way Dad described her. She was so close I could almost touch her. Holding the hem of her dress, her feet bare, her wild auburn hair in whirls down her back, her smile red. She became vibrant colours and shining green eyes, striking a match in the dim light, creating a flame, within which was my mum. She was illuminated and warm in the cold, dark space next to me. And then, when I didn't even know it was going to happen . . . I fell asleep.

Wednesday:
Adversity and Enlightenment

Tom

Last night Angela and I had turned the lights off and opened the curtains in our flat, watching the storm as if we were watching a movie. Sheet lightning had intermittently flashed white through the window all evening, highlighting everything in the world for a bright split second before plunging us into darkness again. 'I love a good storm,' Angela said, taking a sip of wine, just after a particularly loud crack of thunder sounded overhead.

'It's pretty amazing,' I agreed. 'Can you see the purple colour of it?' Another bolt of lightning obliged just at that moment, creating a horizon of black silhouettes against a lilac sky. I took a mouthful of cider and walked over to the window to get a better look, scanning the sky for the next sheet or fork of light, while the world below was taking a massive battering from the driving rain. It was the only time I didn't mind living in a block of flats – being able to imagine a life beyond this town.

As the storm continued, we shared the last bag of crisps in the flat between us. 'It's beautiful. Makes you want to go out and dance in it, doesn't it?' she said as I tipped the last crumbs into my mouth. 'Why don't we? Open the window a bit and put some music on low and we'll pretend.' So we did, we danced slowly with Ed Sheeran and the storm, while I tried not to ruin the moment by thinking of Saffron and how much easier it would be if I hadn't even met her. But I *had* met her. Like finding a freshly minted gold coin in a handful of old money, and a smile that was like a sunburst through cloud.

'That was lovely last night,' Angela said, as I joined her with a pile of toast and a pint of orange juice. She gestured out of the window. 'It looks like the world has been washed clean.' The curtains were still open and the windows still pearled with drops of water, but the steely sky now had a bright strip of silver above the horizon, highlighting where the river flowed and patches of green grew, and where the wild bird in me wished I could live. 'It doesn't change how I feel, though,' she continued as I bit into my toast.

'It doesn't change how I feel either,' I replied, tying the laces of my work boots and grabbing the toast and the bag with my overalls in, then I kissed her goodbye and tried to ignore how the creeping spread of guilt made cracks in my fortress.

Saffron

'Daniel!' I shouted as he walked among a herd of bedraggled teenage boys on his way to school. 'Come here!' I beckoned rapidly, indicating for him to move quicker than his normal lumbering gait. 'Do you *ever* look at your phone?' I snapped, when he got close enough to snap at. I was furious. Not just with Daniel but mainly because of my stolen bag. All my beautiful stuff, gone in one fell swoop!

'Hello to you too,' he answered sarcastically, without a single sniff at an apology. Two of his friends waited beside him and he towered over both of them.

'Yeah . . . you're dismissed,' I said, waving them both away from us before I turned my attention to Daniel. 'I've been ringing you and texting you since yesterday. Where have you *been?*'

'Have you tipped up to have a go at me, or do you want something?' he asked, his gaze following his mates who were now joining another gang of kids.

'If you ever checked your phone you'd know I want something. I've sent you a million texts since yesterday. How can you not know that?'

'I left my phone at Josh's house, he's bringing it today. What d'you want?' Daniel shoved his hands in his pockets and waited with barely a flicker of an eyelash.

'I'm going apoplectic here and you've got no idea what I've been through. I need some money,' I said, just as one of his mates put two fingers to his mouth and sent an ear piercing whistle in our direction. 'C'mon, Hayes.'

Daniel looked over his shoulder at his friends. 'You want what?'

'I want money. Can you give me some?' I repeated.

'It's a Parent Pay school. I don't need money.'

I held the flat of my hand out to him, waiting for him to hand over whatever was in his pocket. 'Don't prat about, Daniel, you've always got money.' I knew for a fact he could always get more.

'I don't have any.' He stood his ground, hands still shoved in his pockets, but I knew him better than that. My brother always had some money on him. How else did he fund the empty crisp and sweet packets that were always stuffed in his school rucksack?

'Hand it over,' I insisted, with my most threatening look, still with the flat of my hand thrust out, then, switching to a more desperate, 'Pleeease, Dan, I really need some.'

Daniel looked me steadily in the eye for the first time since I got there. 'Didn't you nick enough out of Melanie's bag?'

'Yeah. Well . . . I don't feel great about that, but that's gone. It was in my bag, which got stolen. It had everything in it. The money, and all my stuff. My beautiful stuff!' My genuine dismay at being robbed caught Daniel like a fish on a line, as slowly he withdrew a crumpled twenty-pound note, which he placed in my hand. I whipped it away before he changed his mind.

'Is that all you've got?' I asked, putting it in my own pocket next to yesterday's change from the cafe.

'Yes, it is. I need the rest for spends,' he huffed.

'Can you pack me another bag after school? And bring me my ID . . . and get me some more money . . . like a decent amount?' I asked, watching how his face turned from vaguely sympathetic to less sympathetic. 'Pleeease,' I whined again.

He stared hard, then nodded his head up and down as if agreeing to do exactly as I asked, then said, 'No.' I stared hard at him, my frustration building. 'In case you hadn't remembered, I'm going to the Lake District for geography.' My line went slack as the fish swam away. I took in the rucksack by his feet and realised that it was larger than his school bag – the two coaches at the side of the school surrounded by kids also with bags had totally escaped my attention. *Shit!* I'd have to get it myself when the others were out.

'Can I have your key then?' I asked, holding my hand out again. 'I left mine at home.'

'You're pretty useless at this running away lark, aren't you? No, you can't! I left my key at home too.'

Double shit!

'Has Archie got one?' I asked, already knowing that he didn't.

'You know he doesn't! What are you playing at, Saff? Dad and Melanie are going ballistic! They're having to lie to Charlotte and Archie that you're away on a last-minute school trip as well.'

'Well, with their track record, they should find lying easy,'

145

I snapped. We stared at each other then, Daniel looking down, and me looking up, fighting a silent eyeball battle. 'I need to find our mum, Daniel. And when I do, you'll be sorry you doubted her. I'm not giving up and I'm not coming home. I need my ID and some money so I can stay in a B & B or the youth hostel or something.'

He looked down at my stained T-shirt, the sweatshirt now tied round my waist, the socks shoved in my pockets and my badly laddered tights, and frowned. 'So where did you stay last night then?'

'With Tom, my friend when we were kids, remember?' I lied.

Daniel was still frowning. He knew me. He knew that I would never go out in public looking like this. 'And Tom doesn't have water in his house, or washing powder?'

'He didn't have any left,' I said.

'And did . . . *Tom* steal your bag then?'

'It got stolen on the way to Tom's. Took my eye off it for a moment and it was gone!' I crossed my fingers behind my back. The lies, though transparently crap, came easily. I was my father's daughter after all. 'Anyway, when d'you get home? I can't stay at Tom's long.'

'Friday afternoon,' he answered, glancing towards the coaches and seeing that kids were now starting to board. He picked up his rucksack and made to leave. My heart sank. Friday afternoon! How was I going to last another two whole nights before then?

'So you could bring me the stuff on Friday evening then?' I asked, my confidence at this whole running away thing so reduced it was almost in a pool around my feet. He shrugged some sort of agreement that I took to be a yes then I hugged

146

him, like he was now my most favourite person in the world. 'Friday evening, five o'clock at the bus stop near Josh's house. Don't forget!'

Now all I had to do was survive until then.

Having bought some wet wipes, a toothbrush and paste, plus deodorant and black tights from the pound shop, I spent some time searching for a shop or cafe that had a decent sized sink inside a decent sized clean toilet cubicle where I could have a bit of a wash. After several false starts, primarily due to the fact that most places didn't know how to use bleach, I eventually found one that would do. It was in the back of a large cafe where several people were eating cooked breakfasts and drinking hot drinks out of big white mugs. The cubicle was barely the size of a small wardrobe but it was clean and had large shiny white tiles on the walls. The sink was a tiny white rectangle with no plug but there was a dispenser with blue hand soap with a fresh cotton scent. It was OK. At first glance I looked unlikely to contract anything life threatening.

Locking the door I took everything off, hung my clothes carefully on a hook, and placed my feet on two paper hand towels to separate them from the invisible but likely germs on the floor. It wasn't easy washing with soap from the dispenser without a sponge or flannel, and even harder trying to dry myself with paper towels and an ineffectual wall-mounted air blower that kept turning off after three seconds. However, I finally managed it before putting my dirty clothes back on, then with fresh deodorant and clean teeth and my hair plaited into two long thick plaits, I felt a tiny bit better.

147

'It's staff . . . you OK?' said someone with a strong Mediterranean accent, tapping on the door.

I called back at her through the door. 'Yes, I'm fine, thank you . . . hang on . . . just putting on my boots.'

'Are you washing in there?' she asked.

'Yes,' I replied, tying my laces and putting my toiletries stuff back in the carrier bag.

'Could you not have washed before you left your house?' she said, beginning to sound cross, although I didn't have a clue why she should care.

'There wasn't exactly any plumbing where I slept last night,' I replied as I opened the door and pulled a wry smile for her benefit. Stepping out, I noticed the short queue of people who were waiting.

She looked at the stains on my top and noticed the pile of damp paper towels I'd thrown in the bin. 'You sleep rough?' she asked.

'Yeah, well it wasn't a bed of roses,' I answered, suddenly feeling very sorry for myself. I'd hoped she might understand but instead she had a go at me!

'We don't allow homeless people to use these facilities. It puts our customers off – we are not a charity.' The people waiting in the queue were looking fed up. I felt outnumbered and persecuted and pushed past them, muttering 'I'm not homeless' as their eyes travelled over me with disapproval. They'd probably called the waitress because I was taking too long, but it wasn't my concern. My concern was getting out of there before they could see me cry.

Dad: Are you OK? X

His text came through while I was eating my breakfast – an excessive, but therapeutic, pile of chocolate, washed down with Coke, which I consumed while making my way to a cash point to retrieve whatever money I had left on my card. I'd be more OK if Tom would get a guilt trip and let me stay at his. And I'd be even more OK if my mum would contact me. I ignored Dad's text and pushed my card into the ATM and waited for it to tell me how much I had – which, as it happened, turned out to be a massive *nothing*. I stared at the screen, willing it to produce some numbers and give me some cash, but suddenly remembered with a sinking heart the must-have new top that I'd bought on Saturday. That top hadn't even made it into my top-ten items to pack in the hold-all. It had been an impulsive purchase and if I hadn't made it would have left me another thirty pounds to spend right now.

Saffron

'You can't sleep here, you're going to have to find somewhere else to go.' A security guard was ushering Maggie away like she was dirt on the street. The library had suddenly seemed like a great place to go when there weren't many other great places to go: it was free and it was warm and it would have to do because I was completely knackered.

Maggie was waving the security guard away in return as if she was nothing more than an annoying fly. 'C'mon, Maggie, you know you can't stay here. People are trying to access the library,' she said, with no small amount of exasperation. A woman reached for her small son's hand, pulling him sharply away so they could get up the steps without being contaminated in some way.

Something at that moment tugged on me like a child on its mum's coat. This crazy lady had given me a blanket. This crazy lady had tried to help me when I was cold and uncomfortable. This crazy lady was being treated as if she was nothing but a nasty stain on the ground beneath everyone's feet. She only ever knew the tenderness of another human being when they were scraping the dead skin off her feet.

'Two croissants and two spiced lattes,' I said, handing over some of my precious money to the man behind the counter in the cafe next to the library. 'And can you hurry a bit?' I looked out of the window to where Maggie was steadfastly sitting on the steps, one protective hand on her trolley.

'Breakfast?' I said cheerfully as I handed her one of the croissants and plonked myself down next to her on the step. I gave her one of the cups of spiced latte. 'Pretend it's alcohol.' Maggie took both items off me as if we did this every morning, then she sank her rotten teeth into the soft pastry and chewed.

The security guard rolled her eyes at both of us. 'You still can't stay here, however many of you lot turn up.'

'I can't see the sign,' I said, frowning up at her.

'What sign?' she asked, looking around for the sign that I couldn't see.

'The sign that says "No sitting on the steps". You know, like a red circle with a line through it and a picture of a person sitting on steps. Nope. I can't see one.' I finished my looking around then took a mouthful of my drink, trying not to show her how much that latte burnt my mouth.

'She's causing an obstruction. I'm going to have to call the police,' the security guard said as Maggie licked her filthy fingers and pushed the last bit of her croissant into her mouth, along with whatever germ life and filth was under her nails.

'Because the police haven't anything better to do?' I said.

'Because she's causing a public nuisance,' she said.

'Public nuisance. Public nuisance,' Maggie parroted.

'Then why don't you sit somewhere else, if you know you're a public nuisance?' she said to Maggie.

'Because I'm a nuisance everywhere!' Maggie replied, rocking herself backwards and forwards until she'd built up enough momentum to heave herself to a standing position. Then she picked up her spiced latte and placed it in a little holder gaffer-taped to the handle of her trolley. Like William, Maggie seemed to ultimately accept that she was going to get moved on wherever she went.

'Happy now?' I lisped at the security guard with my burnt tongue. 'She wasn't doing any harm. Unless you were expecting a coach load of very fat people to turn up and link arms in groups of five to use these steps, she wasn't actually causing an obstruction at all.'

'No need to make a song and dance about it . . . just move along please,' she said, clearly relieved we were finally going.

'Song and dance,' Maggie repeated. Then suddenly she winked at me as if letting me into her secret world, and started singing at the top of her voice, 'Life is a cabaret, old chum!' This came out unnecessarily loudly but surprisingly tunefully. She was causing a scene. She knew it and was thoroughly enjoying it! Then she waved her hand in the air as she trundled away. 'See you around, firecracker,' she called.

The glass doors of the library swooshed open, revealing a light, bright place that was warm. The big guy who lived in the tent was in there, sitting on a soft chair with a book in one hand and a sandwich in the other. He nodded in my direction, which was quite good of him, considering.

The minute I'd discovered my hold-all was missing, I'd stuck my head through the flaps of his tent. 'Where's my stuff?' I demanded. He was instantly awake, clutching a baseball bat.

'*Jeezus*, kid, are you looking to get lumped?' he asked, breathing heavily.

'I'm looking for my stuff. My bag's been stolen,' I muttered, my eyes already scanning the unexpected sight in front of me. An organised row of belongings lined the edge of the tent next to him – a bag-for-life containing neatly folded clothes; a wash bag and flannel hanging from a bar made out of tree branches tied with string; a mug, plate and water bottle placed on a wooden tray, and a string of battery-run fairy lights intertwined round little hand-made decorative things tied to the centre pole. It was like a mini grotto in there – but no big, black hold-all.

'Yeah, well, we tend not to shit on our own doorstep and as you can see, I haven't got it because it's not exactly palatial in here.' He cast his gaze around him. 'Nice though, hey?' he said with a certain amount of pride.

'Beautiful,' I answered, still peering inside.

'Er . . . but you can go now,' he said, resting his head back on the pillow and frowning at the fact I was still there. 'Nice to chat and all that but I'd quite like a bit more sleep.' Ten minutes later, when he'd successfully untangled my hair from the zip of his tent, and introduced himself as Ronnie, I was able to back out and let him go back to sleep.

I nodded back at Ronnie as I approached the information counter where a man with long grey hair tied in a ponytail

153

smiled at me behind half-moon glasses. 'What do I need to do to use the computers? I don't have a library card,' I added.

'You can use them for an hour at a time and I'll sort you out a temporary card now. You don't need ID and you don't even need a proof of address any more,' he answered, reaching for the paperwork.

'And you should get a job in a hotel,' I quipped. This place was a bargain. No wonder Ronnie was in here – he could sit on that comfortable chair, eating and reading all day until he crawled back into his tent at night.

Logging onto a computer for my allotted hour I typed in the search box: 'How to find missing people' while a little clock in the corner of the screen began unrelentingly counting down the minutes I had remaining – sixty, now fifty-nine, now, fifty-eight . . . Didn't it know how important my mission was? That I couldn't cram ten years of no news about a person into fifty-eight minutes?

'Oh my God, there's an awful lot of you,' I said to the screen as the faces of missing people appeared in front of me. There were so many – hundreds of them. Smiling photos of people, young and old, men, women and children who had been missing for years and years and had never been found, people who had totally slid off the radar. And there was a lot of information to go with it. 'Reasons why people go missing . . . abuse, arguments, kicked out, kidnapped, the slave trade . . . murder! Tell me you didn't bury her under the patio?' I said under my breath to my father. While another minute counted down on the corner of the computer, I half-heartedly entertained the idea that we could have had several family barbeques on the flagged terrace of our old house while she was buried underneath us.

'You said she'd been beautiful, like autumn on a warm, sunny day. So what the hell are you not telling me? What are you hiding? Why didn't she get custody? Or even joint custody? Or even visiting rights?' I leant a bit closer to the screen, scrolling through all the information in front of me. Too many questions. Too many questions that only she could answer.

Suddenly a section caught my eye that made me wonder why I hadn't thought of it myself. 'A private investigator! That's it, we pay someone to find her! You've got the money, Father, and it says here they can find anyone!'

While I waited for him to answer my phone call, it occurred to me with huge relief that if he actually helped me by organising a private detective, all I had to do was wait for however many hours or days it took. I might as well go home, pack another bag and be ready to leave the minute she was traced.

'I'm sorry, Saffy, but I'm not hiring a private investigator.' His words floated out of my phone and hurt me with their unfairness.

'WHY?' I complained loudly, making the man next to me turn sharply to look in my direction. 'They start at only fifty pounds an hour . . . there was five hours of searching sticking out of *her* bag yesterday. In fact, there's about fourteen hours of searching in the cost of the bag alone! I know you can afford it.'

I seemed to have spent the last two days listening to my father take a deep breath while working out what to say and what to avoid. 'It's not about affording it, Saffy,' he said, his voice coming out in a breathy whoosh. I held the phone, waiting for him to elaborate, my hate for him intensifying with every drop of the minute timer on the corner of the screen, fifty-two . . . now fifty-one.

'What's it about then?' I asked, dying to hear the next load of rubbish he was going to invent, but nothing came back in reply. 'You're just not going to do it, are you?' I said eventually, a seething anger making my pulse throb.

'No . . . but . . . Saffy I need to know you're OK . . . Can we meet?'

I pressed end call, leaving his unanswered question in mid-air, and sat perfectly still for a long time, the minute timer dropping from fifty, through the forties and down to thirty four before I was finally capable of movement. The hope I'd felt at finding a solution had been so good until . . . *he* . . . my *father* had snatched it away and there didn't seem to be any justification for it other than that he didn't want to help me. 'I never want to see you again,' I said to my phone, and I meant it. Placing my fingers on the keys, I sat up with new resolve and sighed theatrically. 'I'll just have to do it myself the long way, without your help.' The keys clicked quietly as I typed in again 'How to find a missing person in the UK'.

When 'You must be eighteen years old to use this service' came up on the screen from the fourth agency I tried, I lost the plot.

'Are you all right?' The guy with the grey ponytail appeared by my side. 'Only, you were making a strange noise . . .'

'Sounded like you were being strangled from the inside,'

Ronnie contributed, as he walked past me to put his sandwich wrappers in the bin.

'I would be all right if I wasn't seventeen!' I answered, thumping the keyboard with my fists.

Tom

I'd spent the entire day with my finger hovering over the keypad of my phone, and the fact that John kept having a go about it didn't help. 'Why are you being such a knob?' he said. 'You could put both of them out of their misery plus me 'n' all in one easy move. Angela says she wants to leave and Saffron says she wants to move in. Simples!'

'It's not *simples*, you know it isn't. I'm not ready to force the issue with Angela and if I'd helped Saffron yesterday I'd have risked drowning myself.'

'Instead you told her to go home. You threw her a flimsy lifebelt then turned away without even knowing if she caught it. I can do metaphors too, you know ... And sometimes you've got to listen to the voice of reason with one ear and listen to your heart with the other. I'm the voice of reason and you already know what your heart is saying. Now I'm very thirsty from being all articulate, so stop being a knob and make me a coffee.'

'Stop calling me a knob and I'll think about it,' I said, putting down the screwdriver I'd been using to fit a cupboard door.

'OK, I'll stop . . . but it doesn't mean you aren't one,' John answered, popping his head out from behind the unit he'd been assembling.

Saffron

I tried not to think too deeply about last night not being my one and only experience of sleeping under the bridge. Instead I silently and begrudgingly accepted it. Maggie would be there and so would Ronnie, which, weird as it was, made me feel better. Perhaps even William would be there too. It was a fragile kind of familiar but it was better than nothing.

I'd spent the rest of the day sleeping in the library until it shut at six-thirty. 'C'mon, dear, we're closing now.' A lady with a maroon cardigan nudged me awake, clutching a pile of magazines. 'You were well away,' she added, smiling as I wiped at the trickle of saliva decorating my chin. I squinted at her through the glare of the overhead strip lights and said nothing.

The library doors swooshed shut behind me, and I shivered with the cold October air. Sleeping in the library, dribbling mouth or not, at least meant I stood a chance of surviving the night awake.

Back at the river the man and the woman across from the river had lit another fire and Maggie was trundling her way to the bridge when I got there. 'Home sweet home,' I called, relieved by the familiarity of her.

'There's no place like home, there's no place like home. Still got no ruby shoes?' she chattered.

If I'm Dorothy, then you're the scarecrow, I thought unkindly, but out loud I replied, 'Perhaps I don't want to be back in Kansas.'

Maggie blew a rush of air through her missing teeth. 'There's worse places than Kansas, my lovely.' Parking her trolley up against the concrete pillars, she sighed contentedly as if she'd just come back from a hard day at the office.

'Where do you go all day?' I asked, for the first time curious as to how she survived the endless nomadic hours of a street person. I had endured one day and that was enough to do my head in. She tugged at her bedding, which was wedged among the rest of the rubbish inside the trolley.

'Here and there. Onwards but not upwards. Around and about.' Then she rolled out a mat on top of her cardboard, and placed her sleeping bag and her blankets on top of it. She was like an old hag from a Dickens novel or film, as if she should be wringing her hands and cackling in Victorian slum talk, but instead I couldn't help thinking there was something out of place about her. Something more . . . *delicate* than my preconceived idea of a homeless bag lady. When she'd finished making her bed she looked over at me where I was huddled on the cardboard. 'Did you lose all your things in the tornado?' The *Wizard of Oz* banter was getting tedious now, although she seemed to know the story well. Had this old lady once sat in a cinema, or in front of a television, watching a film like a normal person? Had she watched it with a friend, a sister . . . or a mother?

'No, Maggie, it got stolen. Any ideas?'

Maggie shrugged under her huge coat and passed me the bag with the red pashmina again. 'Why should I know? I'm not your keeper.'

'Because someone stole it while I was asleep! And I didn't ask you to be my keeper.' I reached for the blanket and checked it was still as clean as it had been when I gave it back only that morning, folded neatly and placed on top of all her rubbish. She'd been in a drunk sleep, with only her nose and the tip of her boots visible, and obviously had no idea that I'd frantically tried to wake her when I discovered my missing hold-all.

'Could have been anyone,' she said. 'You look like a newbie to me. That bag didn't look like it had spent more than five minutes on the street, so I expect someone took a shine to it.'

Next she got out a little fold-open stool, reached into a bag and pulled out a few strong beers, tugging at the ring pull of the first one and taking a long hard slug at it. 'Ooh lovely,' she said, smiling lovingly at the can.

I guessed Maggie weaved in and out of crazy depending on how much alcohol she drank. Currently she was able to string whole sentences together and make a certain amount of sense. 'I thought it was that big guy. The one with the beard and dreadlocks, Ronnie. I looked inside his tent. Have you *seen* in there? It's *amazing*!'

Maggie snapped her head round, the swift movement making her cheeks wobble. 'Why did you look inside his tent? Do you walk into people's houses whenever you feel like it?'

I held my hands up to protect myself from Maggie's

annoyance. 'Whoah, Maggie, I was just looking for it, that's all. He seemed like a good candidate. Everyone else was off their faces and he . . . he had somewhere to hide it.'

'Do you think every homeless person is out to mug you? Does adversity *have* to make you immoral?'

'How do I know whether he's moral or not?' I snapped. 'Anyway, whatever he is, he's organised,' I said, picturing the little gathering of belongings inside the prettily decorated tent.

'And does adversity *have* to make you disorganised?' she replied, drinking from her can and stifling a burp. 'Does having a roof over your head make you a better person?' The fading blue eyes landed on me.

'Er . . . I guess not,' I answered. We sat in relative silence for a while after that, with me thinking ahead to the endless hours stretching before me and Maggie occasionally tipping her can to her mouth.

'Sweet?' I reached towards her with my peace offering.

'They get stuck in my teeth,' she answered, without looking my way.

The air was lumpy between us, and I didn't like it. It was bad enough being here without being accused of being the bad guy. 'Look, stop being cross with me, I didn't understand . . . I'm not homeless.'

'You're doing a good impression of it now,' she said.

'I'm not homeless . . . I'm . . . I'm angry.' Even I knew it sounded stupid, as if my own character flaw should put me in this vulnerable position.

'Angry?' Maggie cackled loudly. 'Who with?'

'My father. He lied to me and told me my mum was dead when she isn't . . . and he married an imposter and ruined my life.'

'And no one's actually died?' she added.

'No, it would appear not. Everyone is alive and healthy . . . that's the problem.'

'Then your life isn't ruined,' she said and huffed.

'But it *is* . . . he lied –'

Maggie interrupted me again. 'Then your life *isn't* ruined,' she insisted.

It was with a certain amount of relief that I saw William wandering in just at that moment. Another guy was with him and they both put down their rucksacks and pulled out their sleeping bags, propping up their begging signs next to them. 'Don't you ever use that money to get proper shelter like the sign says?' I challenged, conscious of the fact I was deflecting my bad mood onto someone else.

'I haven't got enough points anyway,' William replied.

'Me neither,' the other guy chipped in.

'What do you mean, points?' I asked.

'We ain't disabled and we ain't registered as having mental health. Therefore we're on our own. *Nil poi,*' he said in a really bad French accent, rolling a joint in the same way William had last night, tipping spice from a shiny packet carefully into a cigarette paper. 'Plus, you're not allowed in anywhere if you're not clean.' He lit his joint and inhaled deeply. 'And it's impossible to get clean when you live like this.'

'This is Chuggy,' William said, introducing me to the guy. Chuggy waved the packet of spice at me as a 'hello' offering.

'Don't give her that rubbish,' Maggie slurred loudly, pointing her can angrily at him. 'It will fry her brains.'

And you would know all about fried brains, I thought, watching her take another long slug before resuming the rhythmic rocking she'd started since her second can . . . backwards and forwards, backwards and forwards.

'Or kill her,' Ronnie called over, appearing round the side of the bridge, carrying his rucksack and a newspaper. He looked directly at me. 'There's a zombie apocalypse going on out there because of that stuff.' Then he disappeared into his tent and re-emerged with a toothbrush and some paste. Using the large bottle of water and the mug I'd seen that morning, he proceeded to clean his teeth.

Maggie was right, this odd little band of down and outs were probably not out to take from each other. There would definitely be all sorts out there on the street but having a house didn't necessarily make you holy, same as not having a house didn't necessarily make you a bad person. But this world I'd found myself in was all so . . . *surreal*, yet so cruelly real at the same time. While Maggie drank herself stupid, and William and Chuggy got off their faces on drugs, Ronnie was meticulously maintaining his pearly whites!

'Why do you do it?' I challenged, imagining the zombie apocalypse Ronnie had said was happening. I'd seen video clips of people having bad trips on this sort of stuff, folded over like puppets with snipped strings, or yelling as if being dragged into the gates of hell. Maggie's route to oblivion seemed much nicer, even if she was mad as a box of frogs.

'You don't understand, little girl,' Chuggy said patronisingly, even though he didn't look that old himself. 'Drugs are the only thing that's great in a world that ain't great . . . they're a love story. You meet, there's instant attraction, you flirt with each other, you 'ave the drug equivalent of casual sex . . .' He took another drag on his joint. 'To begin with you can take it or leave it –' he held the joint in front of him as if talking to it instead of me – 'then you start to want it, next you need it and before you know it, you're obsessed with it. Ain't that right, William?'

William nodded, took several drags of his joint, blew the smoke through his nose, then looked me in the eye. 'Then, like the fishing spider, you shrivel up and die after mating.'

I raised an eyebrow. William was unexpectedly eloquent.

'You're surprised at my analogy?' he asked, while I racked my brains to remember what an analogy was, but if he was talking about the love story and the spider thing . . . yes, actually I was surprised. He nodded again as if he already knew the answer. I felt shame as I realised I had assumed all these people lacked the basic brains and motivation to stay on the hamster wheel like the rest of society.

'What about your mum, your parents? I bet they're proud?' I said, unable to stop my sarcasm finding its way in.

William laughed, a mirthless laugh. 'They were proud when I passed my A levels and got a place at university . . .'

'And then?' I probed, imagining a smiling family with William in the middle, all proud of his success until he somehow mucked it all up.

'And then they stayed proud right up until the moment a lorry hit them on the M25.' It was as if an imaginary lorry had just crashed through my own mind. 'They were taking me back to university after Easter . . .' he continued, my own imaginary lorry still careering through my head. Then, horrified, I realised what he was saying.

'Wait! . . . You were in the car?'

'On the back seat . . . I won't tell you what I saw when I came round . . . it doesn't make for a good bedtime story and no horror movie will ever come close. Suffice to say, the image of it is burnt behind my eyelids for ever.' He closed his eyes and there, in the corners of them, was the evidence of a pain so great it threatened to leak right out of him in front of us all. He wiped it quickly away with the cuff of his sleeve.

I silently and profusely thanked my own eyelids for the memory of my mother's red smile and the four shiny conkers in their prickly green casing. The air became raw with the death of William's parents as if it had only just happened and I really didn't know what to say to him after that, but I felt I should say *something*. 'Do you have other family?' My voice was gentle, as if I was patting him sympathetically with my words.

'Yes. I have a little sister who must be sixteen now and two little brothers, twins, who would be eleven. They went to my uncle and aunt's house after Mum and Dad died.' William's voice petered out, as if his story ended there.

'And you?' I probed again.

'I was nineteen. They didn't have any more room in their house for me . . . they were struggling to fit the others in as it was, and at the time I had digs at uni. If I wanted to stay with the others in the holidays, I had to sleep on the sofa. I became an *inconvenience*. I didn't have my own bedroom or my own home any more and my family belonged to different people. To cut a long story short, I failed my first year at uni, got kicked out, found myself homeless, got into drugs, got banned from coming round to visit the others because I was *unstable* . . . The rest is history.' He said the word 'unstable' while wobbling his head and waving his arms.

William's story lay heavily out in the open as if he'd unzipped his sternum and put all his organs on the ground between us. If I'd stood up and stamped on them, they couldn't have been more damaged than they already were. Whoever treated William after he was pulled out of the wreckage of the car his parents died in hadn't repaired his broken mind. 'I'm so sorry,' I mumbled. I wanted to say more. I wanted to put plasters on his hurt but nothing I could say was going to fix the unfair mess he was now in.

'I've been on the street for years . . . didn't know who my real mum was until a few months ago,' Chuggy suddenly joined in, an ironic grin showing a set of broken and grey teeth. 'She recognised me from a photograph. Came up to me on the street and said, "Is your name Paul?" – cos that's my real name, like – and I said yes, and she said, "I think you're my son!" It's the ears . . .' Chuggy pointed to his ears in case I'd missed the fact that they both stuck out like handles on a jug.

I wondered if I was about to be witness to an emotional story where a mother finds her lost son after years apart. I leant closer to hear more. *Maybe there is hope for me and my mum after all.* 'Yeah, we had a chat an' everything, right in the middle of the job centre. She'd been homeless too . . . on and off for years.' He finished his joint and flicked the end away. 'I went into foster care when I was little because she couldn't look after me. The people gave her photos of me over the years though, and that's how she recognised me. Bloody unbelievable, ain't it?'

'Actually, that's really sad,' I said, meaning it. 'Your poor mum . . .'

'I think she got used to it, cos she did it five times!' His eyelids opened and closed slowly as he eased the grey smoke out from between his grey teeth.

'What? She gave you away five times?' I gasped, imagining that poor woman trying to claim her son, then having to give him up again . . . over and over.

'No, idiot! She got *pregnant* five times and gave all her kids away . . . three of them got snapped up by Social Services and never seen again. I know where she lives now but I don't go there . . . too much grief and bother, like . . . and I'd only bring more trouble to her door.'

Chuggy had a whole dysfunctional family scattered to the winds, landing wherever fate took them – he made my family sound good by comparison. Thankfully neither of them demanded a story from me and I was grateful because while they had no home to go back to, I couldn't say the same.

The night had descended quietly and brought with it a sharper chill. I was sitting on old cardboard, my teeth chattering, while not very far away I had a warm house with underfloor heating, and a kitchen where my dad used to make soup on chilly days and ladle it into little red bowls with little red handles. If we were lucky he would cut the bread with cookie cutters – fish and stars and hearts all piled up ready for us to dip into our soup. That was when it was just the four of us . . . that was when we were OK. I leant my head against the wall of the bridge and shut my eyes, so tempted to slip back into my own house and pretend like nothing had changed.

I put my sweatshirt over my leather jacket again, tucked my hair into my beanie, put the socks on my hands and pulled Maggie's warm pashmina higher up around me, the cold air reaching through the fibre right into the very middle of me, its icy fingers squeezing the part of me that was stubborn. I would *not* go back. That time . . . when it was just us? We weren't OK. We were living a cosy cover-up for his lies. Hate sloshed inside me like the crashing waves of a storm. I was not going to give up and go home, however tempting.

I cast my gaze around my homeless companions. I would find my mother soon and this would all turn into a distant nightmare, but these guys didn't have that luxury. 'Are you clean?' I asked, turning to Ronnie.

Ronnie was still clutching his toothbrush and his bottle of water. 'Yes,' he said.

'Then why can't you go to one of the shelters?'

'I can. When my name gets to the top of the list. Shouldn't be long now. I had a house, and a car and a mortgage not that long ago. I got made redundant, couldn't pay the mortgage, got a loan to cover it, still couldn't get a job, so couldn't pay the loan or the mortgage. Lost the lot! Homeless. Tah-daaah! I'd like to think that one day I'll get back on the ladder though, because I'm not dealing with other stuff. You know . . . like . . .' He flitted his eyes over to the others. 'But these guys . . . and others like them, they don't always have the strength to cope with all the rules . . .'

'Yeah, shelter rules are pretty hard to keep when your head's mashed,' William added, his words now coming slowly and slurred. 'Take them over there.' He pointed to the couple who were sitting round their fire. 'Veterans, both of them. They got post-traumatic stress disorder from serving this great nation and now they, and service men and women like them, are rotting on the streets with the rest of us. If seven thousand heroes can fall through the care system what chance have we got?'

I shrugged, drowning in a total loss of what to say. I'd never really thought about it before. 'What about benefits then?' I asked but Ronnie laughed quietly through his beard.

'Yes, easy as apple pie. You just write your address down and they give you benefit.'

'But you guys don't have an address,' I answered, feeling confused.

'Exactly,' he replied. 'You can use the job centre for an address, but not everyone is capable of getting or keeping a job.' He eyed the others again. 'Drugs and alcohol help them find their happy, only, when they find it, they can no longer live in a world with rules . . . circle complete!'

I felt like I'd just opened my eyes to a whole other reality from the one I'd been living in and it was proving difficult to understand. Ex home owners, university students, service men and women, disillusioned teenagers and people from dysfunctional families. It was all around me and it was all so *unfair.* 'It's all . . . all . . .'

'. . . a bit shit?' he said.

'Yeah! It's all a bit shit.' Not exactly the profound statement I was searching for but it basically said it all.

Ronnie went into his tent to replace his toothbrush and paste, and came out with some feathers, twigs and string. 'It would just be nice if we could live our lives with the cards we've been dealt, without being abused, spat at or sworn at.' He began to assemble something with the stuff he'd brought out of his tent, winding string in the beginnings of an intricate pattern. 'Dream catcher,' he said, answering a question I'd only asked in my head.

Just at that moment something ran across my feet and I screamed, a piercing sound followed by a full, back-rattling shiver. 'Oh my God, something just ran across my feet! A mouse or a rat, something with a tail! Right there!' I tucked my feet underneath me as if they were in danger of being bitten off. 'Did you see it?'

Maggie stirred. 'That's nothing, newbie. Just a little furry thing. You wait until the nightclubs turn out and people come and piss on you.'

'What?' I screeched. 'Tell me that's not true?' I couldn't imagine anyone would do something so disgusting.

Both Ronnie and Maggie gave a resounding 'Yes' at the same time, and Ronnie elaborated. 'They get drunk, think it's funny or think they're paying us back for being lazy.

'Homeless people are nothing more than the shadows of real people.' His words reminded me of last night at the soup kitchen where the hidden people emerged from the cracks in the city, taking handfuls of food from visible people who lived on solid ground. He was right, they *were* like the shadows of real people.

I hoped William was now 'cradled like a baby' somewhere inside himself, deep within his grimy clothes and his shabby sleeping bag, snuggled back in a time when he was real, with a family and a future. Somewhere in his own home, on a glossy white shelf, there should be a photograph of William with his graduation certificate and his parents smiling proudly by his side.

Tom once said it was 'life' that made Maggie crazy. William, Chuggy and Ronnie weren't crazy . . . but maybe 'life' hadn't finished with them yet. I didn't know what Maggie's story was, any more than she knew mine. I didn't know whether she was the victim of any of the scenarios Ronnie, William or Chuggy had just told me, or whether she'd always been an apple destined for the fruit pot.

Ronnie and I sat in companionable silence for a long time until Dad rang again and, once more, I waited, with stubborn determination, unwilling to give him the satisfaction of answering until it switched to voicemail.

'Hi, Saffy. I hope Tom is still looking after you but you know we want you to come home, don't you? We all miss you so much. I wanted to tell you that I loved your mum. She was so . . . energetic. All the things that I wasn't. She took me to festivals, concerts, museums, theatres, cities and mountains. She had all the ideas and I followed. She wanted to try everything, like a butterfly landing on every flower. That's how I saw her. But . . . I saw myself as the one with the net . . . and the jar . . . and . . . I . . . oh

I just can't do this!'

'Can't do what?' I asked the recording. I felt as if each word had physically assaulted me in some way, swatting me with its unexpected loveliness. Stinging and caressing simultaneously. My dad was not like this. He was straight up – not pink and fluffy in the slightest. He must really have loved her to talk about her like that.

For a moment I was transported back to a time before I existed. A time when my parents were young. When they lived a life that sounded – well, it sounded fantastic! But what had happened next? Was it getting pregnant with me? Was I the reason their fun and excitement had ended? Then I heard it. *Her* musical voice in the background of the answerphone message . . . 'You can do it, Teddy. Keep going.'

He was a puppet and she was pulling his strings, and suddenly I wasn't interested in anything else he had to say. I ended the message.

The red bar on my battery life was now reduced to a dangerously thin sliver. I sat there holding on to my silent, almost dead phone, as if all the lost parts of me should be inside it. I was alone. I was very, very alone. Ronnie was no longer sitting with me. I hadn't noticed him leave and bed down for the night in his tent, but in the place where he had been, my hologram mother now sat again, shining with copper and green. I let her tell me about all the things she had done and the places she had visited, then I followed her in my mind across the world, from music festivals to a New York skyline.

I woke to the rustle and shuffle of Maggie heaving herself

from under her blankets, bringing me instantly back to the harsh, hard ground and the cold light of a new day. I was stiff all down one side from the lack of a soft mattress and my eyes were bleary from lack of sleep.

Maggie hauled herself up and made her way to the edge of the bridge where ragged grass grew in small patches and an early mist still lay close to the ground. She coughed repeatedly, slowly at first then gathering momentum as the phlegm dislodged itself from the depths of her lungs and made its way out, like an old machine cranking itself into life. I'd woken up in more appealing ways than this. Being jumped on by Archie and the brat, pulled out of bed by Dad, or threatened with suffocation by Daniel pressing his used underpants into my face. Even the sound of *her* voice trespassing through a gap in my bedroom door was better than being woken by Maggie. Then as if the sound of her inner globules of slime making their way out wasn't bad enough, she lifted her dress and coat up, pulled down everything that was under her dress and relieved herself, farting noisily in the process.

'Pardon me,' she muttered, as if farting in public was wrong but al fresco toileting was OK. 'It gives the belly ease and suffocates the fleas,' she added, for my benefit, when she saw I was awake. But it was at that moment, when she said her delicate 'pardon me', and the anecdote to her peeing that I realised what was out of place about her.

Once upon a time, Maggie had been posh!

Thursday:
Surprises and Ignorance

Tom

6.12 a.m. Three more warm minutes under the duvet before the alarm. My eyes already open, staring into the darkness of the room as if they were peering right inside myself, and there, in the depths of me, was Saffron.

Me: Are you OK?

I pressed SEND, knowing instantly that I was asking for a barrage of abuse in return. Two days had passed since she stormed off when I called her stupid and all I could think of to say is 'Are you OK?' Reaching over to turn the alarm off before it woke Angela, the uneasy feeling that had showed itself yesterday clawed its way up my back and lay heavily on my shoulders. What did I want? Did I really want to tell Angela about Saffron and risk her making those phone calls that would change everything? Was it selfish to want something different from the life I had?

The lamp from the sitting room flicked on, throwing a yellow glow through the gap in the bedroom door and across the carpet. Angela was awake too. 'Couldn't sleep?' I called out, throwing the duvet off and feeling the rush of cool morning air on my skin.

'Yes, I slept . . . most of the time,' Angela said as I padded past her on the way to the kitchen. 'But *you* didn't. You were up twice in the night, you've eaten a packet of noodles and a tin of beans *and* swallowed it down with milk straight from the fridge. That's a mind that is not at peace . . . Eating an entire buffet when you should be snoring your face off.'

'Everything's fine.' I grinned at her round the kitchen door, before reaching for the cereal bowl. 'I didn't mean to wake you, I was just a bit peckish in the night.'

'You always eat when you're unsure of something. What is it? Is it us?'

'I'm unsure whether to have the Crunchy Nut or the Weetabix,' I called back. I wasn't prepared to start something with Angela that I couldn't finish. I needed to see if Saffron was OK first.

Saffron

My dirty clothes felt like they were stuck to me and I was so desperate for a shower I felt like stripping off in the river and using the sad little pile of toiletries I'd bought yesterday to wash myself. The cheap pair of tights I'd bought from the pound shop had already grown two ladders.

Like Maggie, I also had to relieve myself outside but managed to pick a better spot, preferring less of an audience myself. As I picked my way through the bushes, I tried not to think about how many of the people that used this place to sleep also used it as a massive outside toilet.

One more day. I only had to last until tomorrow. I could do this. And maybe my mum would see my social media plea before then.

My muscles were stiff with leaning against the wall all night, and there was still a damp chill hanging in the early morning air. Maggie had shuffled back under her blankets and was now loudly snoring again. William and Chuggy were off their faces still, a sad, dark patch of wet having made its way out from underneath Chuggy, spreading dangerously close to William's face. Ronnie was different. He was still holding on to the idea of life above the cracks in the pavement. No alcohol or drugs for him, just an immaculately tidy tent, with its little decorations and his newspaper, waiting patiently for the outcome of his job applications and his name to come up on the list for shelter.

I didn't know what was saddest, Ronnie trying desperately to cling to normality, Chuggy and Maggie who were so far under the surface they would probably never get out, or the two army veterans and William who, with a bit of help, could be looking at a very different future than the one they currently had.

The tip of my nose and the apples of my cheeks were icy cold, the bags under my eyes virtually hanging off my face but still I wouldn't go home. I pulled Maggie's pashmina back over my knees and hugged myself. The road overhead was already beginning to roar cars and lorries, and the sound of footsteps on the path increased as commuters walked past. I turned my phone on, the thin red battery line offering me the last of its life to check my messages. It was 6.30 a.m. At home I would still have another hour in bed, my head on my pillow, a hot shower only steps away, a clean towel hanging over the towel rack – a choice of perfume, deodorant and body butter lined up ready and waiting in my bathroom cupboard.

Tom: Are you OK?

So now he cares? Two whole days after begging him to let me stay at his house and I get a measly 'Are you OK?'

Me: Two nights under the bridge thanks

At that moment my screen went black. My phone finally dying, cutting off all communication with the outside world and the chance to see Tom's reply. *Everybody* has a sofa and Tom and Angela wouldn't be any exception. If it wasn't for her, Tom would have let me stay and I wouldn't be in such a mess, or feeling so cold, or so horribly on my own in all this. He was a friend and friends should help each other.

I left the bridge before the others had moved and before the morning mist had fully lifted, wandering slowly as there was absolutely no point in walking fast. I couldn't go to college looking like this and I had no agenda other than to find my mum.

Where do people go when there is nowhere to go? Where are the other cracks in this town for homeless people to hide?

Tom

Me: Meet me at 12.15 where will you be?

Oh my God! Saffron had slept under the bridge! Presumably she meant the road bridge on the edge of the park where some of the homeless people hung out. How gut-crushingly bad did I feel right now? I'd cycled under that bridge several times since I last saw her. I should have known that if she said she wouldn't go home then she wouldn't. 'You definitely are a knob,' I said out loud.

'So if you won't listen to me, are you going to listen to yourself?' John asked as I pulled on my work overalls. 'If both of us are telling you you're a knob then we must be right.'

'That girl, Saffron, the one I told you about . . . she's slept rough since Tuesday and it's all my fault. She didn't go home like I asked her to.' I pulled the zip up on the overalls and walked towards the unit I'd been working on.

John whistled through his teeth. 'Blimey, mate. She sounds like a stubborn one. I thought you said she was privileged? Lived in a beautiful house and everything?'

'I did. I can hardly believe she would sleep out all night

over this. She's . . . she's . . .' I fought for the words to describe Saffron.

'She's fucking fantastic, that's what she is!' John whistled again. 'If she can do without all that posh stuff she's the girl for you. Mark my words.' John drained his mouthful of coffee and held out his cup for another.

'I'm riding on a massive guilt trip and you're planning a wedding? Now who's the knob?' I reached for his cup and ladled enough sugar in his to keep a small family going for a week. 'It's not going to happen, John.'

John groaned and slapped his forehead. 'Now you're just being an idiot.'

Saffron

I'd bought myself a bacon sandwich and a strawberry milkshake in the cafe in the hospital and sat at a table half-heartedly looking through a discarded magazine. Going there had been a lightbulb moment. It was a reasonable place to be anonymous and spend the early hours without being chucked out. Staff were far too busy to morph into the toilet police and turf out anyone who wasn't a patient or a visitor.

The hospital was beginning to come alive with people coming and going. An early-morning hive of new activity. Comfortable shoes squeaking on polished floors, arms hugging clip boards; plain clothes, uniform clothes, dressing gowns and pyjamas. It was all there. Warm, dry and safe.

A young girl was asleep, hunched over an open book on her lap. To my newly educated eye, something about her screamed homeless. The fact that she was pretending to read, her feet resting on a very large rucksack and the fact that she was dressed in warm clothes of shadowy, unobtrusive colours. Even her black, tightly curled hair was cropped close to her head as if everything about her wanted to fly under the radar. When she turned up in the toilets a bit later and started brushing her teeth next to the sink where I was brushing mine, before carefully washing her face with a flannel from a little plastic bag out of the pocket of her rucksack, I was sure I'd been right.

They were everywhere, how had I never noticed them all before? Homeless people just trying to get through each day.

I'd left the hospital, and was now carefully using testers to apply make-up in a large chemist in the shopping centre when a commotion happened. Customers all around me straightened up and peered like meerkats, to see what it was about. It was Chuggy, being escorted off the premises by a security guard. He'd obviously revived from his catatonic state under the bridge, made his way into the store and been caught stealing something. He wasn't going quietly and the smell told me he obviously hadn't changed his trousers either.

'Fuckin' get off me, mate!' he shouted, trying to shrug his way out of the security guard's clutches. Chuggy's sandy coloured hair was dark with grease, hanging in limp strands round his shoulders. He wasn't a pretty sight. Combined with broken teeth, bad skin and abusive language he wasn't gaining much sympathy from the other meerkats either.

'What did you do?' I asked as they jostled past me on their way to a room at the back of the shop.

'It was only a bit of effin' electricity for me phone,' he answered, trying again to shrug his captor away. 'Just been done for stealing it, ain't I? Over by the photo bit.'

I almost laughed out loud at how mad that sounded. 'You stole *electricity*?' I repeated as he was dragged past me. 'That's a thing?'

'It's still theft!' said the security guy, pushing Chuggy's

shoulder and clutching the fabric of his coat at the same time to prevent him from running. 'You lot always want something for nothing!'

Behind me a shop assistant tutted. 'He got two weeks last time he got caught doing that.' I didn't know whether to feel sorry for Chuggy or pleased. At least he'd have a roof over his head – and some electricity! Last week I'd have laughed at him, spluttering with all the other onlookers at the scene he was causing. This week, I had no charger either.

Plugging the cable into my phone in the same photo section Chuggy had got arrested for using, I placed my beanie over the top of the phone and pretended to be looking at nearby photo frames. Picking them up, putting them down, making a show of looking at the prices. I knew this would basically be trickle charge and could take a very long time but thankfully the member of staff who was on duty was helping an older lady with the instructions on the touch screen. 'Thank you, old lady,' I said under my breath. She kept calling him back to ask him questions about how to download more photos and get different sizes or effects from the software and every time he turned round, I'd picked up a different frame and was studying it. It took an age for my phone to eventually power up and switch on, but when it did, a message from Tom was there.

Tom: Meet me at 12.15 where will you be?

Despite being upset with him I replied quickly.

Me: Meet me in the library

'Can I help you with this facility?' The guy who'd been helping the lady was now standing right next to me.

'Er, yes,' I smiled, hoping desperately I wasn't about to join Chuggy on his interesting route out of the shop. 'I've got to do a college project about ancestry. I'm looking through my family photos and deciding which ones to print.'

'And do you need any help?' he repeated. 'Only you can't just use this system to charge your phone, you know.' His gaze made its way intently into my own, his eyebrows virtually doing the Mexican wave with his suspicion.

'I told you I'm doing a project and I need twenty photos of relatives,' I repeated, taking a seat and pressing the screen in front of me. This was actually true. Thanks to that briefcase, I'd still not found any photos for my school project in the attic and Melanie was bound to have loads on her Facebook. She was always taking pictures. One big happy family.

Tom

I was really going to do it. In an hour's time, I was going to meet Saffron in the library and tell her she could stay at mine.

'You're as useless as tits on a bull this week.' John snatched away my mug and walked over to the kettle. 'What's the point in having an apprentice if I have to make me own coffee?'

I put down the brush I was holding and rolled my eyes. 'Are you for real, John? No human being can drink what you drink in a day. I'm spending most of my apprenticeship peeing coffee.'

'Two sugars, please,' he called out as I went to fill the kettle for the fifth time that morning. 'It's my responsibility to make sure my staff have suitable breaks. Health and safety.'

'But caffeine addiction isn't part of the contract. I'm buzzing with it,' I said.

'You're far from buzzing with it, Tom. You're working in slow motion and you've stopped making fart jokes. You're hatching something.'

'If I start telling fart jokes again, will you get off my back?'

'Only if they're as good as this one,' he said, farting so loudly we both laughed.

'Now *that's* a health and safety issue,' I said, taking my mug and moving quickly towards the open window. 'Anyway, I'm sorting it. I'll be back on the planet by tomorrow. Promise.'

Saffron

There were five albums on Melanie's profile.

'Family, Charlotte, Archie, Daniel *and* Saffron. You've got one for me?' I said to the screen.

I opened it and there, going back nine years, to the age of eight, was me. I was in colour, black and white, special effects, they were all there. 'So many,' I breathed, staring hard. Every birthday, every school concert, every prize giving and virtually everything else I'd ever done, snapped, downloaded and shared. There was even a recent photo of me in my prom dress labelled 'Sweet sixteen. Beautiful Saffy ready for prom'.

I could feel my heart tumble and I didn't like the way it made me feel. 'Beautiful Saffy,' I whispered. Why had she taken all those pictures of me? Why had she labelled me? I was horrible to her. She'd even put a frame round the prom photo – a string of white daisies with little green leaves that circled me in my beautiful satin dress, the colour of burnt umber.

Several times, I'd Photoshopped Melanie's head onto animals or other inappropriate things and labelled them with funny comments. I called her Smellanie, or 'my step-witch bitch', yet here she was simply calling me 'beautiful Saffy'.

'Are you going to print that?' a woman's voice asked from nearby. The old lady the guy had been helping was looking over my shoulder, smiling at the screen of my phone. 'That's a really lovely photo. You've got the most *amazing* hair, and that hairstyle you're wearing there looks fabulous with that dress.' *Melanie* had done my hair, taming it into shiny curls that hung down my back, weaving thin plaits into the side until I looked like an elfin princess.

'I don't think so,' I answered and scrolled quickly to the next photo. Now there was one of me and Melanie together. I remembered the exact moment, she'd leant in towards me and swiftly taken a selfie, just after she'd finished doing my hair.

'Ah that's nice. Is that your mum?' the woman said, leaning in closer. I had smiled automatically for the camera, so pleased with what she had managed to do with my hair. Melanie was smiling too. Her hair almost touching mine.

'No! My step-mum,' I mumbled, wishing this woman would go away. I wanted to say, my real mum wasn't like her. My real mum had green eyes and hair like mine and she shone like a butterfly. She was exciting and vibrant and didn't take other people's husbands.

'She's lucky,' the woman said, looking between me and the photo, and despite myself, I could feel my eyes widen with surprise as I waited to hear what was lucky about it. 'Yes, it's really hard being a step-mum. Whatever you do . . . however much you love, you never quite get back as much as you give. But there you two are, looking so beautiful together.'

I wanted to put her straight. To tell her there was nothing beautiful about the relationship between me and my stepmother, but as I scrolled to the next picture and the one after that she kept commenting on how lovely they were. They were all captioned with a title, a date or something funny or mushy. Saffy on her birthday, Saffy on her first day at senior school, Saffy in the snow. You name it, I was doing it. In front of me were moments caught on camera that I never realised existed yet Melanie had uploaded them for everyone to see, including apparently, the woman by my shoulder.

Being unsure of the way it made me feel, I waited for the assistant guy to turn away, then I unplugged my phone, smiled briefly at the woman, and ran out of the shop with my phone that was still only on thirty percent.

Saffron

Having spent more of my rapidly dwindling money in the pound shop on tights, underwear, and the cheapest phone charger it was possible to buy, I was back in the library, charging my phone, having changed in yet another public toilet.

Ronnie was back, working at a computer, and the girl from the hospital was now in here too. Her open book was again on her lap, her feet resting on her bag, protecting it from being nicked, her head heavy in her hand while she slept. I reckon she had it the right way round. Sleep all day, stay awake all night. That's probably why she still has her bag and I don't. I tapped her on the shoulder and pointed to the orange juice and sandwich I'd bought and placed on the table beside her. 'I guess you need this more than me,' I said, trying not to notice how desperately grateful she looked, and trying not to notice that I now hardly had enough money left to survive until I met Daniel tomorrow.

I was so tired of this week, and wanted so desperately to leave this world of homeless people behind and forget they ever existed. It was all Dad's and *her* fault and no amount of happy photographs and apologies could ever make up for the way I felt. I checked my phone again for any news of my mum and yet again there was nothing, only more well-wishers or more stupid messages from opinionated or weird people. The photo of me and Melanie however would not leave my mind, like a nasty stain, pasted behind my eyes like a permanent reminder of their lies and how I'd fallen for them. I wiped the angry tears that were tickling my jaw and blew my nose, which was throbbing with snot. This resulted in an impressive amount of nose-blowing, which the entire library must have heard. My tissue filled with so much sticky wetness that I had to use my sleeve to finish the job.

'Are you entering "the loudest snot blow produced inside a library" competition?' Tom's voice said in my ear, as he shuffled his seat over next to mine.

'Why do you always appear at the worst possible time?' I moaned, quickly rolling the wet tissue into a tight wad and shoving it in my pocket. 'You'd cry too if you had a bastard for a father,' I snarled.

'I'd have to know who he was first,' Tom replied. 'In fact, technically speaking, I think that makes me the bastard.'

'Lucky you,' I mumbled insensitively.

'Er . . . thanks . . . if you say so,' he said, looking mildly surprised, then changed the subject. 'I've wangled two hours off work. I've brought sandwiches.' He held up a small, paint-spattered rucksack with pride. 'We'll spend a bit of time in here then you can help me eat my lunch. But first you can tell me why you didn't go home and why you thought sleeping under the bridge at risk from perverts and murderers was a preferable option.'

'Firstly, it *was* a preferable option,' I said. 'Secondly, when I gave my father a chance to explain, he couldn't, and thirdly . . . I hate him . . . and *her*! Oh, and in case you've forgotten, you wouldn't help me, so there you go. It was the bridge for me!'

'How did you survive under that bridge?' he asked, serious for once, a T-shaped frown deeply embedded in his forehead.

'It was *awful*. I was surrounded by alcoholics and drug users . . . and *Crazy Maggie* was there being all crazy . . . she went to the toilet in front of everyone! I didn't need to witness *that* in my life I can tell you!' I knew I was embellishing the reality of the characters I'd met over the last two days, but my nights had been cold and awful and if there was any chance Tom would change his mind and let me sleep at his, he needed to feel bad about turning me away.

'I can't believe you did that. Is that why you wanted my credit card?'

'Yes. I *had* money, but the hotels wanted a credit card as insurance, but now it's not an issue because I haven't got any money now either. It was stolen when I was asleep – along with my bag.' I paused to let the horror of my time on the streets effectively sink in, to further tighten the tiny screw in the 'you should have let me stay at yours' scenario. 'It had my favourite stuff in it and now someone's either wearing it or selling it.'

'It must have been someone with muscles to lift that thing up,' he said.

'You're not funny. It had some pretty nice stuff in it, plus the rest of my money. Whatever you say, I'm not going home . . . I'll sleep under the bridge tonight again if I have to . . . with the weirdos.'

Tom examined his hands, then gave a dramatic sigh. 'I've been thinking . . .' I squeezed my fingers together and hoped with all my might he was going to say what I thought he was going to say.

'You can stay at mine.' Out popped those five precious words and I loved each one of them. Halleluiah. I had a bed for the night. 'You can't spend another night sleeping rough. You can come round later, when I've finished work. Come about seven.' There were no dimples. He didn't look wildly happy about having me over, but I was past caring.

'Thank you!' I squealed, then despite the fact that his lack of enthusiasm was vaguely insulting, I hugged him, impulsively, until the dimples appeared. 'Where do you live? I've never even been to your house!'

'I'll give you a grand tour when you get there, if you've got a spare . . . thirty seconds,' he answered. He sounded almost apologetic but I didn't care. Small was beautiful as far as I was concerned, especially when you compare it to the great, freezing, outdoors. Angela must be very dominating if it took him this long to get the courage to ask her if I could stay.

Tom

For one brief moment, I had the scent of perfume and the softness of copper curls against my cheek. Her hug of gratitude remained wrapped round my neck long after she sat back down, and it made me feel so guilty about Angela. Angela would use this as her way out without a doubt. I'd warned her, 'We don't have a sofa, or a garage, or even a bath . . . but we do have a spare bed.'

'Is the bed made of concrete and piss?' she asked, grinning still.

'Well, no . . . but I can make arrangements if that's what you'd like,' I laughed.

Saffron

After the huge relief that Tom had finally agreed to let me stay at his, I was left with the awkwardness that came with knowing that Tom and Angela had no real space for me. I was jealous of a woman I'd never met, because a boy I wasn't going out with was living in a cupboard with her. My mother needed to see my advert quickly, or Daniel needed to bring enough money for the youth hostel, otherwise I was going to be an unwelcome guest for more than just one night.

Tom turned to the computer next to mine and put his fingers on the keyboard. 'You need a library card to use the computers, but we can use my temporary one,' I said, pulling my chair closer to him.

'I've got one,' he said, logging in. 'I've always had one. I like a good read.' I glanced at him to see if he was joking but he wasn't. He never talked of pubs or clubs and now I knew why – he was probably getting all adventurous down at the library with his library card. 'Right, what have you done so far, in terms of searching for your mum?' he said, cutting into my thoughts.

'Mainly adverts on social media. We could have got a private investigator except my father won't pay for one and I can't get one because they're too expensive and I'm only seventeen. There isn't much I can do until I'm eighteen except hope that the social media gods will answer my prayers.'

Tom tapped away at the keys, basically calling up the same information that I'd done yesterday. 'It's only a few months until you're eighteen, Saffron, then you can do some proper hunting. You can't stay away from home for that long if your mum doesn't see your messages.'

'But I'm not prepared to live with a cuckoo,' I said, thinking of Melanie.

'What is it exactly that you hate about her?' he asked, his eyes fixed on the faces of missing people coming up on the screen.

'Everything.'

'Does she shout?'

'No, but she's got a very grating voice . . . a Welsh accent that gets on my nerves.'

'That's not exactly a crime, Saffron. I quite like a Welsh accent. Very musical.' Tom glanced at me briefly as he spoke. 'What else? Is she mean?'

'Well, no . . . not mean . . . more annoying. She cleans, all the time . . . like she's got OCD or something, it's really intrusive.'

'Mmm, cleaning, hey?' A dimple appeared on Tom's cheek. 'Dreadfully intrusive!'

It was beginning to sound all wrong. 'I mean, like, in my bedroom . . . touching all my stuff, which, for your information, *is* intrusive. And she calls my dad Teddy. That is so *not* his name. It makes me cringe every time she says it.'

'Teddy?' Tom repeated. 'That's positive abuse.'

'It is and stop making everything I say sound so insignificant.'

'What about real abuse, like . . . can she cook? Because if she can't cook, I'll call Social Services.'

I could feel my cheeks in flame. 'Yes. She can cook, but that's not what I *mean*.'

'What *do* you mean, Saffron?' he asked.

'She isn't my mum and she is the reason my mum isn't with my dad.' Every time I thought of her another wave of anger swelled into my throat.

'She may just have . . .' Tom stopped moving. His finger remained in the air over the mouse pad and his jaw was unattractively limp and his mouth open. A fly could have gone in it, buzzed around for a bit and left unnoticed.

'Just have what?' I asked. Tom remained silent, staring intently at a photo of a girl on the screen. 'She knew that Mum wasn't dead and that *was* a crime. Did I tell you that Daniel doesn't even care? . . . Tom?' Tom did not move a single muscle, except for the deep T-shape that had reappeared on his brow. 'Are you listening?' I poked at his arm to catch his attention.

'Uh-uh,' he mumbled through his gaping mouth. I looked at the picture he was staring at. A smiling girl with long brown hair stared out from the screen through vivid blue eyes.

'What's so fascinating?' I asked him. The girl was wearing an old-fashioned outfit from the late eighties. Her hair cascaded over her shoulders in an abundance of brown waves and her face was *very* pretty. 'Nice outfit,' I said sarcastically, taking in the huge shoulder pads and the vibrant blue of her shirt, which matched her eyes.

'*Look* . . .' He pointed to the screen.

'I'm *looking*,' I answered, seeing nothing except the enviably pretty girl from a different era smiling out at us both.

'Forget the outfit, Saffron, look at the face,' he urged.

'I *am* looking at the face!' I answered, feeling totally bewildered at his interest. 'She has a nose and eyes and a mouth . . . like most faces.'

'And she's young,' he added, 'and pretty . . . and happy.'

'And . . . so what?' I asked, not getting the point of this charade at all.

'And . . . it's *Maggie*,' he said.

I almost fell off my chair, trying to get a closer look. 'No *way*!' I screeched so loudly that everyone within a twenty-metre radius looked over at me.

'*Way!*' Tom answered, as we both leant even further forward, both our mouths open and our noses almost pressed against the screen to study the photograph. 'Crazy Maggie was not always crazy, it seems,' he uttered eventually, '. . . or old.'

'Crazy Maggie was beautiful,' I whispered, trying hard to visualise this young girl in front of us as being the same person who walked round stinking of her own urine, with her whole life in an old shopping trolley.

Tom snapped out of his trance and scrolled down the screen. 'It's this site where people try to track long-lost relatives. I thought I might see if there was anything about your mum. But Maggie's on there. Her family were still looking for her at the same time your mum went missing. It's definitely her. "Alexandra Margaret Barrington". What a posh name . . . "Distinctive by three moles on her cheek".' The frown smoothed out and the dimples appeared on his cheeks as he grinned at me. Trying to imagine how the beautiful *Alexandra* in front of us was our Crazy Maggie was difficult, but those three moles were definitely hers and the eyes, although faded now, were the same.

'They're in for a shock when they see her. Those moles are the only things left of her that haven't changed,' I said.

'The moles . . . and her underwear,' Tom added, and we both spluttered.

'She was nineteen when she ran away. That means she's fifty-five now . . . Doesn't look it, does she? More like a hundred and fifty-five. That's what a life on the streets does for you.' Tom whistled through his teeth.

'Fifty-five,' I echoed. 'That's only eight years older than my mum. I hope my mum looks better than that after all these years.'

'Just think, your mum could have a beard too.' Tom put his hand under his chin and wiggled his fingers around like long curly hairs.

'Drop the beard thing, Tom. It makes me feel ill, and that's my mother you're talking about. Anyway, does it say how we send Maggie's family a message to tell them we know where she is?'

'Whooah, you can't do that!' he answered, almost before I got to the end of my sentence, becoming deadly serious. 'We need to go and ask her what she wants us to do.'

I grabbed his arm. 'Are you joking? We could put them out of their misery right this second.'

'It isn't as easy as that. You can't just crash into people's lives like that – being a clumsy do-gooder.'

I didn't understand and thought of my own agony at trying to find my mum. 'Is putting her family out of their misery being a do-gooder? There's no point asking Maggie, she's nearly always off her bananas on booze, Tom; she probably won't even know what she wants us to do.' I felt a bit bad describing Maggie like this. She wasn't off her bananas all the time, only some of the time. I'd glimpsed the person beneath the fathoms of booze and dirt and odour that still existed, even after all these years. 'Her family will have worried about her for years and we know where she is. It isn't right.'

'It's right for Maggie,' he said, as if this was the final say on the matter. 'Plus, these sites have a policy they need to stick to.'

'If someone knew where my mum was, I'd never forgive them for not telling me. Imagine if I had to spend the rest of my life wondering where she is and never be told . . . It doesn't bear thinking about.'

'And are you prepared for what you might learn if you do find her?' Tom remained fixed on the screen, as if confronting me and avoiding me both at the same time.

'*When* I find her!' I added. Surely there was only one scenario? My mum missed me and I missed my mum: what else was there for me to learn?

'And would you like it if someone told your family where you are right now? So they could come and drag you back home?'

'Stop being so . . . so . . . sensible,' I snapped.

Tom read the rest of the plea out loud from Maggie's family. '*Alexandra Margaret Barrington, born 1964, left her home in Cheltenham in March 1983 aged nineteen. Distinguishable by three moles on her cheek and vibrant blue eyes. She is 5' 4" and a talented singer and pianist.*' To them, Maggie had simply vanished. I couldn't imagine what had happened to make her want to leave like that.

'*Had* vibrant blue eyes,' I corrected. Maggie's eyes, ten years down the line, were no longer how I remembered them when I found her on the street when I was seven. The white bits were now yellow and cracked with veins, and her face was so blown out of shape it was hard to see how pretty she could ever have been when she was nineteen.

'She was a talented singer and musician. Can you imagine?'

I remembered her bursting into song outside the library and how it was surprisingly tuneful. It was funny at the time. Now it was almost horrifying.

'What if my mother took to the streets too, Tom? What if my mother is rolling around a pavement somewhere wetting her knickers and shouting at people?'

'Bollocks!' he said loudly, noticing the time. 'C'mon. We won't get any lunch if we don't hurry.' Then he closed down the computer and pushed back his chair.

'We can eat in the library if you like? They allow that now,' I said.

'What? When there's a blue sky and a whole world outside?' he answered, already making to leave.

Tom

'Did Angela make these?' Saffron asked, referring to my homemade sandwiches.

'No. I made them myself. I'm house trained,' I replied, through a massive bite of sandwich in my mouth.

'You have a kitchen then . . . in your house that doesn't have anything else?' she asked.

'Yes, we have a kitchen, and a shower so you'll be able to wash after you throw more food down yourself.'

'But no sofa?' she quizzed.

'No sofa,' I confirmed.

'*Everybody* has a sofa, Tom,' she said. 'How come you haven't? Do you live in a cupboard or something?' The smile was momentarily replaced by a frown that travelled down her forehead and nestled in little crinkles on the bridge of her nose.

I was honest . . . well, partially honest. 'I don't have a sofa because Angela has moved into the lounge.' I didn't want to tell her any more because I wanted her to see it for herself and in truth I wasn't good at saying it out loud.

'She *is* your girlfriend, right?' she asked, looking confused.

'No!' I answered, equally confused that she even thought

that. 'I've never told you I had a girlfriend or led you to believe I had one. You made that one up all by yourself.'

I watched another wave of confusion cross her face, making the freckles on her forehead wriggle. 'Your dog?' she probed.

I shook my head. 'Na-ah,' I responded, beginning to find this amusing.

'. . . Your grandmother? Daughter? Sister? Friend?' She kept asking and I kept shaking my head.

'My aunt,' I said, putting her out of her misery, while I wondered how two tiny words could carry such weight.

'Oh,' she said quietly. Her expression was unreadable. Almost forced composure. 'What do you even do at work?' she suddenly asked, changing the subject, noticing the speckles of red paint on my hands and work shoes.

'Don't become a journalist, will you?' I said, swallowing hard at an insufficiently chewed mouthful of food.

'What are you talking about?' she asked, her own sandwich now halted on the way to her mouth, causing more lumps of tuna mayonnaise and sweetcorn to fall down her top and onto her lap. 'You over-stuffed this thing,' she complained, flicking the bits away from her clothes but not before dark speckles of grease appeared on the fabric.

'I like tuna mayonnaise,' I said, casually scooping a blob of mayonnaise off the front of her jacket and wiping it on my jeans, sucking the residue from my fingers.

Saffron

I found the whole mayonnaise finger sucking thing slightly . . . intimate and tried not to let it show that it had ruffled me. For a second it felt like we were closer than friends, but he would never go for me in a million years. He was always so busy, so casual, so indifferent. When he nudged me for an answer, I realised I'd been staring at him. 'What do you mean, don't become a journalist?' I asked.

'It's the *first* time you've asked me a question about . . . me.'

I stared at him again, cocking my head like a confused puppy. Was it really the first time I'd asked him anything about himself? The more I thought about it, the more I realised he was right. As children, we were always immersed in our imaginary lives as pirates or soldiers or explorers and he never invited me back to his house, saying he preferred to come to mine or hang out in the park. Plus, since the moment I tried to lunge in for a kiss at the duck pond, he had never hung around long enough for a sensible conversation. I tried to hide my embarrassment by fumbling desperately for something to say that would take the blame away from me. 'I thought you were . . . you know, *private*, that's all. I offer stuff about myself to you all the time but you never offer anything back. If you don't talk about yourself, that's your problem.' I knew I was getting prickly but I was embarrassed that he thought I wasn't interested when in truth I was so very interested.

Tom looked thoughtful but said nothing. 'So what *do* you do?' I asked, instantly hearing how pathetic I was being at 'interested' conversation, as if we were merely acquaintances at an adult dinner party.

'I've got an apprenticeship in joinery. I'm at college part time and the rest of the time I work with a cool guy called John and he gives me two-hour breaks for emergencies . . . which happen frequently, it would seem.' He was making a dig at me and my soap-opera life.

'So what are you making now?' I asked, ignoring his dig, and glancing at the deep red gloss on his hands.

'*Another* question? Steady on, Saffron. At this rate you'll be doing the full interview in . . . let's say, forty years?' I was doing my best to appear fascinated in whatever it was he was building, so he could at least appreciate it, but actually I *was* fascinated. I suddenly wanted to know who my friend Tom was when the spring tide was out.

'Very funny,' I said, giving a sarcastic laugh. '. . . So?'

'We are making a kitchen for a client.'

'A red one?' I asked, pulling a face. 'Bit bright.'

'Oh no, it's an oak kitchen – the red is for a personal project of mine.'

'Oh, what's the project?' I asked, my spark of interest growing.

'Blimey . . . anoth—'

'Yes! I know it's another question! I'm being *interested*.'

210

'It's a narrow boat.' His eyes twinkled as they followed the ripple of surprise that must have been playing across my face. Out of everything he could be painting, I wasn't expecting him to say that. 'Like one of those boats you see on the canal. I bought it. It's mine. I've been saving up since I first started earning money on a part-time job . . . when I was fourteen.'

So, that's why he never talked about getting drunk in pubs and clubs or had much money to spare – he was working and saving! And now he owned a canal boat. Which was pretty amazing! 'What's it like? Other than narrow, and red?' I asked.

'Run-down. I bought it cheap . . . for a few grand with the help of my boss, John. It needs an awful lot of doing up, but the skills I'm learning from my apprenticeship will go a long way to helping me make it beautiful.'

I looked into his chocolate-button eyes – I could see they were soft with the intensity of his enthusiasm for this boat. I imagined him, bowed head, paint-speckled hands, working meticulously and carefully, sanding and painting.

'John has been a saint, helping me find and secure it, complete with mooring licence, which is like gold dust round here. He's also sent things my way like tap units, or a sink fitting, or parts of apparently surplus kitchen units. It's amazing how many "unusable" things he claims to come across.'

'He sounds like a great boss,' I said.

'He is! Daft old bastard.' Tom grinned, then his voice turned down a couple of notches. 'He's helping me turn something that's a bit battered into something less battered.'

'It sounds romantic. Like . . . a floating sanctuary.' I sighed, suddenly wanting to be on the receiving end of all that Tom had to give. He wasn't just a golden-haired superhero who always appeared when I needed him, he was clever and resourceful and he had a lot of love to give, if you happened to be a boat. He obviously had many layers to him and I wanted to fall all the way through them until he caught me.

'You like the idea?' he asked, leaning forward a little as if what I was about to say mattered.

Tom looked proud, and capable and achingly lovely and I so wanted him to open up his paint-spattered arms and take me in them. The glint in his eyes stabbed me in the heart and I knew that if I didn't do something or say something I was in terrible danger of letting it show that in the last few minutes I had fallen a little bit more in love with him. 'Yeah, why shouldn't I?' I replied over-casually, looking away from the intensity of his gaze. 'I could stay in it. From what you say, it's bigger than your flat.' In that sorry moment, I noticed with shame how his cheeks snatched his dimples clean away.

'Well done, Saffron, you made it all about you within . . .' He looked at his wrist to check the time on a watch he wasn't wearing, '. . . oh, all of six minutes. Like I said, don't become a journalist.'

A silence gathered between us like an uncomfortable lump. I childishly tried to turn it back on him but I only made it worse. 'I only said it because you've made it obvious your flat isn't really big enough for me and it took you three days to get around to letting me stay with you.'

Tom checked the time on his phone and stood up, throwing his wrappers in the bin. He was a very noticeable fifteen minutes ahead of his two-hour curfew.

'I'm sorry,' I said. 'It's just that . . .' What was it? What could I say that would excuse me behaving so selfishly and crashing through his dream? I could hardly say it was the first thing I could think of to stop you guessing what you mean to me? 'It's just that I don't think before I open my mouth.' I stood up and threw my own rubbish in the bin.

'At least you'll always be surprised by what you have to say as well as everyone else,' he said, his small smile hopefully forgiving me. He unpadlocked his bike and put his rucksack on his back.

'Will you help me buy some cider . . . for Maggie? I want to soften her up so that I can tell her what we've found,' I asked. Tom had made it clear he didn't have a lot of spare cash to throw around, and I guessed buying Maggie some booze wasn't in his budget either.

'Is that a good idea? Booze for an alcoholic?' he asked, walking slowly and wheeling his bike as we talked.

'You think us buying a can of cheap cider is going to change anything for Maggie? Do you think we will save her from what she's become by buying orange juice now?' I thought about William and Chuggy living in a world that had let them down. 'Society needs to change things for people like her and all the others out there!'

'Fair point,' Tom replied, picking a bit of sweetcorn off my chin and trying not to smile when he showed me what he'd found. I frantically brushed at the rest of my face and apologised for wearing my food.

'Take it easy on her,' he said, handing over two ciders in a bag as he came out of a shop. 'You'll be scraping the scabs off a very deep cut, which she might not thank you for. I'll see you tonight, yeah?'

'Yeah. I hope your aunt doesn't mind me coming,' I added, more as an afterthought than a question. I felt as if I'd pushed them both into a corner and forced them to come to this decision – and something about their relationship seemed so *complicated*.

'She won't mind at all, that's half the problem,' he replied cryptically.

'And the other half?' I asked.

'Well that's . . . that's the other half of the problem.' He climbed onto his bike. 'Gotta go,' he called and cycled off, leaving me wondering what on earth he was talking about.

Tom

Saffron was right. I had probably never offered anything back about my life. Not when we were children and not in the few times we'd met since. I'd happily listened to her peculiar life; missing mothers, ill mothers, dead mothers, replacement mothers, resurrected mothers. Or her latest decoration ideas for her bedroom: blue carpet or cream? Leather or cloth for the sofa in her bedroom? Blinds or curtains for the windows? Lemon accent or pink? I'd been unwilling to chip in with my own bedroom decoration ideas . . . whether I should let the mould in the corner grow right up to the ceiling or keep spraying it with mildew treatment? Should I move the bedside cabinet to the left of the headboard of my single bed with its ancient rocket-ship-patterned duvet cover, or to the right? Should I tie the matching rocket-ship curtains back with string or just let them stick to the condensation on the glass?

And then there was all the other stuff I couldn't tell her before. My mother. My aunt. My absolute vulnerability.

My boat was my future, and telling Saffron about it would be like exposing my innards. For a beautiful second, I thought I could see a glimmer of what I felt about my boat reflected in her eyes. I thought she could see what I saw in a different kind of life, a life on the water – a huge world under a massive sky and the ever-changing seasons draping themselves across the landscape. I thought I could see more than I could.

One day, I would live on the river and with the chug of the engine I could go anywhere I wanted, like a human water-snail, and leave Saffron to a life I could never compete with. My kind of life was so far removed from hers that it was stupid of me to think I could offer her more. When I found a bit of sweetcorn on the corner of her mouth, and she'd grimaced as she frantically wiped her face with both hands, I assured her that she looked fine.

Because she always looked fine to me.

Saffron

How stupid can one person be? Tom had worked for years on his boat, the excitement of his achievement positively radiating out of him, and all I could say was 'I could stay in it'. I wanted to tell him that I, too, was caught up in his dreams. That for a moment I'd floated away on them, become part of them. I wanted to tell him how happy I was that after all these years, he was finally giving me a peek into his world, yet I didn't. Instead I waved goodbye as if he was just a friend who'd simply offered me a room for the night.

'Good afternoon,' I said as I sat on a park bench next to Maggie, tipping my head to the flimsy kind of warmth the sun was offering as it hung limply over the buildings on the west side of town. I was almost used to Maggie's green haze now, prepared to breathe in a way that didn't send it via my nasal receptors. 'Can I join you?'

'Got to go, someone else is calling me,' she said to an invisible friend, turning to me as if I were no more real or imagined than her not-real friend.

'It's me, Saffron. I'm the person you gave your red pashmina to. The person who gave you a drink and croissant this morning,' I said.

'Of course, the firecracker! I'm not blind. Or stupid. Or a goldfish,' she muttered.

'I've brought you some cider,' I said, jumping slightly as she grabbed hold of the bag. Then I fished in my pocket and offered her the cereal bar I'd insisted Tom also buy her. 'Something healthy . . . ish to go with it?' I proffered.

'I'm way past being healthy! . . . Even "ish",' she snorted. And her snort became laughter, and her laughter became another bout of hacking coughs, which made her eyes water and a strand of spittle hang from her mouth. 'And besides, look at these.' She wheezed, turning her face fully towards me, scrunching her lips apart to reveal very few teeth, blasting me with the foul odour of her breath at the same time.

I managed not to react like a cat sicking up a hairball and put the cereal bar back in my pocket. I wouldn't be eating it either, especially not now. In fact, I wasn't sure if I could ever eat anything again after that display. 'Anyway, Maggie.' I tried to swallow the hairball back down. Suddenly I didn't know where to begin. How do you begin telling a homeless drunk person that her family would like her back in the folds of their Cheltenham post code? I couldn't work out a way to tell her that I knew she was once a very pretty girl from a well-to-do family – a girl with a whole future ahead of her. It was difficult to compare the two Maggies but as I sat next to the current one, I searched for the one she had started out life as. For the lost blue colour in her eyes. For the shape of her face behind the sagging folds of skin, and the three moles still visible within the weather-worn mesh of red veins on her cheeks. Those moles were now the only hint of the long road that linked her two lives.

'Have you come to tell me about the party?' she asked. I was getting used to her haphazard conversation, and although a few days ago I would have laughed, this time I knew I was about to snatch her away from the invented party in her head and chuck her into real life.

'No, Maggie, although I'm sure it will be a good party.' I took a breath. 'I've come to tell you that I know you have family that are looking for you.'

My words were unwelcome. 'I don't have any,' she snapped, folding her arms aggressively, her eyeballs instantly disappearing behind tightly shut fat eyelids.

'But you do, Maggie. I saw them on a website. You've been missing for years.' Her eyes remained shut, her body becoming motionless, sagging like a rag doll, her head dipping low. What was she doing? I wondered if she'd dropped into some sort of catatonic state, but unexpectedly she emitted a loud rumbling snore. Then another. And one more after that. 'I know you're not asleep. Don't pretend.' I was amazed by this strange reaction. I was sure my mum would be wild with relief if this was, God forbid, the sort of life she was living when I found her. 'Your family, Maggie, they want you back. Your advert is still on the internet.' The conversation was very one-sided. I don't know what I expected from her but it wasn't this theatrical snoring she was currently doing.

'I'm thirsty,' she snapped, with her eyes still tight shut and arms folded over her belly. I pulled the ring pull off one of the cans and watched as she drank it, fascinated at how desperately she needed it. I had dragged something to the surface and she wanted to force it back down below the waterline as quickly as she could. What on earth had happened to this woman? I wondered if, like me, she'd once had an argument with her parents. Had she also once packed a very large hold-all and somehow ended up in this mess? It wouldn't happen to me though. I'd never let this . . . this . . . *awfulness* happen to me.

'I found out my dad had been lying to me about my mum,' I offered. I thought maybe if I told Maggie why I'd left home she'd open up too. 'He told me she was dead when she wasn't . . . *isn't*. I hate him for it but I *am* in contact with him – at least he knows I'm alive.' Maggie said nothing. 'Why did you leave home?' I prodded.

The silence that followed told me that Maggie did not want to talk about it – or maybe she'd forgotten why. Maybe years of alcohol had pickled her memory and she didn't know who she used to be any more. We both sat watching water from the fish-head fountain fly into the air, briefly reflecting the world around it before plopping loudly into the pool beneath. 'Don't you miss it? Your home?' I said, trying to push away the sudden realisation that I missed mine. 'Not just the comfort, but the familiarity . . . The not having to try so hard just to tackle every hour of every day? Opening the fridge and finding lovely food? Having people talk to you, asking you about your day?' Still Maggie said nothing. 'I miss my brother Archie, even him showing me his latest bogie collection. I miss fighting with Daniel over the remote control and I even miss the splashes of colour that follow Charlotte everywhere – toys, clothes, paintings. The humming of my father as he slips off his work shoes and loosens his tie, and even . . . even . . . the warm, fresh smell of the undeniably delicious banana bread that *she* bakes.'

Maggie moved. Her foot in its many socks and old boot tapped the wheels of her trolley. 'This is my home.'

'But it's . . . um . . . it's . . .' I couldn't think of a kinder way to tell her she was pushing a massive pile of toot around.

'I've got everything in here I could ever need – bedding, clothes, cutlery, shoes, radio. What more do I need?'

'Don't you want a house?' I asked.

'Don't *you*?' she suddenly accused, and she had a point. 'Anyway, I've got a house.'

'Oh, you have?' I answered, curious.

'Yes. It's in my pocket.'

I stifled a laugh. She was so funny. Her head was full of so many odd things. She unbuttoned her overcoat to reveal a large inside pocket. 'I was given it by a little firecracker who jumped right out in front of me from nowhere.'

'Oh?' I replied tentatively, eyeing the piece of folded card she fished from her pocket. It was blue and crumpled, and showed a child's drawing of a house with yellow curtains and a red front door.

'I've had it a long time,' she murmured. But I knew exactly how long she'd had it. She hadn't even looked at it on the day I gave it to her, putting it straight in her pocket before Dad had dragged me away.

'You kept it?' I asked.

'It was a present,' Maggie said, as if it was obvious. She studied the now crumpled and discoloured card as if it was an expensive work of art. Then she smiled. 'It was a lovely present.'

I wondered why she'd shoved it in her pocket so quickly that day. Why she hadn't looked at it at the time, yet kept it with her all these years. 'Why didn't you open the card when the firecracker gave it to you?' I asked, touched that something I had done so many years ago had been that important.

'Because I was saving it for later,' she answered. 'I hadn't been given a card or a letter for years. Something that precious is not something you rush, firecracker.'

'Do you call everyone . . . firecracker?' I asked softly.

'No,' she answered.

I was amazed that she'd remembered it was me after all this time. That I had touched her in such a way. She tipped up the cider and took another long drink. Maggie's beauty had long since slipped off her face and the gorgeous brown hair had paled to a dirty grey. Something had damaged Maggie. 'You were musical when you were young, weren't you?'

'Alexandra was. She could play the piano quite well and loved opera.' She tipped her head back and closed her eyes, not pretending to be asleep this time, but perhaps contemplating the distance between Alexandra and Maggie. The fountain continued to spew water, constant and mesmerising. Two children held their hands out like starfish, hoping to catch some of the droplets before they disappeared. A man with a wire-haired dog jogged past and an old lady staggered to the next bench with three heavy bags of shopping.

Maggie, her eyes still shut, began to emit a thin noise. It grew into a long note that gurgled a bit and made her clear her throat several times before she tried again. A couple walking out of the market pointed at her, laughing, and I gave them my best 'eat shit and die' look. Gradually, a tune I recognised, in words I didn't understand, came out of her mouth, quietly at first, then louder and more confident, eventually building into a proper bit of park-bench opera. She was turning heads again but this time no one was laughing. Maggie was *amazing*! She was probably no longer pitch perfect, but even so, who would have dreamt it? Maggie, the town's drunk, could sing beautiful opera. It was Italian! The foreign words died out when Maggie raised her can and took another gulp, bringing her back to the moment. 'O *Mio Babbino Caro*. Alexandra loved that one the most,' she said, burping slightly, as a huddle of people clapped their hands in delighted surprise.

'Why did Alexandra run away?' I asked, realising too late that I had opened a painful portal into her past. Just as with William, two tears slid their way down her cheeks. I had pried the top off her scabs, just like Tom said I would.

'She didn't mean to do it,' she whispered. 'Alexandra was babysitting. She ran the bath. She left him . . . just for a tiny moment.'

'Who? . . . Who did she leave?' I asked almost as quietly, something awful finding its way into the pit of my stomach.

'Little Eddie. He was only two. The doorbell rang . . . Alexandra answered it . . . she took her eye off him . . . and he climbed in the bath. She was *responsible*.' Suddenly the story was halted. Whatever Alexandra was reliving from all those years ago was halted by a barrier that Maggie threw in her way. She wasn't crazy, like everyone thought . . . like I had so unkindly said so many times. Maggie's mind was simply protecting her from the awfulness of what was in it. A long,

long time ago, a little boy had died and Alexandra Barrington had died with him.

The strawberries on Maggie's hat swung gently with her laboured breathing and her tears shone brightly against the age-old dirt. 'I'm sorry,' I said, and placed my hand on hers.

Maggie stared at my hand. 'Touch,' she whispered, before slowly curling her fingers round mine.

Saffron

'Hey.'

I hadn't got far after leaving Maggie sleeping peacefully, when a deep voice calling out made me stop. I looked up to see the guy from Tuesday walking towards me. The dark-haired guy with the grey eyes who'd rescued me from face planting the pavement.

'Hi,' I responded, mentally groaning. I didn't want him to notice I was still wearing most of the same clothes from two days ago.

'You OK?' he asked.

'Why wouldn't I be?' I answered, as cheerfully as I could muster.

'Look, I don't mean to be funny, but I know you didn't have anywhere to stay the last couple of nights. I know you haven't been home . . .'

All internal bodily functions came to a complete standstill as I eyed him cautiously. 'Why do you say that? Why would you even think you know that?' This guy must have been sent to spy on me by my dad and I wasn't happy.

'It's OK, don't panic!' he laughed. 'I'm Mike. A volunteer

for the local shelter and support group for people in the town who might need our help. I know most people in this part of town and I know you've been sleeping rough. I'm skilled at spotting it. It's my job to show people how to access local services if they need it. I know a day centre that will help you. It's got showers, a washing machine, cafe, help with finding accommodation. Everything . . . and it's a really friendly place.'

I continued to be cautious – stranger danger and all that – but if he could take me somewhere that could help me find accommodation, I wouldn't need to worry Tom and Angela. It was obvious I was going to be an inconvenience to them and this could be the solution for all of us. 'Will the day centre try to phone my dad and tell him?' I asked.

'Of course not.' He smiled. 'Not if you don't want it. If you like, they will just let you shower and wash your clothes and help you with whatever else you want.' I tried not to smile at his name. *Mike*, the name I made up for my boyfriend . . . the non-existent body builder. 'Shall I take you?'

I looked at his smile, the way it stretched across his crooked teeth, happily quirky. He was wiry framed and definitely not a body builder, like my imaginary boyfriend, but he was quite fit and seemed to know what he was talking about.

A wave of excitement overtook me. 'Independence!' I grinned. 'How will they help me get somewhere so quickly?' remembering what William and Chuggy had told me and aware that even Ronnie hadn't got somewhere to stay yet.

'Don't you worry about the detail,' Mike said confidently. Then he led the way through town while he told me about his volunteering work for the homeless and I told him all about the briefcase in the attic and my dad and why I'd spent two nights on the street. Eventually we crossed a small humped bridge over the river where, on the corner, was an old Victorian house. 'Here it is,' he said, as we reached the tall, white building. There was a huge sign on the front saying River Street Homeless Day Centre, and the front area was edged with black iron railings which had two bikes chained to it. The door was open and I could see several people inside. It did look welcoming . . . if you were down and out . . . which I wasn't. I was not one of them. 'They don't look homeless,' I said to Mike, indicating the people I could see from where I was standing outside. Down the side were tables and chairs with men sitting having hot drinks and smoking cigarettes.

'That's the whole point of this place,' he answered. 'Clean clothes and a chance to get back on the wheel. Most homeless people don't sleep rough, they sofa-surf, or stay with friends, in shelters . . . anywhere they can while they try to rebuild their lives.'

'But I'm not *homeless* as such . . .' I began, as I put my foot on the first step up to the door, about to tell him about Tom's offer.

'Indeed. But you are eighteen. Right?' he said, catching hold of my arm.

'No,' I answered, feeling the first flutters of disappointment. I'd told him the other day that I was at school, but he must have forgotten.

'Oh *Christ*, sorry, Saffron. I didn't think. You have to be eighteen to use this service. They don't allow children here.'

My heart sank to my chunky boots. 'No shower?' I asked. The thought of not washing properly after another night on urine-stained concrete! I'd been so close to not having to rock up to Tom's looking like this.

'No shower!' he replied with an apologetic look on his face. 'Sorry, Saffy.'

I shrugged. 'That's OK. I'd have liked a shower but beggars can't be choosers.'

Mike pointed at a cafe over the road. 'How about I buy you a drink? We'll see if we can find another way to help you with accommodation.'

Tom

Stepping out of the shower, the cold shower curtain sticking to me, my feet landing on the thin bath mat, I wondered how grateful Saffron would have been for my shabby bathroom over the last two days. And picking my way over everything in the living room on my way to the tiny kitchen, I also wondered guiltily how grateful she would have been for the roof over her head on the night of the storm.

'We've got a bit to do round here, Angela. Saffron's going to get here for around seven.' I shoved the second half of a Snickers in my mouth while pacing in a small circle on the carpet.

Angela swallowed a mouthful of her tea. 'I'm looking forward to meeting her already. And stop pacing, you're making me dizzy.'

'It's not exactly what she's used to,' I said, through nuts and caramel.

'Aren't you proud of our palace?' Angela grinned, sweeping her hand across the paraphernalia in the room. Then she took another sip of tea and pulled a serious face. 'All the more reason for me to leave now, Tom. You need to start again.'

'See! There you go. I knew you'd jump in the deep end with this whole thing. She hasn't even got here yet and you're already packing. She'll run for the hills if you start ranting on about her and me having a relationship. There is nothing between us. She'll stay in the spare bed and then probably after one night she'll get the hell away from us as fast as she can.'

'Surely not. What's there not to love about this?' she joked again. '. . . Or you.' Her laugh turned into an indulgent smile.

'Seriously, I don't want you embarrassing me in front of her.'

'I would never do that.' She looked at me with pretend hurt eyes and a huge sealed grin, pretending to zip it shut in front of me.

'It's important. *Really* important. Not only is she in a mess at the moment but she's used to a different kind of life from anything I can give her. She wouldn't want me.'

Saffron

Mike and I drank from glass Coke bottles through a straw. 'I wouldn't be in this mess if I had ID. My bag got stolen because I didn't have any ID to get a room. My beautiful stuff, all rifled through by someone who's probably already flogged my designer labels on a street corner for a couple of quid. My brother is bringing me my ID tomorrow though.'

'Your brother? Couldn't you stay at his place?' Mike asked.

'His place is a dungeon that stinks of cheesy feet and underpants. He's thirteen!'

'Won't *he* tell your parents where you are? You were worried the shelter would phone them.'

'Parent,' I corrected. 'He won't tell my dad anything because I have his life on the end of my fingers. He wouldn't dare.' I tapped my phone knowingly. 'And my mum . . . well that's a whole other story.'

Mike thanked the waitress who brought over two plates of pancakes with ice cream and cherries. 'So once you get ID you're sorted . . . you can pay for accommodation?' Mike queried.

'Um . . . well . . . my money got stolen too. It's been a

stressful couple of days. But Daniel will bring some money too . . . hopefully.'

'And if he forgets . . . you won't go back to your parent?'

I was unwilling to go into detail, so I sucked in my breath and said, 'No I won't. It's a long story but basically I told my dad that I'm staying with a friend so he won't send out the search party. I am staying at a friend's house tonight but it's not ideal. They didn't want me to stay when I first asked, hence the sleeping rough, so my guess is they don't really want me there at all.'

'So you've run off into the sunset and it's not going well.' Mike balanced a large amount of pancake, cream and cherries onto his fork and scooped it all into his mouth.

'Pretty much,' I answered.

Tom

'You didn't have to make that call now!' I said, shoving her make-up bag off the chair and onto her lap, and sitting down next to her. 'Everything could be like it's always been. Just for a bit longer.'

'Everything changes, Tom. This is just one of those changes.'

I picked at some paint that was stuck to the hairs on my shin. 'Saffron is not a *thing*, I keep telling you. She's just a friend who needs a bed for the night. When you leave this flat, I have to leave this flat, and I haven't finished my boat yet so I can't.'

Angela rooted through the make-up bag for her little hand mirror and some lipstick. 'That's because you're starting from the outside on that boat and working your way in. You're stalling for time – you know it and I know it. But I know you could clear a space and have a bed in there by the end of the month if you put your mind to it. Do I look nice?'

'You look almost pleasant,' I said, avoiding the swipe of her hand aiming for the back of my head as I stood up and stretched. 'Better get on, she'll be here in an hour.' I looked around me to see what Saffron would see when she arrived. It was now tidy enough, but the kitchen was still minuscule and the two bedrooms weren't big either. The living room was now Angela's bedroom, full of Angela's stuff, but at least it meant Saffron could have the one decent bed. The windows still had a touch of black mould clinging to the edges and corners but there was nothing I could do about that now except hope she didn't have a serious mould allergy.

Saffron

'I'm going to take you to the youth hostel. They know me there so you won't need ID. I'll sign you in and arrange through the voluntary service for you to stay for a few nights. It's not really protocol to do that but I'll bend a few rules. All I need for now is your mobile phone number and your full name, then when you get your money from Daniel you can take over from there. How about that?'

'You hardly know me,' I stuttered, giving him my number. 'What about rules? You'd put yourself on the line for me?'

'I know you well enough to know that you need a place to stay and no one is helping you, are they?'

'I have a place for tonight,' I reminded him. 'With my friend Tom.'

'And Tom was OK with you sleeping rough the other nights, was he?' Mike asked abruptly.

'To be fair, he didn't know. He assumed I'd gone home.'

'He didn't check though, did he?' Mike said. I looked at the ground. Tom hadn't bust a gut to find out if I was OK. It was true.

Mike took my elbow and propelled me down the path. 'I

do this stuff all the time, Saffy. I'll make sure you're safe. And as you look eighteen, you can pay me back by coming for a drink.' We reached a bar by the river, where people were sitting at wooden garden tables or leaning against the wall edging the river. 'What do you fancy? I could get you a glass of wine or something . . . no one would know you weren't eighteen if I was paying. I'll bring it outside.'

Mike was treating me like an adult and I loved it. Music was filtering out from inside the pub and the idea of being independent and being treated like this was very appealing.

'Thank you. I'll have a vodka and lemonade please,' I said, making my way towards the wall where hopefully no one would ask any questions. I was small for my age and although I had put make-up on that morning in a department store, I knew I didn't look eighteen. When Mike emerged from the pub he was carrying a pint of beer and my drink, which he handed to me with a big grin on his face.

'You don't have to sip it like it's the last drink on earth, I can get you another one afterwards,' he said.

'It's strong,' I said, taking another, larger sip.

'Double! Like I said, you've been let down by everyone and I'm just showing you not everyone is that bad.' He grinned at me again and took a glug of his beer, making a smacking sound against his lips. 'Why do you keep checking your phone?' he asked, as I was swiping my finger across the screen.

'I'm waiting for news . . . of my mum . . . I'm looking for her.' I peered up at him to test his response.

Mike balanced his glass on the wall. 'Wow. When you didn't mention her before, I thought perhaps she'd died. What do you mean you're looking for her? Don't you have any contact with her?'

It came out then. The whole thing. Like vomit, and I couldn't stop it. 'So you see, it's really important that I hear from her.' I studied his face, waiting to see his reaction to my dysfunctional life. His face was serious and he touched my arm.

'You poor thing. How awful that she just disappeared like that. And your dad? How could he have kept such a secret from you for all this time? That's abuse, that is!'

I sighed. 'Isn't it just.'

By my second double vodka and lemonade, the sun had almost disappeared and street lights were starting to pop into life. A string of glass bulbs hanging outside the pub came on and the dark river became splashed with little white pools of light. The alcohol made me feel relaxed and confident and everything in my world seemed infinitely brighter.

When we eventually left the pub to go to the youth hostel, I was not only slightly drunk but I realised with horror that it was almost eight o'clock. I hadn't told Tom I'd found somewhere else to stay. As Mike got us a taxi to take us to the youth hostel, I quickly tapped out a text.

Me: Thanks for your offer for a bed tonight but Mike
is able to get me a room at the youth hostel. So sorry
if you went to any trouble. I'll contact you tomorrow x

I guessed Tom would be pleased to get my text, he hadn't really wanted me to stay anyway and maybe he would think that my body builder boyfriend called Mike was real after all.

His text came back almost immediately.

Tom: Cool. Hope it works out x

So he was cool with it. Probably massively relieved that I wasn't putting him and his aunt to any inconvenience. Mike paid the taxi fare, which was generous of him because it came to over ten pounds, and we made our way up the steps to an old building. Several lights were on inside, giving it a welcoming look. I could hardly wait.

Tom

I'd sorted stuff, moved stuff and thrown stuff away. Sprayed, vacuumed and scrubbed as if the queen was coming to visit. By seven o'clock I'd prepped Angela over what she was and wasn't allowed to say. 'I've got it, memorised the whole script, won't put a word wrong. You can trust me,' she said, checking the time and putting another smear of lipstick on.

'That's just it, I can't trust you! You've got a runaway mouth and it's going to get *me* into trouble.' She scoffed, as if what I was saying wasn't important.

Her smile slipped then. 'Why do you insist on building a fortress around yourself? You can't keep shutting people out.'

'I'm not.'

'You are.'

We looked at each other for a whole minute before she eventually said, 'Why won't you risk your heart on her?'

Another minute passed while her blue eyes fixed on mine and I wrestled with the answer, finally settling on half of the truth. 'Because it's the prince who wins the heart of the princess, never the peasant who wins the heart of the princess.'

Then Angela reached out her hand and tapped mine. 'But

when the princess kisses the peasant he turns into a prince.'

'It's a frog, Angela. The princess kisses a frog, who turns into a prince.'

She laughed then, a crinkly, smiley laugh and tapped my hand harder. 'It doesn't matter, this girl will find the prince in you. I know she will. If you'd only give up on building that fortress . . .'

We were still there, waiting, when the closing music to *Eastenders* blared into the room, telling us it was eight o'clock. There had been no clank of the lift outside, no knock on the door, but a fresh cover on the spare bed and a single flower pinched from the bunch I'd bought on Monday still waited patiently for our guest. Then my phone buzzed with a message from Saffron.

Saffron: Thanks for your offer for a bed tonight but Mike
    is able to get me a room at the youth hostel. So sorry
    if you went to any trouble. I'll contact you tomorrow x

'She's not coming. She's found somewhere to stay.' I looked across at Angela, and she looked back at me and neither of us said a word. I couldn't help thinking that if this Mike was real, why couldn't he have helped her out two days ago? But then, I supposed, I was real, I was her friend – yet I hadn't helped her out two days ago either.

Saffron

The staff at the hostel were really friendly but it still didn't change the fact that the youth hostel was full.

'We're nearly always busy because it's such a popular town,' the guy said, smiling at me apologetically through his red-rimmed glasses, then he pushed them back up his nose while looking at the screen in front of him. 'We've got a bed free on Sunday. Do you want me to book you in then? You can have it for four nights?'

I could feel a prickle creep up my back and neck, burying itself in the roots of my hair. I knew the red thing was going on again, but I was past caring because I was going to have to text Tom again and look like a complete idiot. 'There must be something going on in town for it to be that full otherwise they would have been able to squeeze you in somewhere,' Mike complained as we walked heavily back down the steps. 'Sorry about that, Saffy. I feel really bad.'

After everything he'd done for me, the last thing I wanted him to feel was bad on my account. 'It's OK. I can grovel to my friend and hope he forgives me but he's quite a long way from here. I'd better start walking.'

Mike sighed a long, thoughtful sigh. 'Look, I shouldn't do this, but I do know somewhere you could stay for now.'

Hope revived itself as I stopped mid-text to Tom. 'Mine!' he said. 'I share a flat with my girlfriend and we don't live far. She has . . . stuff . . . scented, girly stuff you can freshen up with. There are even fluffy towels,' he added.

I was unsure. It seemed like such an imposition and alarm bells were ringing. I hardly knew this guy but it did sound appealing, and better equipped than at Tom's. 'I'm a volunteer for the homeless, Saffy. This is what I do . . . I help people. My flat has a big spare bedroom and you can stay until I get you your own accommodation,' Mike encouraged.

'Do you have WiFi?' I asked eventually with a hopeful smile.

'We have WiFi. Come on, the shower and fluffy towels are waiting. You'll be fine, I'll look after you.' I fell into step beside him, relieved. Tomorrow suddenly looked a whole lot brighter if I could spend the day using Mike's WiFi to look for my mum.

'If you don't want your family bugging you at my house, you'd better turn location services off on your phone,' Mike advised.

'Don't worry, I turned that off ages ago,' I answered.

Saffron

The shower was . . . reviving. There was, as Mike had said, stuff I could freshen up with – shampoo, shower gel and deodorant – and I was grateful for that. I tried not to mind that the towels weren't exactly fluffy, that they had that sour smell washing gets when it hasn't been aired properly. But most of all I really tried not to mind that Mike didn't actually live with his girlfriend.

He showed me into his spare room, which was sparsely decorated and although it had a double bed in the centre, I could see that the sheets were thin and faded and not the clean, crisp cotton I had on my own bed at home. The pillows I'd longed for while I was under the bridge were flat and obviously hadn't ever seen a single feather in their lives.

Mike stood in the doorway next to me and surveyed the scene. 'Is it OK? I rented this place with my girlfriend . . . *ex*-girlfriend, and we were going to do it up together, to make it really nice . . . until I found out that one boyfriend at a time wasn't enough for her. I still find it hard to admit to myself or anyone else that she left me. She really hurt me.'

He stared at me with pained eyes and I immediately felt so

sorry for him. 'It's OK,' I replied, deciding not to go into detail about the massive bathroom in my own house or the size of my bedroom with its cream sofa, fitted wardrobes and en-suite. 'It is a damn sight better than the bridge . . . thank you.'

Mike made me a huge bowl of soup with some bread, while I curled up on the sofa under a blanket wearing a T-shirt nighty his ex-girlfriend had left behind. 'This'll warm you up,' he said, pouring me a drink and offering me a tumbler glass. I took a sip and immediately the heat hit my throat and made me gasp. 'Blimey, Mike, what is this?'

'Sorry. It's whisky. I don't have any wine or juice,' he answered. 'You'll start enjoying it after a couple of mouthfuls. Trust me.' I trusted him, and he was right, before long I was enjoying the burn and the effect of it as it flowed through me. He got up to pour me another and the little flat began to look more homely as the strong alcohol joined the remaining vodka and lemonade in my system. The living room had a balcony and his television was huge. And he was being very kind. Very kind indeed.

My phone vibrated with a message.

Dad: I'm still here for you. I've always been here for you.
Please can we meet? x

'Message?' Mike asked, eyeing my phone.

I deleted the message. 'It's my dad. He's trying to suck up to me but I'm not interested. He wants to meet but I'm not going to and it's his own fault.'

'Tell him you're safe and you're with a friend. It will put

his mind at rest and get him off your case for tonight,' he said, pouring another drink for himself. 'And you'd better give me your number as well so I can contact you about accommodation.' We sat in silence for a while, staring at the muted television until my phone screen flashed at me again. This time, an unknown number and a smiling yellow face appeared on the screen. I looked across at Mike, confused. He laughed. 'What? I was beginning to feel left out. You spend all your time looking at your messages,' he joked. I sent him one back of an upside-down smiley face. He sent one back of a laughing smiley face.

'So, I'm not being funny or anything, but your dad's a bit of a prat to keep your mum from you all this time, isn't he? I'm not surprised you don't want to go home.'

'Don't forget my step-witch. She's a bit of a prat too. He got rid of my mum and replaced her with Smell-an-ie.' I was beginning to feel the alcohol take over my tongue, stopping my lips from working properly.

'Yeah. You're not her own child, that's the trouble,' Mike said. 'I had a stepmother and we never got on. Nothing I did was ever as good as what her own sons did.' I nodded enthusiastically when he said that, but then I remembered the lady from that morning telling me that step-mums always give more than they ever get back. The picture of me and Melanie smiling at the camera wavered in front of my eyes and my head filled with confused thoughts that I tried to push away. I held my tumbler out and Mike obediently filled it. My phone flashed again and it was another smiley face from Mike and a hug emoji. 'I wanted to make you feel less sad,' he said.

The whisky made my head really heavy and my arms go all loose, like I was immersed in a deliciously warm bath although in reality I was curled on a brown, slightly sagging leather sofa in Mike's flat. Conscious that I mustn't do that 'all about me' thing again, I decided to ask him questions but I could hear the words come out slow and laboured. 'Who do you volunteer for? You know . . . the people you help on the street?'

'The church,' he answered. 'We go out and about looking for people who are sleeping rough. Help them find accommodation, food, hot drinks and stuff. We help many people that way. It's very rewarding.'

'The church? Are you a vicar?' I giggled, imagining Mike in a dog collar holding a Bible, then I giggled some more, like it was the most hilarious thing. 'How come you weren't working this afternoon . . . if you're very busy helping all the shadows of real people?'

'The what?' he asked.

'The shadows . . . of *real* people. One of the homeless guys I met calls them that. It makes sense – I've always believed everything bad that happens to us, slips down into a puddle of dark at our feet. Obviously some people fall right into that puddle and become the shadow.' I was slurring now but I'd got to that point where everything you say sounds really profound.

'Are you drunk?' Mike asked.

'Absolutely,' I answered, draining the last of my glass, still giggling until my mouth stiffened and, totally unexpectedly, a strangled sob came out. I pulled the blanket tighter round

246

my legs and curled into the sofa, clutching my empty glass to my chest. Mike put a hand on my ankle and squeezed gently, and leant forward to refill my glass.

'A new beginning,' he said, holding out the bottle.

Saffron

I tried to be sick quietly but it wasn't working. The vodka and lemonade plus the whisky came out of my mouth in a loud gush accompanied by lumps of half-digested pancake and some chunks of cherry, followed by a horrible burping and retching sound.

'You OK in there?' Mike asked through the closed door to the bathroom. I groaned and spat out some bile, in reply. 'I'll get you some water,' he called. I wasn't used to quite that much alcohol, hence my stomach now projecting its contents into Mike's toilet.

I'd got myself to the bathroom shortly after noticing that the dusty lampshade hanging from the living room ceiling was creating circles above me. The floor started moving when I tried to get across it. I was now on my knees with my head in the pan. My hair was dangling in splashes of sick and the sight of sticky yellow drops of Mike's urine dried onto the seat was making me retch more. This was not the cleanest toilet, or bathroom, I'd come across, and my face being only inches away from it all was making it worse.

'I'm so sorry,' I said, looking up at him with embarrassment as I staggered out of the bathroom. 'I'm not used to whisky. I think I'd like to go to bed now please.'

'You should have said,' he answered. 'I'll get you something different next time.'

I groaned, pulling the thin duvet over me, resting my sick-infused hair on the biscuit-thin pillow.

Friday:
Castles and Warriors

Tom

'You OK, Maggie?' I asked as I slowed to a halt on my bike. She was hacking up her guts as I was cycling to town, wincing and holding her side as if in great pain. 'You don't look great.' She'd unbuttoned her coat and there was a sheen to her forehead, despite the cold. Maggie never looked special at the best of times, but this morning I'd say she was looking extra un-special.

'Never mind that. I've been looking for you,' she puffed, shaking her head so hard all her chins wobbled. Then another huge hacking cough came almost from the toes of her boots and I could hear phlegm crackling its way through every millimetre of her lungs, the strawberries on her hat bouncing wildly.

A sprig of plastic sunflowers poked out of the side bars of her trolley and round her neck was a garland of flowers worthy of a Hawaiian beach party. 'Your ... trolley looks nice ... and, er, so do you,' I complimented. Despite the bloating, the smell and that beard, there was something very feminine about Maggie. All flowers and polka dots and brightly coloured trinkets, but despite that she still looked particularly awful this morning, as if whatever illness or decay was going on inside her was beginning to show through her skin. She was almost transparent behind the high circles of rouge on her cheeks and the blue of her eyes was even more faded against the eyeshadow she'd recently plastered up to her eyebrows.

'The firecracker went off with that twat and she wasn't under the bridge last night. I saw you with her in town, she's your little girl, isn't she?' she puffed, gaining control of herself just enough to convince me that she wasn't about to die right in front of me.

'I assume you mean Saffron, but she's not my girl . . . she's staying at her boyfriend's now and there's not much I can do if he's a twat. Sorry, Maggie . . . got to go, it's my day at college for my apprenticeship, I've got a lesson on hinges and brackets in half an hour.' I pushed down on the pedals of my bike and made to leave.

'He's a twat,' Maggie called out. 'The firecracker went off with that twat.'

I placed a foot back on the pavement and laughed. 'You can't call someone's boyfriend that, Maggie. Though I kinda like the fact that you have.'

'He's not her boyfriend!' Again, she shook her head until the strawberries almost bashed her in the eyes.

'Who is he then?' Instantly, the fact that I was going to be late for my first class faded into insignificance when I realised I might just have stumbled upon yet another of Saffron's disasters.

'He's not nice, that's who he is. He gets drunk, gives us street people a hard time. He's relieved himself on me more than once.'

My heart beat rapidly. 'Sounds like a lovely bloke,' I muttered. 'Do you know who he is?'

'No,' she answered, 'but I do know he's a wrong'n!'

Saffron

The sky was the colour of steel. The kind of sky that made you want to stay in bed all day. I'd woken to the vibration of my phone alerting me to another message and my head feeling like it was about to cave in.

> Dad: I've just remembered something about
> your mum that you'll like. She loved mornings.
> She believed they held exciting secrets that
> would be revealed as the day rolled on xx

The thin curtains in the room were half open, allowing the grey light from the grey sky to enter. I opened them fully and squinted out. The view was . . . uninspiring, but I forced myself to reach beyond the buildings and houses in front of Mike's flat. *She loved mornings.* I wanted to be like her and look for the exciting secrets. What would the day bring? Would it bring her? All it had brought so far was a mouth like the bottom of a bird cage and a bad head.

As I carried on squinting with the light hurting my eyes, cloudy rememberings of Mum coming home with armfuls of nature began to form in my mind. Archie in his cot, Daniel and me waiting for her to come back from her many long walks. The picture frame in the hall that still displayed a photo of us children. I passed it every day. A wooden surround with a multitude of feathers varnished into it, collected in her treasure bag. *Waiting for her to come back . . .* A fine crack opened in the clouds, issuing a slice of morning sunlight, beckoning me to peek inside for a clearer view of my memories, but I just couldn't quite grasp them.

My phone buzzed again. It was Mike sending me another emoji. Three, in fact. A kissing face, a bunch of flowers and a cup of tea. I started to respond but my phone rang with Tom's name across the screen.

I climbed back into bed, pulled the second biscuit-thin pillow behind my head and propped myself up. The duvet felt old and cheap beneath my fingers as I drew it towards my cold shoulders, like it was stuffed with lumps of bread. I guess not everyone could afford feather but whatever kind of bread was inside it, it was definitely better than cardboard and Maggie's blanket. 'Saffron, who's this guy you're with?' Tom's voice came urgently down my phone.

I lowered my voice so that Mike couldn't hear. 'Good morning, Tom. I'm sorry about last night . . . but I didn't think you'd mind.'

'So who is it? This guy? Do you know him?'

'I told you, it's Mike. He's helping me.'

'Maggie said he's dodgy. Can you meet me . . . like now?' His words rushed their way out of his mouth as if he was in a hurry.

I whispered harshly into the receiver. 'No. I'm not even

dressed. What's the panic? He's not "dodgy". He bought me dinner and put me up in his spare room for God's sake!'

'Ever heard of grooming, Saffron? Maggie said he's a wrong'n. He even pis—'

Mike knocked on the door and I quickly put the phone down. How on earth would Maggie know if Mike was no good and why on earth was Tom even listening to her? I shoved the phone face-down on the covers and fumed. Mike had been nothing but helpful. He'd really put himself out for me, paying for taxis and trying to help me find accommodation. He'd had a million opportunities to put a bag over my head and spirit me away into the underworld and hadn't. I was offended on his behalf.

The door swung open before I managed to say 'Come in' and Mike was grinning and carrying a large mug of tea, some toast and an orange flower, which he ceremoniously gave to me. 'I nicked it from the garden outside. Do you drink tea?' I didn't but I'd have rehydrated with anything right at that moment. He put the cup on the bedside table, and stood by the edge of the bed as I gripped the duvet tighter around my shoulders to prevent it from slipping down and revealing my bra-less chest through the thin cotton shirt I was wearing. Mike had put all my clothes in his washing machine when he gave me the shirt and blanket last night, and as I couldn't bear the embarrassment of handing him the knickers I'd been wearing, I'd washed them through in the sink and hung them over the window handle to dry overnight. They were still there, the only form of decoration the room had.

'Got messages?' he asked, eyeing my phone face down on

the bed. 'From family . . . or your mum?'

'I got yours . . . but there's nothing else, you know, about my mum or anything.' I smiled up at him through my headache and thought about Tom and Maggie calling him dodgy.

'Isn't mine enough?' he joked. 'You'd think they would all be contacting you all day to see if you were all right. People let you down, don't they?' I nodded. 'They should be making you feel like you're the most important person in the whole world.' I nodded again. As he said those words, I experienced a sudden hollow feeling where my family and friends should be. They *had* let me down. And they *hadn't* made me feel as if I was the most important person.

'You should be made to feel like a princess,' he continued. He was right! If just one of the people I knew had cared enough about me to help, I wouldn't have had to risk my life by sleeping outside.

I felt my phone vibrate on the duvet and I picked it up. Tom's name lit up the screen again but I shrugged at Mike. 'It's no one,' I said.

'I'll leave you to your cup of tea then,' he said kindly, and made his way out of the room.

'Are my clothes dry yet?' I asked. 'Only, I'd like to get dressed, and I'm meeting my brother later.'

Mike smacked the side of his head, chastising himself. 'Oh sorry, Saff, I forgot to take them out of the washing machine last night. They'll be wet. I'll hang them out to dry now.'

However nice Mike was being, I wasn't happy wearing someone else's clothes any longer than I had to . . . or having to put on the awful limp dressing-gown that was drooping off a single hook on the back of the door. My dressing-gown at home was powder blue and as soft as a summer cloud – I missed it desperately. 'Can't you put them in the tumble dryer?'

He smiled apologetically and made to leave the room. 'I don't have one, only a washing machine. I'll hang them over the radiator and I'll go out and get some nice things for you to eat and you can stay here and relax while I'm gone.'

'Don't you have to go to work? Or the volunteer thing?' I asked. Mike reached for the door handle and grinned at me again.

'Not today. Hang on . . . I'll get you one of my sweatshirts and a pair of my track-suit trousers. They'll be too big for you but at least you won't get cold.' Then as he shut the door behind him I reached for my phone and checked Tom's next message.

Tom: Can I meet Mike?

I deleted Tom's message and drank the sweet tea, which was horrible but helped clear my head, then wearing his clothes and enjoying the delicious independence of his flat and wanting to impress him, I set about tidying it up a little. It was fun to imagine a different kind of life where I didn't have to answer to Dad and I didn't have to live with his wife, or find the brat touching things in my bedroom or have Daniel and Archie farting on me at every opportunity. Maybe he would let me stay until I found my mum.

I'd even begun mentally decorating the place when he eventually came back. 'Wow,' he gasped, looking around him when he entered the flat. 'You're quite the home-maker. My

girlfriend, my *ex*-girlfriend, didn't like doing housework, and I'm useless at it. Normally too busy at work or helping vulnerable people to find the time, but this is great, Saffy. You'll have to stay!' He unpacked a pile of food onto the kitchen counter. Chocolate, chocolate spread, bread, diet lemonade, a fresh carton of milk, biscuits and two bottles of wine.

'Not much good at meal planning either,' I added jokingly.

'I don't know about you needing my help, I think *I'm* the one who needs help,' he joked back. 'I've been on my own for a long time . . . it's quite lonely.'

I frowned when he said that. 'I thought you said you only recently split up with your girlfriend?'

'Oh . . . no . . . it *has* been a while but I haven't been admitting it to myself . . . that's all.' He opened the loaf of thick, white bread and reached for some plates and knives. The idea of a chocolate-spread sandwich for breakfast was actually quite a good one. 'This is fun, isn't it?' he grinned. 'I bet you wouldn't have had chocolate sandwiches at the youth hostel.'

'Did your ex-girlfriend like this sort of stuff for breakfast or was she healthy?' I asked.

'She was *lazy*!' he answered, frowning at the memory of her. 'I had to do everything for her and when that wasn't enough . . . she left.'

'Oh,' I answered, lacking anything more profound to say. 'How mean.' At home I didn't have to do a lot apart from clear up after dinner with the others or help put out the washing. *She* was such a clean freak that nothing had the time to get dirty or messy anyway. I wiped the crumbs off the counter top into my hand and tipped them into the bin, then took the dirty knives and placed them in the washing-up bowl. 'Breakfast!' I smiled, picking up both our plates and leading the way into the sitting room. I needed him to believe it was a good idea to let me stay.

'What do you do about drying your clothes in a hurry?' I asked as we both ate. 'Only, the radiators are on so low mine are going to stay damp for ages.'

'I don't. I just don't expect them to be dry in five minutes,' he answered.

'I want to get dressed though. I'm meeting my brother and I can hardly go in wet clothes.'

'Maybe you could meet him tomorrow?' he volunteered but I needed to meet Daniel at the given time. I'd waited so long for my ID that I wasn't going to chance it by rearranging.

'I could try ironing them dry?' I suggested hopefully.

'In the cupboard in the kitchen. Put the kettle on while you're there . . . I've got biscuits for dunking.' He crossed his legs and pushed a cigarette out of a carton and lit it. My clean clothes draped over the radiators would stink in no time but it wasn't my place to tell him not to smoke in his own home. I would just have to put fresh stuff on when Daniel brought it.

The ironing board was behind the kitchen door, a yellowing cover sliding off it, with a burn mark in the middle, but the iron was nowhere to be seen. 'Er . . . Mike?' I called as I kneeled on the floor to look in the cupboards and found myself at eye level with the dials of his washing machine. 'I think you have a drying option on your washing machine . . .'

'I do?' He appeared in the doorway within seconds, making

me jump. 'I told you I was useless at housework. To think I've had a tumble dryer hidden in my washing machine all these months and I never knew.'

'And your girlfriend never knew either?' I said, slightly puzzled.

'I told you, she never did anything around here,' he said as I loaded my damp clothes into the cylinder.

'Mastered!' I said triumphantly as a low whir began and the drum began to turn. 'They'll be dry in no time and so I can meet Daniel in my own clothes.'

'Great,' he said. 'I'll come with you when you meet him. Then as you'll have some money, we can buy something for dinner on the way home,' Mike said.

'You don't have to chaperone me . . . I'll be fine. It's only Daniel.'

'I'll come with you anyway and help you bring your stuff back. You can repay me by cooking dinner. It would be fantastic to have something decent for a change.'

I suddenly wished I'd joined in more when Dad and Melanie were cooking at home. Even Daniel, Archie and Charlotte had got involved more than I had, forming a little band of chefs on pizza night or pot-luck dinner Sunday while I isolated myself in my room and waited to be shouted to the table. 'OK, as long as you think noodles or pasta count as dinner,' I said.

Tom

'I'm a total knob, John.'

'We both already know that, so why are you phoning me?' John's voice came out of the phone.

'I'm an effing pussy and now I've put her at risk.'

'Stop swearing, Tom, it makes you sound like a fucking wanker. Now it's the one day I have some peace from you because you're supposed to be at college and you phone me. What's up?'

'Saffron didn't come to mine last night in the end – instead she's gone off with some dodgy guy by all accounts . . . Well, Maggie's account, but I think she knows what she's talking about for once. I don't know what to do, he sounds like a right arsehole.' I waited while a silence came down the phone before rapidly removing it from my ear when John emitted a loud burp directly into the receiver.

'*Pardon donemwah,*' he said by way of an apology. 'You mean . . . there's someone who's a bigger arsehole than you?'

'It's *pardonnez-moi.* And I'm serious, John, she was all set to come to mine and then sent me a text to say she was staying with someone called Mike.'

'So you're jealous?'

'No, this is not about me, it's about Saffron. Maggie says she saw her go off with someone who gives all the homeless a hard time . . . He takes a *leak* on them. And now she won't answer my texts.'

'Maggie?'

'No, Saffron! Stop being a prat, John. I don't know where this guy lives and there's nothing I can do.'

'Then there's nothing you can do,' John replied unhelpfully. 'Except when she next gets in contact with you, act like you actually give a shit for once and act like you want her in your life because I know it, Angela knows it, and it looks like even bloody Maggie knows it.'

'But what if she doesn't get in touch,' I said, listening to John slurping at his drink.

'Listen, Tom, and listen good. If Saffron is stupid enough to stay with the arsehole then she was never yours to have. But very soon she's going to realise that you're a good lad and there ain't many good lads like you. I love you like a son so I should know. You're solid gold boy, and don't you forget it.'

A pool of unexpected water collected across my eyes as I listened to John speak and I struggled for something to say, but John, in his true John style, said it for me.

'Now fuck off and I'll see you on Monday.'

Saffron

'Blimey, Daniel, it's almost as if you care!'

Daniel lolloped his way slowly to where I was waiting, the overhead street lamp throwing shadows in the hollows of his face. Despite everything, I tried to push away the rush of warm familiarity. Mike stood a few metres away, leaning against a nearby wall. He said he'd hang back and I didn't need to be told twice. I didn't want Daniel asking if he was Tom in front of him.

'No hurry,' I uttered as he grunted a Neanderthal-style greeting and handed me a half-full plastic shopping bag. 'Where's my stuff? Where's the rest of it?' I asked.

'You said "pack me a bag". Well, I packed one. Be grateful,' he replied as I took it off him and looked inside.

There were two T-shirts, a pair of socks, one of his own sweatshirts, my passport and a screwed-up twenty-pound note. 'Well done, turd features. I meant a *proper* bag. Like a hold-all or a suitcase. You haven't brought proper money, or even packed me any underwear.'

'I wasn't going to touch your skidders,' was all he said as an apology. 'And I had to get the T-shirts out of the laundry room because Dad was upstairs right near your room. If you want your stuff that badly, come home and get it! I'm not being your mule any more . . . and by the way, this is totally unfair on everyone else especially Archie and Charlotte. They're missing you and they've got wind of the fact you're not really on a school trip.'

'Tough!' I replied. 'I'm missing my mother! Doesn't the fact that I've been missing her for ten years count for anything? You're all traitors, the whole lot of you. You'll see. When I find Mum, you'll realise that their sordid affair cost us our childhood.'

'It didn't cost us our childhood. You did that all by yourself.' The street lamp shone bright orange on the top of his head and our shadows spilled over the pavement beneath us. Was my shadow darker than his because I remembered her more?

'Did you know that Dad was in touch with her after she left, otherwise he wouldn't have been able to get a divorce? He never told us that, did he? A whole year after he told us she was dead, her dead body managed to sign the divorce papers. That's a pretty impressive thing to do, by anyone's standards, don't you think?'

Daniel looked hard at me for a moment, his eyes glittering in the orange light, before glancing at Mike, who was lighting a cigarette. 'Who's that? That's not Tom.'

'He's Mike. I'm staying with him.'

'I thought you said you were staying with Tom.' He said this loudly, causing Mike to look over at us.

'Well, it's *Mike*. You . . . misheard,' I said.

Daniel frowned. 'So how *old* is Mike?' Emphasising the word as if Mike was a hundred or something.

'Shush! You're very loud,' I said, putting my fingers to my lips.

'So how old is he?' Daniel asked – if anything, even louder.

'I . . . um . . . twenty-eight,' I replied, snatching an age out of the air. I really didn't have a clue how old Mike was. I'd not asked him. Tom was right, I really shouldn't become a journalist.

'More like thirty-eight!' Daniel sneered. 'Where did you pick him up from? He looks like a right creep.'

'Shut up, Daniel. He'll hear you,' I hissed again.

'Like I care?' Daniel shrugged. 'Why's he standing over there anyway, like he's hiding or something?'

'He's just keeping out of my family affairs, that's all.' Daniel was annoying me intensely and his effort at packing a bag was useless. I held it up towards him. 'This is rubbish. Thanks for the ID but I need way more clothes and money than this. Meet me tomorrow at the same time?'

Daniel looked down at me and like the other day he nodded his head then dished out a negative. 'You know what? No!' he said simply, and glanced back at Mike. 'I'm done with it all. Dad and Melanie think you're with a friend. They think you're safe . . . working things out, that you'll be home when you're ready, and all the time I have to live with the fact that I know you slept on the street for two nights and now you've hooked up with a paedophile.' Then he gave me a last look, the orange reflection of the street lamp in his eyes almost lasering my face off with his disappointment before he turned away.

'I've got it!' I waved the bag at Mike and smiled, trying to ride out the fact that this was all I was apparently getting from my useless brother.

'He made an effort then?' Mike scoffed sarcastically. 'Did he say anything?'

'Daniel? Like what?' I replied.

'Like were they looking for you? Or ask where you were going to stay now that you've got ID?'

'It's fine. The rest of the family still think I'm with Tom and that I'm OK. Like I said, he's only thirteen and he's got the sense of a fruit fly who was at the back of the fruit-fly queue when God was giving out teeny-weeny little brains.'

'Did he bring your ID?' he asked.

'Yes.'

'And some money?'

'Twenty pounds.'

'Hardly enough to replace all that lovely stuff you had stolen. Doesn't he care?'

'He's just stupid. I told you . . . fruit-fly brain.'

We fell into step with each other, with only the sound of our footsteps and the rustle of the pathetic carrier bag for company until he eventually broke the silence. 'So Tom didn't want you to stay at his, your dad has been lying to you for years and your brother can't be bothered to make sure you've got clothes or money?' Mike draped an arm round my shoulder and I hoped desperately he couldn't feel my shoulders shaking beneath it.

Tom

'Answer the *phone*!' I yelled down the receiver.

'I've answered it, Tom. You're screaming in my ear! What do you want?' Saffron was whispering as if she didn't want whoever she was with to hear her.

'Are you OK? Where are you? Are you still with that guy ... Mike?'

'Yes, I'm fine. Stop worrying. He's fine and he's *not* dodgy.'

'So, are you going to let me meet him?'

'No! Why? So you can vet him? He's OK ... really!'

'But Maggie said –' I didn't get any further before Saffron interrupted.

'You listened to the town's drunk and thought I didn't know what I was doing? That I'd be stupid enough to go off with just anybody? He helps vulnerable people who are on the street and you don't get much better than that. He's a good guy, trust me.'

I didn't trust her. 'Does he offer them all a bed for the night ... or just the young ones?' I snapped.

'You're vile, Tom. He's not like that. We've got separate bedrooms and he's made no attempt to touch me. You're just

270

trying to ruin it because I'm not flattering your ego by asking you to help any more.'

John's words echoed in my ears. *Act like you give a shit.* 'I care, Saffron, I really do, and I'm sorry I didn't help you when you first asked me.'

'Yeah, now you're sorry! I spent two nights, freezing cold . . . alone.'

'I know and I really am sorry, but Mike? I think he's . . .'

My words were met with the dull tone of a disconnected line before I had the chance to mention the word *grooming* again.

Saffron

'Is everything OK?' Mike's voice came through the bedroom door. 'Only, you sound upset.' I'd been *whispering*! The walls of this flat must be very thin.

'Yes, I'm OK, just fed up with my so-called friend.' I'd laid out the meagre contents of the bag on my bed and my phone was beside it, the screen not yet gone into hibernation.

'What's she doing?' he asked.

'It's *he*, and *he's* decided to get all funny because I'm staying here in your flat . . .'

'Is it Tom?' Mike opened the door and came in.

'Yes,' I said.

'Is he your boyfriend?'

'No!'

'Do you want him to be?'

'No way! He's just a friend.'

'A friend who didn't want you to stay with him when you needed help but likes to be in control of you?'

I'd never thought about Tom wanting to be in control. Was that what he was doing? Had Maggie really warned him against Mike or was he making it up?

I nodded slowly in agreement, feeling uncomfortable about not being entirely truthful to Mike and also being a traitor to Tom. But Tom had virtually accused Mike of being a paedophile, so in the light of that, I resolved not to feel too bad.

I'd cooked pasta in the end, with pesto, cheese, garlic bread and a side of salad, plus a tub of ice cream for dessert. The pot I'd cooked it in was still on the hob, a greasy colander sat on the counter top and strands of cheese that never made it into our bowls were scattered everywhere. 'Our family rule is whoever does the cooking doesn't have to do the clearing up,' I called. The sound of the television filtered through quite loudly from the living room as I stood at the sink next to it all, squeezing and twisting the water from the two dirty T-shirts that Daniel had brought me. Mike had said the washing machine was too expensive to use on such a small wash.

He didn't answer. I put the washing powder back in the cupboard next to the washing machine and placed the T-shirts on the draining board. If I could live here, I could be independent. I'd get an evening job to pay my way, until I finished college. I remembered how Mike had squeezed my ankle last night before he poured me another drink. If I could live here, I could go home, pack all my things myself and move in, and no one could stop me.

I wandered into the lounge to ask Mike for hangers for the T-shirts, but he was asleep, his pasta bowl on the floor and his empty glass beside it, tipped over on the carpet. Canned laughter from the comedy he'd been watching burst out of the speakers, as if the television itself was laughing at me.

I hesitated in the doorway to Mike's bedroom. I needed

hangers for my T-shirts and there weren't any in my bedroom. It felt wrong to creep in and look in the wardrobe without asking him but he'd walked into my room this morning. It was only a wardrobe after all.

It might only be a wardrobe, but there, shoved in the bottom of it, was a surprise. A big, black, shocking surprise. My hold-all! The zip undone. My clothes and belongings jumbled inside, all my stuff pulled about, a pair of my knickers on show. My stomach fell out of my ribcage and landed on the carpet next to the T-shirts I'd just dropped. My ears rushed with Mike's words of yesterday: '*I don't mean to be funny, but I know you didn't have anywhere to stay the last couple of nights*' and '*Hardly enough to replace all that lovely stuff you had stolen*'. Visions of the people at the youth hostel not having a clue who he was and him plying me with alcohol now became so glaringly obvious.

Mike had stolen my bag. Mike had caught me like a fish. Mike was a complete creepy pervert! He'd run his filthy hands over everything inside my bag, touching my underwear, stealing my money. No wonder he could pay for pancakes, alcohol and taxis.

Canned laughter burst out of the living room again, mocking me, telling me how stupid I was. Saliva rushed from my cheeks and pooled in my mouth, the sound of roaring air filled my ears, my heart now the size of a watermelon, wedging itself in my throat. Everyone knew he was bad news – Daniel, Tom and Maggie . . . everyone apart from me. How could I have been so gullible?

'All right, Saff?' Mike had woken and was calling over the top of the noise from the television. I shut the wardrobe doors

274

quietly, grabbed my T-shirts off the floor and hurried back into my room.

'Yeah, just sorting my washing out,' I called, my words sounding strangled by my watermelon heart.

'Just going for a shower,' he called back, walking into his room and coming out again with shorts and a towel.

'OK!' I squeaked, spending an unnecessarily long time pretending to hang my clothes over the dusty, luke-warm radiator. The door to the bathroom clicked behind him and the clank of pipes sounded through the wall as he turned on the shower.

My fear turned to fury. How could he be so . . . *pleasant*, when really he was a controlling, manipulating, thieving, lying pervert? Rushing into his room, I slipped on my boots, grabbed the hold-all and ran for the front door, turning the handle frantically. The door was locked! Shit! Where was the key? It wasn't where he kept it, in a pot on a little table by the door. He'd said it wasn't a good neighbourhood round here but now I realised he was probably locking me in, like his princess in a tower. '*You should be made to feel like a princess,*' he'd said. Had he even deliberately lied about his tumble dryer? Keeping my clothes damp to prevent me from leaving?

'Tom?' I whispered into my phone. I'd moved the hold-all onto my lumpy duvet and shut the door behind me, the sound of the shower competing with the television Mike had left on.

'Are you OK?' Tom's voice came urgently out of my phone.

'I've just found my hold-all!' I whispered again. The sound of a shampoo bottle or something clattering to the floor made me hold my breath.

'Where? What do you mean?' Tom asked, unnecessarily whispering back himself. The voices from the television went quiet and I could hear the rings on the shower pole rattle. I held my breath. 'Saffron? Are you there?' I was frozen, expecting to be caught out at any second. The shower rings rattled again, another burst of canned laughter came from the television, and my rapid breathing started again.

'Yes, I'm here. I'm in Mike's flat . . . *he's* the one who stole it. You were right. He must be a total freak and now I can't get out because he's hidden the key somewhere. What shall I do?'

'Where is he now?'

'In the shower. I haven't got long.'

'Has he done anything to you?'

'No. He made me tea, and breakfast in bed . . . *separate* beds. But he gave me alcohol . . . an awful lot of alcohol –'

'Sounds wonderfully romantic,' he interrupted. 'The police are hardly going to blue-light their way to *that* crime.'

'He's creepy . . . controlling. He told me he didn't have a tumble drier.' As I said it out loud, all the little strange things Mike had done continued to crowd in my head.

Tom continued to whisper urgently into his phone. 'I would ring the police but they're never going to listen when I tell them you're with a man who made you breakfast in bed and hasn't got a tumble drier! Where are you? I'm coming over.'

'I'm in Cambourne Flats . . . but I don't know which one!'

'What's his surname?'

'I *don't know.*'

'Jeezus, Saffron, what are you like?'

'I'm like stupid, I know. Just get me out of here, Tom.'

'Can you get out of a window?'

'No, the flat is too high. Think, Tom, think!'

'I *am* thinking! Will he let you out if you tell him you need something . . . something from a shop?'

I thought about Mike escorting me to meet Daniel. How he didn't want me to go alone but still let me go. 'Yes, I think so . . . but he'll want to come with me,' I whispered.

'Is there a shop near the flats?'

'Yes, right outside. What could I need?' I hissed. The noise of the shower came to an abrupt halt. 'Oh my God, Tom, he's finished in the shower. I can't talk.'

'OK, just listen to me. Tell him you need . . . tampons! You're having a massive period and you've got to get girlie plugs and stuff for it. No man in their right mind would argue with that. I'm coming over now!' I had to admit, it was a good idea, even if he was more descriptive than he needed to be. 'Oh, and Saffron?'

'What?' I whispered, in my most whispery whisper.

'Don't forget to act really . . . periody. Trust me on this . . . he'll let you go to that shop in a flash! I'm already on my way.'

I knew Tom was already on his way. I could hear the sounds of his breathing, feet on steps, doors closing behind him, but it would still take him a good while to get here. I opened the bedroom window and managed to shove my bag out, watching it hurtle down five floors into the bushes below, jumping out of my skin when I heard Mike call through the door.

'All right, Saff?' It was all I could do to hold myself back, not to fling the door open, launch myself at him and tell him what a total freak I thought he was. Instead I breathed out slowly and opened the door to face him. He was weedy without clothes on and my stomach turned with the sight of him in this new light. Two pale nipples sat on his skinny white chest and a horrible line of dark hair ran down from his belly button and disappeared into the towel round his waist. I knew I was staring at him.

'You OK? You look like you've seen a ghost. Were you leaning out of the window?'

'I . . . I . . . I don't feel good,' I stuttered, rushing into the bathroom and locking the door behind me.

'Is there anything I can do?' he asked through the door as I leant against it, chest heaving, the toilet in front of me where I'd projected the alcohol-drenched contents of my stomach the night before. A couple of spots of my own sick were splattered up the wall behind it. I tried to calm myself. As long as I could act normal, I'd be OK. Whatever he was planning, he was probably in for the long game.

'Saffron?' Mike turned the handle of the bathroom but I pushed against it.

'I'm fine. Sorry. I've . . . I've got my . . . period . . . only I haven't got anything for it. I'm going to have to go to the shop.'

'Oh. Can I get the . . . er . . . stuff for you?' he asked.

'Um, not really. I like to choose. Er, it's embarrassing, Mike. I don't want you getting it. I'll be out in a minute.'

'OK. Let me get dressed quickly. I'll come with you.' He had called *Tom* a control freak? He was definitely the control freak. I unlocked the door of the bathroom, clutching my stomach and trying very hard, under Tom's instructions, to look 'periody'.

'God, you look awful.' Mike rushed into his bedroom to find some clothes. The hold-all! He would realise it was gone and then God knows what would happen. I had to stop him looking in there. Following him to his open door as he pulled off the towel, unashamedly drying things I really didn't want to see, I pointed to the bed where he'd left his clothes from before the shower. 'It's *really* bad. Please can you just put them back on, like, *really* quickly and let's go.'

Mike took a key from a drawer in his bedside cabinet and opened the front door. I ran, taking the steps two at a time. 'What about the lift?' Mike panted, trying to keep up with me and grabbing my arm. 'You're not *dying*, Saffron.'

I was losing my cool rapidly and didn't like the fact that he had hold of my arm. 'I'm not dying, Mike, but I'm . . . I'm . . . *leaking.*' This time it was his turn to pull a face, instantly letting go of my arm and if he hadn't been a sad, pathetic loser, it would have been funny.

Tom

I didn't think it was possible for my legs to cycle any faster. Maggie was right! Some creep had gone off with the firecracker and I wanted to kill the bastard.

'Turn left in five hundred metres.' The voice on my phone navigation sounded so calm – didn't she know it was an emergency? Cambourne Flats was over four miles away so I just had to hope Saffron knew how to stall so I could get there in time.

It's my fault, I thought as I snarled aggressively into the oncoming wind. *I let self-preservation stop me from doing the right thing by her. If this prat has laid a hand on her, I'll never forgive myself.*

'Turn right in two hundred metres.' The voice hadn't told me to stop at the two red lights I'd cycled through, or not to cut all the corners, or to watch out for the lorry that sounded its horn so loudly I nearly fell off my bike, and she wasn't going to say this when I reached Cambourne Flats: 'You have reached Saffron Hayes – she is your destination.'

Saffron

'Where are you, Tom?' I looked over the aisle I was standing in and mouthed the words as if he could hear me across the city.

Mike was beginning to wonder what was taking me so long choosing a packet of tampons after I'd been so desperate to buy them. 'I'm not sure whether to get the applicator type or not. What d'you think?' I asked, watching the various expressions of horror that flitted across his face. 'And I probably need these, and also these.' I picked up an extra-large packet of pads and tucked it under my arm. *Hurry up, Tom!* 'I need chocolate too,' I told Mike. 'It's a thing . . . a girl's gotta have chocolate at a time like this.'

Mike was beginning to look openly distressed or disgusted, I wasn't sure which, as I went through the same pantomime picking various chocolate bars up, putting them down again, reading the labels. 'I like a high percentage of cocoa. I just can't make up my mind – the bar or the packet . . . or both?'

He clutched another bottle of wine. 'Have both,' he said, beginning to sound short of patience. 'Then when you're . . . sorted or whatever, we could have this.' He raised the bottle for me to get a clear view of the cheap label and smiled indulgently.

'You bought one this morning,' I reminded him, wondering at how much alcohol this guy thought it was OK to give a seventeen-year-old girl.

'Yes, but we've already had some with dinner,' he said. This man had lassoed me, masquerading as my saviour, convincing me that my family and friends had let me down, that no one cared like he did – and I had fallen for it. If he hadn't made the mistake of keeping my bag, I would have stayed with him until I was well and truly duped . . . or worse.

'I need a fag. I'll wait just outside the door. Get this too,' he said, handing me the bottle of wine.

'I'm seventeen!' I said, loud enough for the woman behind the counter to look over. As Mike went in this place all the time, from now on she'd hopefully know he was the kind of sleazy, needy weirdo who likes them young. For the first time since this nightmare began, those words 'I'm seventeen' made me feel powerful.

'And these things are expensive, you know,' I called as I headed towards the cash desk, indicating the various packets I was holding. 'I don't have enough left from Daniel's money to pay for it all.' I held my hand out. It was my money he was giving me back, after all. Mike unwrapped a ten-pound note from a small roll and offered it to me. 'I said they're expensive . . . and I need painkillers.' He frowned deeply, but gave me another ten-pound note, pushing the rest back in his pocket.

'Want a bag?' the woman behind the till asked as I handed over the money bit by bit, counting it out really slowly, panicking about how long it was taking Tom to get here.

Then a wonderful screech of bicycle brakes made me turn as Tom rushed in and I flung my arms around him. 'I have never been so relieved to see anyone in my entire life,' I mumbled into his neck.

'Take your things,' the woman behind the till said, pointing to my items and opening a bag for me.

'Tena Lady?' Tom asked, with huge, familiar, wonderful, dimples appearing in each cheek. 'You told him you were *incontinent?*'

I grabbed the packet and shoved it in the bag along with the chocolate and painkillers. 'I'd have told him I was doubly incontinent if I had to . . . I wasn't paying attention, I was *stalling.*'

Mike looked startled when we got outside. He looked even weedier next to Tom, who had suddenly become so . . . solid and reliable . . . soft round the edges by comparison. He put both his arms round my shoulders and looked Mike in the eye. 'Ever heard of groomers?'

I don't know what I was expecting but what actually happened was a desperate show of pathetic, defensive and aggressive behaviour. 'What are you doing, Saffy? I've done *everything* for you . . . *Everything.*'

'We know about the bag. Saffron found it,' Tom said.

'What bag?' Mike answered, looking innocent.

'The hold-all? Saffron's hold-all. The one you *stole* from her to lure her in.'

Mike shot me a look . 'I . . . I have a bag that I *found* but I didn't know it was yours. I found it dumped on the edge of a road so I brought it back to see if I could find its owner.'

I found myself gasping in disbelief at his lies. 'You *saw* me with it. You *helped* me with it when I tripped over the kerb. It was full of clothes in my size and I told you my bag was stolen. You took money from it.'

Mike tried to change tack. 'I couldn't think of any other way to help you. I needed to get you off the streets.'

'So when the police arrive, you won't have a problem telling them a thirty-something-year-old man stole a bag plus a load of money from a seventeen-year-old girl?' I said, craning my neck, pretending to scour the streets for the police car that wouldn't be coming.

Mike then amazed us both with his ability to articulate a constant stream of foul swearwords with hardly taking a breath as he walked, defeated, back inside his block of flats. 'Did you get all that or would you like me to repeat it?' Tom asked with a serious expression before a small smile worked its way onto both our faces. Then he picked up his bike and tied my shopping bag round the handle with his red-paint-speckled hands. 'Did he hurt you in any way?'

I looked up at him, relieved and embarrassed. 'No, I told you he didn't.'

'Did he threaten you in any way?'

'No.'

'Did you go to his house willingly?'

'Yes! Because I was stupid and fell into his trap. He's a creep.'

'Then it shouldn't be this way but unfortunately I don't think the police are going to be interested unless he forced himself on you.'

'But he stole my bag and took my money.'

'Yeah, and you and the bag spent the night in his flat, totally unharmed. Nothing can be proven so we just need to be thankful that you didn't stay long enough that it could. And the other fact is you're seventeen – it's not illegal.'

'Of course. Good old seventeen,' I said, rolling my eyes and heading for the bushes to retrieve my hold-all, which I'd thrown out of the window. Tom didn't understand what was so strange about being seventeen . . . but then he hadn't just had the week that I'd had.

'What are you doing?' Tom called as I rustled about in the bushes before dragging my bag out from the middle.

'I didn't want him having my things . . . My mother's photograph is in there. My *underwear* is in there . . . *This* is in there . . .' I said, pulling a bright yellow jumper out of it before handing the bag over to Tom.

'*Everything* is in there,' Tom sighed, heaving it up, a handle round each shoulder, grunting as he tried to adjust it to a better position. 'Well, it doesn't feel like he took anything. It still weighs a tonne.'

'Get me out of here,' I said, feeling suddenly weary and like my back was covered in grease, as if the whole awful experience was clinging to me and needed to be scraped off then washed away under a hot shower.

'You OK?' he asked.

'Do I look OK?' I answered, pulling on the yellow jumper as the tears suddenly fell down my cheeks.

Tom

'You look like a bunch of marigolds,' I said as Saffron pulled on the bright yellow jumper, releasing her hair from the confines of its collar. The copper of her hair and the yellow of her jumper, combined with the orange glow from the street lamp reflecting in the tears on her face made her look startlingly beautiful. *Marigolds?* What was wrong with me? Couldn't I have simply said: Saffron, you are startlingly beautiful.

'Er, thanks . . . I think,' she replied.

I tapped the cross-bar of my bike. 'Come on. Hop on, my trusty steed will take us out of here.'

Saffron tipped her head towards me, showing the yellow and copper now in her eyes. 'Are you joking?'

'If the Dutch can do it, so can we.' I held the bike still until she was balanced on the cross-bar, then attempted to pedal fast enough to keep us both balanced until I could get a proper momentum going. My arms were either side of her as I held onto the handlebars of my bike, her hair catching in the breeze, the curls brushing against my face. The hold-all throwing me totally off balance. The bike wobbled to start with, making her scream, then unexpectedly laugh out loud.

I laughed out loud too. 'The faster I pedal, the faster you can leave it all behind you,' I called as the road sloped downhill and the air rushed in our faces.

The evening was chilly but dry and the river was close, so close that I knew without a doubt that I was going to take the turning that ran along its edge. I was about to show Saffron Hayes a piece of my heart.

Saffron

Sitting on the cross-bar of Tom's bike, the wind in our faces, his arms either side of me, made me wonder why I'd ever thought it was OK to tell Mike that Tom was 'no one'. Regardless of what happened in my life, however awful I felt, Tom always let the sunshine in, he always made me feel a whole lot better.

Landing in an ornamental hedge in someone's front garden happened quite suddenly. 'Did you hit a rock or something?' I grunted when I finally got my breath back.

'I'm blameless. That rock jumped out and hit us,' Tom answered from where he was lying next to me. We were sprawled, half in a hedge and half on a lawn, with the bike and a large hold-all tangled between us and a whole lot of sanitary goods scattered on the grass. A security light came on, followed by a man opening his front door to see what the noise was about. 'Are you guys OK?' he called, the white light illuminating us and everything around us. We didn't move. He walked up his path in socks, until he was standing over us where we lay on our backs.

Tom looked up at him, suddenly pointing to the sky. 'I can see the big dipper and the little dipper.'

Loud, uncontrollable laughter forced its way through my closed lips, followed closely by similar from Tom. We just lay there, the upside-down face of an old man hanging over us, and laughed until we thought our sides would split. 'I guess you're all right then?' the guy muttered crossly, bending down to take hold of the bike in an effort to help.

Tom pulled himself together first and stood up, reaching out a hand to me and pulling me upright. He heaved the hold-all back onto his shoulders while I quickly gathered my shopping and ineffectually patted the dented ornamental hedge. 'Thank you, yes we're fine,' he said, taking the bike off the man and stepping back onto the path. 'Sorry about your hedge.'

'Yes, sorry,' I added, giving it a final pat before we both walked away. Tom pushed the bike with one hand and picked off a bunch of leaves that were caught in my yellow jumper with the other.

'We'll walk the rest of the way. It's probably safer,' Tom said, grinning.

'Probably,' I answered, grinning back. 'Do you live near here? Are we going to your flat?' I asked.

'Not yet,' he answered cryptically, turning down a side road towards a cut-through at the bottom, which led to the river. 'I'm taking you home to mine via a detour. Via the love of my life.'

'Your boat?' I asked, then almost inaudibly echoing: 'The love of your life.'

'My boat!' he repeated, shining the light from his phone on the path ahead of us as we joined the unlit towpath.

There was something quite romantic about the idea of a riverboat. Lined up nose-to-tail along the edge of the water, each one slightly different. Some were dark, boat-shaped silhouettes, visible against the orange of the sky, and others were inhabited, their lights casting strips of yellow or white across the towpath in front of us. 'These are called cabin cruisers,' Tom explained, pointing towards traditional-shaped boats, their white fibreglass bodies a stark contrast to their dark removable covers. 'And these are narrow boats – like mine, only bigger,' he said as I shone the torch from my own phone over each one, noting the paintwork of the narrow boats – ornate and colourful, like floating, old-fashioned gypsy caravans.

'Which one is yours?' I asked.

'I'll tell you when we get to it. Don't blink though, or you'll miss it.' A clear moon followed us, floating silent and silvery on top of the water, its light creating a bluish aura in the dark air. The bushes and trees lining the river dipped their dark reflections into the moonlit water. Something rustled in the grass nearby and when I jumped, squealing, a dog barked in a nearby boat.

'It's just a water vole, or a cat or a badger or something. You get used to nature being on your doorstep when you're here long enough. It's like living inside and outside at the same time.' Tom smiled again.

We kept walking, my torch highlighting all that river life had to offer. Television aerials on roofs, little chimneys billowing clouds of steam, tarpaulins and flower pots and herb gardens, mooring ropes and log stores and bicycles tethered on decks. Many had their shutters closed but in a couple they were open with the lights on, so I could see all the tiny sinks, sofas, wood burners and tables. They were all adorable and I could see why

Tom had spent years making this dream come true. There was something exciting and free about it. Was he planning on floating away on it one day, never to come back?

'Here she is,' Tom exclaimed, halting on the path and looking towards a boat. I shone my torch over it and tried to conceal my shock – it was awful! He was right. If I'd blinked, I would have missed it. It was a tiny thing with a small outboard motor, not much bigger than a row boat. It had once been white but was now covered in dirt or mould or moss, or all three. Its cover was a sagging dark canvas, surely hardly able to keep the rain out. The curtains in the cabin, no bigger than a washing-machine-sized box, were ripped and the whole thing looked like it would be better off sinking to the bottom of the river. 'What d'you think?' he said, sounding nervously hopeful.

'Um . . . well . . . I'm sure it will look great with a bit of a clean,' I said, trying to sound positive.

'Not that one, shit for brains . . . *This* one!' he said, grabbing my hand and shining my torch on the one next to it.

'Oh!' I gasped, letting out a shout of laughter as I stepped forward to look at the boat next to it. You could see it was very much a project because there was a clutter of things piled on the deck and some on the grass beside it – tins of paint and old bits of wood presumably pulled out from the old design, along with fresh lumber waiting to be installed. It was, as he said, one of the smallest narrow boats on the water, but it shone with a freshly painted bright-red gloss like a boat-shaped ruby. 'So . . . now we're looking at the right one, do you like her?'

'Her?' I asked.

'Yes, all boats are female, that's why you don't see any *Colin of the Canals* or *Bilge-water Brians*, only names like *Priscilla*, or *Emma-Louise* or *Moonbeam* or *Princess Beatrice*.' There was a panel on the side where I guessed the name should be, but there was a cover over it. 'Each boat has a name,' Tom continued, pointing to the panel. 'This was called *Baby Duck*, such an awful name! I've renamed her but I can't take the cover off until I've asked Neptune to wipe the old name from his records.'

'What are you talking about?' I stared at the covered panel.

'It's a boat thing. It will bring bad luck if I don't rename her properly. I'm going to perform a ceremony and everything.' Tom was actually serious.

'And what are you going to call it – her?' I asked.

'You'll see, if you perform the ceremony with me. You could be my witness – I have to have one for the ceremony – and once it's done I can give her her new name.' He smiled at his boat and then at me, and I could see in his eyes, even in the dark, that he *adored Baby Duck* or whatever she was going to be called.

'She's wonderful. Can I see inside?' I asked, and I took his hand as he helped me step over the gap between boat and land. Tom lit a portable light, then opened two small double doors that led us inside, down some steps. Instantly, I could see why I couldn't have slept in there. It was tiny and full of tools, decorating cloths, paint pots and bits of wood. There wouldn't be room for anything in there until it was properly built – but there was more to it than that . . . it wasn't just the lack of space, I understood now – this project was *love*. I shouldn't have asked to crash in it before it was ready, before he had experienced the completion of all his hard work. 'It's really cute, Tom. What you've done is amazing. It's going to be absolutely beautiful.'

I opened a narrow door to my side and peeked in. 'Oh look, a tiny toilet . . . and the shower is actually hanging above it! And there's shelves for toiletries and everything.' I ran my hand over the tiny things. 'Little boiler. Minuscule sink. There's everything you need in here.' I turned to look at Tom as if I was showing him something new.

'Yes,' he said, grinning with pride.

'What will it be like when you've finished?' I asked, stepping out of the bathroom and into the main room, casting my gaze around the small living space crammed with building materials.

'I have it all worked out.' His eyes were shining. 'This area will hold a bed and over here I'll have a wood-burning stove, under here there will be storage for clothes and bedding etcetera, a bench seat here, shelves there for books and stuff, cooker there, drop-down table along this bit . . .' He showed me his entire plan with his hands and his imagination – he had really thought this through. 'There's more storage at the back and in good weather you can sit outside and watch the world.'

'You're so clever,' I said and I meant it. He was going to build this whole thing by himself and, quite frankly, it was brilliant. Making our way back on the deck, he suddenly grabbed my arm, halting me in my tracks. 'Great crested grebe.'

I glanced at him. 'Same to you,' I said.

Tom tilted his head to the river. 'The bird call . . . *listen*. It's a great crested grebe.' We both tilted our heads to the sound: a rapid chucking noise came from somewhere along the edges of the river. 'It's a water bird. Long neck. Funny tufty head. Elaborate mating display.'

I glanced at him again, unable to tell if he was making certain comparisons between me and the wildlife but he wasn't.

'This . . . is . . . awesome,' I said, tilting my face towards the moon when the chucking finally stopped.

'Do you think so?' he asked, an earnest tone to his voice.

'It makes me feel . . . uncomplicated,' I said, realising that it actually did. When for some time he didn't pass comment, I turned away from the moon to find him staring at me, his curly hair, the tip of his nose and his fingers lit up by the silvery glow. He was leaning in slightly with one hand, reaching for my hair as if he was going to touch my cheek. My heart ramped up a notch and I waited, hardly daring to move. Then Tom reached for a curl of my hair and held it in the cup of his hand, studying it before lifting his gaze again, searching my eyes with his. The little bird flapping in the cage of my chest morphed into a giant thing, its wings beating hard against my ribs.

Suddenly he made a violent flicking move with his fingers, almost yanking my hair clean out of my head. 'Bug!' he said, snatching his hand away.

'Ow!' I yelped, holding the side of my head yet aching inside with a different kind of pain. What happened just then? How could I have read him so wrong . . . *again*!

Tom immediately leapt up and ducked inside, leaving

me sitting alone on the deck with my complete and utter embarrassment. I could hear him boiling a kettle and banging stuff inside the boat until eventually he emerged, bringing out two mugs of instant hot chocolate in bright red mugs. We sat silently side by side on tiny inbuilt wooden benches, an awkward atmosphere between us, and sipped from our bright red mugs, the light from the portable lamp behind us throwing our black shadows across the towpath. 'Your hair makes your head look huge,' Tom said, unable to keep serious for long, wiggling his own head around so his smaller shadow head could prove his point. I used my shadow hands to make a shadow middle finger at his normal-headed shadow.

'I always thought my shadow was blacker than everyone else's. That our shadows are where all the awful things in our lives go,' I confessed.

Tom's shadow head tilted towards mine. 'Everyone has a shadow, Saffron, but if you look deeply enough you'll find the colour in them.'

'You mean, like, every cloud has a silver lining and all that?' I asked.

'I mean, like, however bad we think our life is, there's always something good there if we look hard enough for it.'

'I'm not seeing any colour, Tom. Just a black shadow with a giant head full of very black things. Maybe your shadow isn't as shadowy as mine.'

He looked at me again, an unreadable expression in his face. 'Well?' I persisted. 'What's the colour in your shadow then?'

Bats swooped around our heads, their tiny silhouettes fleeting across the moonlit sky and that great crested thingamabob chuckered his call again. A river-scented breeze brushed itself across our faces and something made a rippling sound in the dark water behind us. 'Come on,' Tom said, completely ignoring my question and securing his boat for the night. 'I'll take you to meet Angela.'

Tom

Saffron had sat on my boat with her hair lit up by the moon, silvery spirals heading in every direction, the colour of her eyes transformed into gold under the light of the lamp. I wanted to touch her hair, to bury my hand in its soft glistening spirals that in daylight were the colour of everything warm – fire, spice, sunshine. And then I nearly flicked her eye out pretending there was a bug, but it was the only way I could stop myself from lifting it to my cheek, inhaling the scent of it. Making a fool of myself. After everything she'd been through with that creep, the last thing she needed was a friend coming on to her – burying his hands in her barnet.

I wanted a different kind of life. A life away from the council flat I lived in, its windows looking down on an urban jungle below, its walls suffocating the living breath out of me. It was here that I could breathe again, the river pulling me to it like an enticing mystical force. Sitting on my boat with Saffron, our hands clasped around my new red mugs, I'd let her peek through the door of my dream and for a wild, wonderful moment, she was part of it. Yet I couldn't leave the flat . . . I couldn't leave Angela.

'What is the colour in your shadow?' Saffron had asked me as we were looking at our shadows on the towpath in front of us. Thankfully I managed to avoid the question. Otherwise I'd have had to tell her that she was. She was the colour in my shadow.

Saffron

Standing in the doorway of Tom and Angela's flat, I managed to stretch my face into a smile. Tom had warned me his place was a far cry from mine, but he could have won the 'understatement of the year' award for making the biggest understatement in the history of understatements.

I could see a small galley kitchen and two bedrooms leading off what was supposed to be the lounge. Through the open doors of the bedrooms I could see a small double bed in one, squashed between an old-fashioned brown wooden wardrobe and chest of drawers. In the other room there appeared to be a single bed with the biggest mountain of *stuff* next to it. Floor to ceiling *stuff*! Boxes, bags, cushions and even a sofa turned on its end.

And there, propped up on pillows, in the room that should have been their living room . . . was Angela.

Tom

Saffron stood in the doorway of my flat looking around, her smile huge and fake. I'd warned her it wasn't exactly a penthouse suite. The flowers I'd bought Angela earlier in the week were still just about alive, in a blue glass vase. The vase I'd bought from a charity shop, for Angela's birthday when I was fourteen, the pink and white flowers peeping out, trying valiantly to hold their own against the turmoil.

I put Saffron's hold-all on the spare bed, but Saffron remained standing where I'd left her, near the front door, unable to enter into the reality of my world. Now more than ever I was aware I should have said something before, explained maybe – but I could never find the right words.

'Tom, my mum is dead,' she'd said, all those years ago. I'd wanted to say 'So is mine'. I'd wanted to say 'I miss my mum so much my heart is sore with the hurt of it'. Instead I'd simply said 'Shit!' and squeezed her hand. Then when she'd described her new, apparently awful huge house, and how she'd had to leave behind the memories of her mother in the walls of their old home, I wanted to tell her then that I'd once had to do the same. Only my move was to a block of flats that suffocated me every minute of every day. But when she said, 'I hate my stepmother because she took the place of my mother,' I wanted to tell her, the person who can step into a mother's shoes should get a medal for giving unconditional love against a tsunami of resentment. And when she said 'My father lied to me about my mother' I wanted to say, then your father probably loves you very much.

Saffron

The entire lounge was consumed by the jumble of paraphernalia needed to cope with someone who was dying.

My 'lucky spring-tide friend' was a carer, and the truth came crashing in on me as I realised that the warm southern wind that I always believed made him so carefree, was in fact commitment and responsibility. In the centre of the room was a hospital bed and Tom's An-ge-la was young – maybe only forty, it was hard to tell – almost transparent against the fat pillows behind her, the smile on her face far more real than mine. 'I'm sorry we were so long,' Tom apologised. 'My rescue mission was over the other side of town, then we went to the river for a bit.' He made it sound so simple. Mike and my naive stupidity was discretely brushed away.

Tom pushed me gently forwards, before turning to Angela. 'This is *Saffron*.' He pulled a chair forward, and placed it close to Angela's outstretched hand, indicating for me to sit down, which I obediently did. The resulting squeeze, as I placed my own hand in hers, was stronger than I expected. Her nails were painted a clear gloss, and her cheeks were rosy with pink rouge against a pale face but it couldn't hide how her skin was all papery and thin, like it was leaving this world in thin, silent layers, before she did.

She held onto my hand tightly while I hoped desperately she was unaware of the entire ocean of shame positively flowing out of me. A vision of me in the toilets of the cafe came to mind, me sulkily sounding out the syllables of her name, 'An-ge-la'. How could I have been jealous of this? Of her? I'd automatically assumed she was his girlfriend, a threat to me and my feminine ego, and now here I was drowning in my own mortification. 'My aunty Angela,' Tom introduced, looking back and forth between us both. 'My mother's younger sister . . . she took me in when I was five years old.'

'I thought you said you knew where your mother was?' I said.

'I do.' He lowered his voice. 'She's in Thornbury Road Cemetery. She died . . . of cancer.'

The last two words he added so quietly. Cancer was obviously going to rob him twice over and there was nothing he could do about it, and I had spent all this time going on about my own mother while he hadn't breathed a word.

'So you've come to stay for a while?' Angela asked smilingly, smoothing over the crater created by the C-word. I nodded my head slowly.

'Only one night, please . . . if that's OK? I'll be very quiet . . . I'll go to bed soon . . . you'll hardly know I'm here.' My voice trailed off as I ran out of ways to shrink myself out of their way.

She instantly looked perplexed. 'Oh no, Annie, we have a spare room – my old bedroom. Tom refuses to use it for himself. Stay as long as you like . . . please.'

'It's Saffron! . . . Remember, I told you?' Tom reminded her.

'The medication is making her doolally . . . isn't it, Aunty?' Angela laughed. They were sharing a joke, but for the life of me I couldn't think what was so hilarious about cancer taking your memory away.

Tom

Six years ago I'd found myself holding Angela tightly, late into the night.

'I'm fine,' she'd said. 'I'm losing weight, which means I've regained a whole load of clothes I haven't been able to wear for years.'

'But you'll disappear,' I'd replied, hiding my own tears in her shoulder, forcing myself not to shudder with the weight of them.

'I won't completely disappear, Tom. Not ever. I'll be in everything you say and do. Everything you love and enjoy. Like your mum is. She's up there now, making sure you're OK.'

'But I'm not ready for you to go too.' My grief fell out of me in great wracking sobs. Angela had pushed me gently off her, holding her hands either side of my head, her thumbs wiping my face.

'Then I won't go until you're ready. I have a pact with the Big Fella. There's a world out there, Tom. A big wide world full of beautiful things, so your side of the deal is, as soon as we've got you good and ready, you go and you grab it by the bollocks.'

'What if God is a girl . . . or the world is a girl?' I'd asked, trying to make her laugh.

She did laugh. 'Even better. Only, telling you to grab the world by the muff doesn't sound so . . . impactful.'

With our jokes, for brief moments we could hold the awfulness of it at bay. When I told her about the day I met Saffron, and how she looked like little orphan Annie, she knew that despite all the cold, broken bits inside me, I'd found sunshine. She also knew something happened the day Saffron had tried to kiss me at the duck pond. Something that had forced me to close my shutters to keep her out. Sunshine was one thing, but love? That was a whole different ball game and one I couldn't bear to lose again.

Now here she was, holding hands with Angela, in our living room.

Saffron

Tom and I stood side by side in the kitchen as he poured juice into two glasses and a small tumbler of brandy for Angela. 'Why does she keep calling me Little Annie?' I whispered.

Before Tom could answer Angela called out from the living room, 'I'm dying but I'm not deaf! He's called you that since he first met you. Said you looked like little orphan Annie.' I raised my eyebrows at Tom, biting back a splutter. 'Orphan Annie?' I questioned.

'The hair,' Tom answered, tugging his own hair but looking at mine. 'The kid in the film with the red hair and freckles?'

'Oh yeah . . . *that*,' I groaned. 'Unlucky genes, I guess.'

'Not unlucky . . . lucky! He absolutely adores it,' Angela called out again from the living room.

'That's enough now,' Tom hurriedly called back. 'You don't know what you're talking about.' Tom had pink splashes on his cheeks, which told me more than he wanted me to know. *He really did like my hair.*

'He said you were not only called Saffron, but you were the living representation of the saffron spice itself . . . a vibrant tangle of crimson and yellow.'

'Oh, God. I knew it was a mistake to bring you here. She's HALLUCINATING!' Tom said the last word extra loud as he poked his head round the door to the living room and gave Angela an iron stare. Then he groaned. 'Sorry, Saffron.'

'No, it's fine . . . more than fine. I *hate* my hair. Do . . . do you really like it?'

'Yes!' came the voice from the living room.

'It's all right . . . nice . . .' He shrugged.

'Is that the best you can do, Tom? You said it was the most beautiful colour hair you'd ever seen in your entire life,' Angela called out.

'I'll take that,' I called back.

'Don't even get me started on the eyes!' she said, at which point Tom marched into the living room and hovered over her bed. 'You promised,' he said. 'Does that mean I don't have to keep my side of the bargain? Does my promise not count now either?'

'You absolutely *will* keep your side of the bargain. Anyway, I had my fingers crossed under the covers so my promise doesn't count.' Angela raised both her hands with her fingers crossed as proof.

'Then you cheated,' he complained. But he leant his face towards her hands, which she reached out to him and, uncrossing her fingers, he allowed her to press them against his cheeks. I watched them both from the door into the kitchen, aware that I was intruding on a moment but unable to turn away from it.

'Let me give you this one thing. You are ready to go your own way, and you and I both know it,' she said, dropping her hands tiredly back on the bed. 'Now go and get me that little drink. All this talk is drying out my mouth.' Tom came back into the kitchen, prised two cubes of ice out of a white plastic ice tray and plonked them into the tumbler. I followed him back in with the glasses of juice, placed them on a small table in the corner of the room and searched for a third chair. There wasn't one.

'I'm going into care,' Angela announced, as I sat and Tom stood, almost as if she'd triumphantly won something.

'Oh,' I answered lamely. 'Is . . . is that what you want?'

'It's not what *I* want,' Tom interjected.

'But it is what *I* want. And you *weren't* crossing your fingers when you gave your promise, so you have to keep it.' Angela turned to me and added conspiratorially, 'He'll get his boat done up any day now, then he needs his own life. Not this . . .' She cast her eyes round their flat as if it was holding them both back. 'Anyway, I've had enough of him . . . he's a pain in the bum. Keeps bringing me flowers. Plus, he's got a girlfriend now,' she added.

Tom

Well, that went worse than I expected.

'Sorry,' I said, leaning against the bedroom door where Saffron was pulling stuff out of her hold-all . . . so much stuff, like a scene from *Mary Poppins*. 'You could probably hardly wait to disappear in here.'

'Ah, my pyjamas,' she grinned, pulling a neatly folded pair of PJs out of the bag and waving them at me. 'I'm fine, Tom. It's me that should apologise. I didn't understand . . .'

'You weren't expected to understand. I kept it from you. It's just a bit complicated, that's all. Do you want to stay up for a while with us?' Saffron shook her head. She took out a large comb and some face wipes and began wiping her skin clean. 'I'll be in the way. There's nowhere for me to sit.'

'I'll sit on the floor. I don't mind,' I volunteered.

'It's fine, Tom. You spend time with Angela. All I really need is to get out of these clothes and have a shower and an early night, and I'm dying to re-do my nails.' She showed me her fingernails with their dark, chipped nail varnish. 'I'm grateful, I really am, that you've both let me stay . . . and I'm sorry I didn't understand before.'

Later, when I was alone with the flickering blue light of the muted television, Angela next to me, breathing rhythmically in sleep, barely detectable beneath the covers, my phone flashed with a message.

It was a message that would quite possibly trigger the end of any further role I had to play in Saffron's life.

Saturday:
Love and Hate

Saffron

The morning brought with it many things.

I'd woken in the early hours and glimpsed Tom, tousled hair and crumpled cotton shorts, helping Angela to the commode. Beside me, on a small wooden cabinet, an assortment of photo frames jostled for attention. 'You were cute,' I said, to the small boy wearing little blue shorts with red wellies, holding a fishing net, looking intently into a bucket. Next there was a boy in school uniform with a cheeky grin and golden curls. A woman with white-blonde hair and a curly-haired toddler in her arms, both smiling at the camera. The same woman wearing a tell-tale headscarf smiling next to a slightly older child. And then there was Angela – light brown hair, falling to her shoulders in waves, a blue and white stripy slash-neck jumper and white jeans, red polish on hands that were clasped round Tom's shoulders. There were about seven pictures in total, and they all told a story that broke my heart.

Tom continued to sleep in the single bedroom. A room just big enough to hold a single bed, rammed up next to all the boxed up items that should have been in their living room. Items that should be making it cosy instead of practical. Two unused lamps, an oscillating fan, and several ornaments were piled on top of the boxes, plus the sofa on its end, which matched the armchair still in the living room.

Not for the first time this week, I thought about my own bedroom at home with its cream leather sofa, placed several paces from my king-size bed, across my paradise-blue carpet. The fitted wardrobes, containing hundreds of clothes, shoes, toiletries and jewellery, which lined one wall, shining with floor-to-ceiling mirrors, now seemed outrageously decadent by comparison. Tom woke every morning to clutter and another day off Angela's life, yet they both seemed to laugh their way through everything – while I had spent my life living in the past.

I was awake for ages after that, until the faintest mist of a new day sprayed itself across the horizon. Standing at the window, the cold night air clinging to the glass, an urban greyness below, all blocks and lines, roofs and fences, I suddenly knew why Tom loved the river so much. The colours, the scent of everything green, the huge sky overhead and the space. So much space.

I leant closer to the glass, my breath making steam between me and the outside world, my fingers drawing clear patches in the mist. Maggie was out there somewhere. No one had rescued her like Tom had rescued me. I could hardly imagine how hard all those years had been for her, surviving alone, without anything more than her world in an old shopping trolley. How cold she must have felt, how damp or uncomfortable – how lonely. How many Mikes had tried to abuse her? How many people had spat on her or relieved themselves over her? In the same way my seven-year-old self was still hurting inside me, her nineteen-year-old self would be doing the same.

316

The overnight clouds rolled themselves into balls, leaving gaps of colourless sky that would eventually turn blue. I slipped my yellow jumper over my cream and grey pyjamas and pulled on my multicoloured socks with the toes in. I needed a drink. Angela was lying on her back, eyes shut, the rouge long gone from her cheeks. Almost pantomime style, I crept past, lifting each foot carefully and placing it down slowly, quietly, vaguely wondering if she had, in fact, already passed away, as she was so still.

'Good morning, lovey.' Her voice broke the silence, making me halt mid-pantomime tiptoe.

'Shhh, it's still early, Angela. Go back to sleep. I'm sorry if I've woken you,' I whispered.

'Pffft! Daytime, nighttime – it's all just time.' She smiled at me and I found myself smiling back. It was hard not to.

'Can I get you anything?' I asked, still whispering so as not to wake Tom again.

'I'd love a cup of tea. It's so nice to see another young face, and such a beautiful one at that.' I shook my head ruefully. I'd piled my hair on top of my head last night, as I always did, to prevent it suffocating me in the night, but much of it had worked its way free and now I resembled a badly groomed poodle. 'No sugar,' she added, whispering loudly, reaching out to turn on a lamp then trying to prop herself up on her pillows. I quickly reached behind her, moving them to a comfortable position, feeling the bones of her back against my hands. 'Thank you,' she sighed gratefully as she leant back into them. 'Make yourself a cup of something and come and join me for a bit.'

I made two drinks and handed one to Angela. 'Tom always

does this for me when he wakes up, but we're a bit early for him,' she said, as I placed the cups on the little table beside her and sat down in the armchair nearby. 'Move closer, I don't want to wake Tom,' she ordered, reaching a skinny hand out as I pulled the chair nearer. I was expected to hold it. I felt awkward by her eagerness to accept me being there. Even though she wasn't that old it was like meeting someone's over enthusiastic grandma, the type that loves to kiss any passing child. I took her hand, wrestling with how it made me feel and knowing instantly why Tom loved this lady so much. 'I love your nails.' She held my fingers out to study my varnish. A long shower and a fresh application of Black Grape Ultimate Shine had gone some way to getting rid of all traces of Mike. 'Tom does mine. He's such a good boy. He really is.'

So this was Tom's life. He worked, he cared, he painted nails, he built a boat and cared some more. 'Do you have other colours?' Angela broke into my thoughts. 'I want something . . . decadent.' I disappeared into the bedroom for my bag of things and within minutes, she was drinking her tea with one hand while I painted Emerald Dazzle carefully on each nail of the other.

'How do you manage when Tom's at work . . . or doing up his boat?' I asked.

'I have carers. They come in the morning and again at night. But that's going to change as soon as he finishes that boat. Tom feels guilty. He wants me to stay at home here but it's no life for him and to be honest it's no death for me either.' She laughed unexpectedly and something about the way she did that at something so *unfunny*, made me laugh too. I paused,

318

varnish brush mid-air, to sip at my milky coffee. 'I've got a great hospice to go to and they'll probably paint my nails better than Tom can.' We shared a brief moment of eye contact then, and we both know it wasn't true. There would be nothing anyone could do for Angela that would match what Tom does, yet she was going to give it up, for him. 'He's doing it all himself, you know . . . the boat, that is. He builds it with love, every square inch of it comes from the very soul of him.'

'I believe you,' I whispered. 'I saw it in his face yesterday evening.' Her face, which I'd imagined so differently over the last few days, was soft and pale, surrounded by short, thin, light brown hair, the downy ravages of chemo sessions, now a thing from a once-hopeful past. 'It must be wonderful to be loved that much,' I said, unsure as to whether I meant the boat or this person whose nails I was painting.

Tom

They hadn't seen me standing behind the gap in my bedroom door watching them.

I'd woken for a pee. Saffron was sitting in our bunged-up living room, as yellow as a buttercup, painting Angela's nails like it was the most normal thing for them both to be doing at the crack of dawn, and I didn't want to spoil the moment by walking across the lounge to pee in a bathroom that had paper-thin walls. I was fascinated by an unexpected tenderness that Saffron had about her, as if I was peeping into the Saffron I knew before she reinvented herself. Here she was in the early hours of the morning before the rest of the world was awake, carefully painting the nails of my dying aunt, all bright and yellow and beautiful.

But by lunchtime she would be gone.

'Why do you think he's worried?' she asked.

I knew what she was getting at, what she was angling for. 'Because . . . he loves me,' I said, sighing heavily. 'I know he does, but it doesn't change anything. He still lied and denied me my mother, and I'll never, ever, trust him again.'

'And how do you think Daniel and Archie and Charlotte feel?' she continued.

I thought about my brothers. Archie with his mad hyperactivity and Daniel with his pretence at couldn't-care-less, and then there was the little honeysuckle weed, Charlotte, who hugged me even though I tried to cut her back. 'They'll be missing me, I guess.'

'And how do you think Melanie feels right now?'

I remained silent for a while at this question. *Who cared how Melanie felt?* I fidgeted under the scrutiny of her questions. 'Glad!' I said eventually.

But Angela was relentless. 'What makes you say that?'

This was getting more than uncomfortable now. I was pinned between the front door and a dying woman and I wanted to bolt. To get the hell out of there. To leap over the commode, weave between the packets of incontinence pads, to run away from the woman who used to have thick, wavy light-brown hair and a blue and white slash-neck stripy jumper and the sun on her face.

'I don't want to talk about her,' I replied, tight-lipped.

'Is she a bitch?' Angela asked. I raised an eyebrow at her but she raised one back. 'You think dying means you can't say fuck and bitch any more?' Angela laughed, her face lighting up. 'Actually, dying *is* a right fucking bitch,' she added, and this brought a hard-earned smile to my face.

A silence followed in which I placed the brochure back on the little table and drew up my knees until I was sitting cross-legged on the chair, pulling at the toes of my socks and folding them into little coloured knots. I sighed heavily, my inner self answering for me. 'She's not a bitch. But she's not my mother either. I . . . I . . . can't forgive her for that.'

'And I'm not Tom's mother. He couldn't forgive me for that either . . . in the beginning. Always bunking off school, hanging around the street or the park instead of coming home to me. He was a complete git when I first had him.'

So that's why he was always around like a wild animal. 'But it's different. You loved Tom because you're family,' I said.

'No, I loved him because I *wanted* to. Love is an honour not a right. Plus, he's much less of a git now.' She drained the dregs of her now-cold tea into her mouth. 'You're both on a path to destruction. *He's* building a fortress and *you're* wallowing in misplaced anger.'

'It's not misplaced. I'm angry at my dad, for very real reasons.' My whisper was struggling not to reach a much louder volume.

'You don't think you're angry with your mum? Because she was out there, somewhere, all along?' She said this sentence very softly, so it would land on me in the gentlest way possible, but regardless of how softly she spoke, each word sliced a little incision in my chest and slipped inside like a razor blade.

'I told you. I'm *excited* about my mum. I've got to go and get ready.' I scooted the chair away with the backs of my knees and disappeared into her bedroom before she could see that I was going to cry.

Tom

'Uh oh.' The two tiny words came out without warning. I'd been waiting for the moment Angela's questioning would cause a red-head explosion, a stomping of feet and bouncing of hair, and here it was. She'd picked up the biggest, most ugly piece of Saffron's inner mind and moved it into the light when she asked the fatal words, 'You don't think you're angry with your mum?'

Now, from the bedroom, came the sounds of stomping and banging from someone who'd just had their beliefs challenged. Angela was good at doing that.

But on the bright side, I could now leave my bedroom and take the pee I'd been hanging on to for an hour.

Saffron

'Daniel!'

My brother actually answered his phone! Wonders would never cease. 'I've found her!' I almost shouted down the phone, screwing up Angela's hurtful comment and shoving it into my internal bin. I physically had to stop myself from jumping up and down as I said the words, 'She wants to meet up . . . today, at eleven o'clock . . . in the centre of town, on a bench by the massive tree.' An underwhelming silence came out of my phone. 'Daniel?'

'That's good,' he answered sluggishly.

'Good? It's fantastic! I thought you'd change your mind about not caring if you knew she wants to meet us. What's wrong with you?'

'Duh . . . I was asleep?' he said.

'Well, don't be. Get dressed and meet me in town. We . . . are . . . meeting . . . our . . . mother!' I was so excited I had to savour every single word and how wonderful it sounded out in the open.

Daniel yawned. I could hear the rustle of his bed-covers move, the sound of him stretching lazily after sleep. He let

326

out a big, after-stretch sigh, farted loudly and spoke at the same time. 'I'm busy.'

My brother was basically an amoeba with gas . . . an amoeba who had just successfully wiped my very wide grin completely away in two words. 'You want me to tell *our mum* that you're *too busy* to meet her? I can't *believe* you.'

'Yeah. Do me a favour . . . ?' His voice was unfamiliarly deep through the phone, having made a smooth transition from kid to man in relatively few warbles and screeches.

'What?' I snapped back.

'Don't let your idea of who she is stop you from seeing who she *really* is.'

'Listen, I don't need your amateur psychology as well. Last chance, are you coming or not?'

'Not,' he grunted, then added 'Laters' before putting the phone down on me.

'Guess he's not interested,' I huffed, turning to Tom, who'd appeared and was now sitting on the end of the bed, next to me. His arm was touching my arm, his thigh touching my thigh. The message on my phone in front of us.

'I think he cares in a different kind of way,' he replied. 'You just don't know what that way is yet.'

'Great! I'm surrounded by amateur psychologists giving cryptic messages. I don't care what you all think.' Then at that moment an unwelcome shard of doubt penetrated my confidence. 'Do you think it's really her? What if it's another Mike who's tapped into my social media?' The profile picture on the message was a tiny kitten sitting in a tea cup and although I confirmed to 'friend' her, there wasn't much on her profile either.

'You'll find out this morning. I'll come with you,' Tom said. 'Till she arrives.'

'I've changed in ten years. What if she doesn't recognise me?'

Tom snapped his head round to look at me. 'What are you talking about? You haven't changed at all. You look exactly the same. All you need is a pair of stripy tights like you were wearing when I met you.'

'You sad case!' I laughed, bumping his shoulder with my own. 'What kind of freak would remember that level of detail?'

'I would,' he said and looked quickly away.

'What fortress are you building?' I asked, remembering Angela's words, my heart beating a little faster.

Tom

I couldn't help it. Her eyes were only inches from mine, pulling me into their ocean of greens that swirled with ripples of grey and ribbons of golden yellow. Her molten copper hair was burning me with its loveliness, the sprinkle of cinnamon across the milk of her skin, her breath warm and sweet against my face. I didn't want to tell her that the reason I'd built a fortress was because sooner or later the people I love leave me. That I'd tried so hard not to love her from the first moment I met her. That I'd known she would break my fragile heart if I let her in.

Kissing Saffron was like falling through the defences I'd built up around myself. Like landing in waterfalls and meadows, blue skies and sunshine, music and dancing, cake and donuts, with nothing to bring me back to sanity. Nothing to protect me from the absolute certainty that I'd left the drawbridge open. Saffron had made her way inside my fortress, and in a couple of hours she would, without a doubt, break my fragile heart.

Saffron

'You're beautiful,' he said, his hands cupping my face, his lips still shining from our kiss, his expression unbelievably sad.

'I'm ginger . . .' I began, but his thumbs reached across my face, pressing themselves lightly on my lips to prevent me saying any more.

'You are every shade of ginger and more. You are auburn and copper, yellow gold and rose gold, caramel, burnt umber, cinnamon and magnolia. You are every shade of warm.'

I tried to speak. 'You . . . make . . . me . . . sound . . . like . . . a . . . cake!' I forced my words past his thumbs until he slid both hands round the back of my head, pressing my face to his chest.

'You *are* a cake. You're a ginger fruitcake.' Then he let me go and stood up, the joke conflicting with the sad expression on his face. 'Come on,' he said. 'You've got a while yet. Let's go and find Maggie and tell her I rescued the firecracker from the twat.'

'Let's bring her another drink?' I said.

'For breakfast?'

I knew Maggie would want it for breakfast, lunch and supper

if she could. Time had no agenda for her. I'd sampled a tiny little bit of life on the streets. I knew how each hour dragged on, how the cold crept into your bones overnight, how the unforgiving ground stole your sleep, how the only warm hug Maggie would ever get now was in a bottle.

'Yeah . . . for breakfast,' I answered. 'She'll love it.'

We found her plonked right in the middle of a wooden seating area on the edge of the shopping precinct. Last night must have been cold as she'd finally swapped the straw hat for her winter woolly one. A grey knitted version of her straw hat, a red knitted flower now pinned to the brim, several badges pinned to the main part of it and a memorial poppy poking out of the top.

'The firecracker,' she said brightly when we reached her. 'You didn't get abducted then?'

'Yup, the firecracker,' Tom said. 'She's safe, Maggie.'

'Thank you for caring!' I said, handing Maggie a large bottle of breakfast cider, noticing her grey pallor beneath the bright make-up she'd applied, and how a sheen appeared on her skin when she coughed violently. Then we sat in a row. Me and Tom with our Coke and Maggie with her cider. Two teenagers and a homeless lady lifting our drinks to our lips simultaneously, watching the world go by.

Maggie coughed again, the harsh sound of it in her chest. 'The best cough medicine ever,' she said, saluting me with her bottle. She had obviously forgiven me for raising the subject of her family.

'I'm going to meet my mum, Maggie,' I announced. 'I haven't seen her for ten years.'

'I'm pleased for you, lovey,' she said.

'You don't look pleased,' I replied, feeling slightly cheated.

'Some things are better left alone,' she said, her words drowning in another gulp of cider.

Saffron

Tom's breathable mesh uppers pointed the same way as my own size-three boots, as he sat himself next to me on the bench in Jubilee Gardens. He was wearing the same knitted green jumper he'd worn when he took me for hot chocolate at the beginning of the week and even though it was cold, he still wore his shorts and work boots, his curly hair loose and catching in the breeze.

It was a cold day, and the earlier clouds that had rolled themselves into balls were unfurling – billowing across a sky that had turned blue. A breeze blew in and out of my hair, lifting it in curly chunks as I sat on the bench nervously looking left and right over and over again for the first glimpse of my mother. I hoped I looked good for her. I'd chosen carefully what to wear from the clothes in my retrieved hold-all. Dark-red skater skirt over thick black tights and my chunky black boots with the silver buckles, a thick cream jumper and a dark-red and grey woollen scarf wrapped round my neck, and my grey beanie.

I pressed my knees and ankles together and fiddled with my fingers, which poked out from a pair of grey fingerless gloves, wishing I knew which direction she might be coming from.

A swarm of little stinging things were filling up my ribcage, stirring up the past with their wings. 'When I go, I'll be at my boat if you ever need me,' Tom said eventually.

'If I *ever* need you? That sounds a bit final,' I said, still fiddling with my gloves, my eyes scanning the whole of Jubilee Gardens every few seconds.

'Everyone loves you, you know. We're all here for you.'

'Thank you,' I mumbled, nibbling at the knuckles of my fingerless gloves.

'Remember, sometimes things don't turn out how you think they will,' he continued.

'YES! Thank you, Tom . . . You're beginning to piss on my chips now!'

Tom held the palms of his hands up in mock surrender. 'Just saying.'

'Would you mind . . . sort of . . . disappearing? I'll text you later – tell you everything. It's just . . . you're acting nervous and you're making me nervous and I want this to be perfect.'

'I'll wait over there then,' he said, pointing to another bench about a hundred metres away, 'then I'll go . . . promise.'

I checked my phone again. Another minute had gone by since the last time I checked it. 10.56. These minutes were the slowest in history. I checked the message again.

My darling Saffron, I would love to meet you.
There is such a lot to explain about the last ten years.
I love you. Mum. PS Meet me today in Jubilee Gardens
at 11 on the bench by the massive oak tree xxx

It would be fine. No internet pervert knew how long it had been since I'd seen her. 10.57.

The park was busy. I could see Tom sitting on the other bench, looking back at me. People were playing, walking or running across the park, forming a cat's cradle of human jet streams. The day was moving at a normal pace for all these people but I was stuck in slow motion. 10.58. I continued to nibble at the threads on the knuckle of my gloves, staring hopefully along paths, between trees, across grass, all the way to the street at the opposite end, checking every car that parked, and back to Tom, who waved – not at me, but near me . . . at someone else.

An ugly ribbon of doubt twisted itself around my insides. The bench creaked, making me turn to see who had sat down next to me. Two pink shoes faced the same way as my chunky black boots. I could feel hot tears start instantly, building up and sliding down my face until they mingled with the wool of my fingerless gloves. Next to me, horribly, touchably, close, was *her* – Melanie! 'What are you doing here?' I demanded, my heart exploding in all directions around my body – painful splinters catching in my throat.

'It was the only way,' she said.

'What was the only way?' I asked, the ugly ribbons twisting hard, pulling too tight.

'This,' she said, simply. 'Finding you. I saw your hold-all under your bed on Tuesday morning. I knew you were going and I knew you wouldn't listen to me if I asked you to stay. I hoped you would go to your gran's, that I could persuade your dad to meet you there and tell you everything. But then you didn't go to your gran's and we didn't know where you were. I felt responsible.'

'Was he involved with this plan to "find me"?' I asked, pointing to Tom's now-empty bench a hundred metres away.

'Him and Daniel, yes. Like I said, it was the only way.'

'She's still coming though, right? My mum is still coming . . .'

'. . . under the massive tree at eleven o'clock . . . ?' She spoke too softly considering how much it wounded me. I couldn't speak. I was too preoccupied with the pain of it ripping holes inside me. I sniffed repeatedly, running a fingerless-gloved hand under my nose. *She* opened her Prada handbag with her long shiny nails and pulled out a small packet, offering me a tissue printed with little birds. I didn't take it. 'She's not coming, Saffy . . . She will probably never be coming. The message was from me.'

Tom had listened to me reading the message over and over, yet he'd known all along it was a trap. My friend . . . my only real friend had done the dirty on me. He'd been a collaborator, a conspirator . . . a traitor, joining ranks with all the other rotten traitors. He'd kissed me this morning knowing he was letting me down more than anyone had ever let me down before.

I turned on my phone and punched out a text.

Me: You are out of my life!

336

Tom

And there it was. Saffron's text telling me in no uncertain terms that she no longer wanted me in her life. Her smiling face contained within a circle next to her words, the kiss we shared this morning, still lingering on my mouth, the red mugs we drank from last night still stained with the traces of chocolatey lips, my chest still warm where I let her in, my heart in pieces within it.

Cool light cast down from the October sun onto the water and a leaf floated lazily through patches of shade. The recently finished gloss of the paintwork on my boat dipped into the river, spreading ribbons of reflected red along every passing watery ripple. There was such a lot to do, a bed to build, a kitchen to make, shelves to put together. Angela was right, I'd deliberately started from the outside in – delaying the moment it would be finished. Delaying the moment Angela would insist that it was time to let me go. And now she had made that phone call to the care home and there was no changing her mind.

Daniel was a pretty awesome brother in my book. He'd confessed about something that would apparently go down like a turd in a fruit bowl once it got out, yet he'd done it to help his sister. Unfortunately for me I played a big part in his plan to bring his family together.

I knew from Melanie's profile picture what she'd look like. She wasn't a step-witch, hunched and old, wearing a black cape and holding a poisoned apple, but a stylish lady who looked nice . . . pretty and smiley with blonde hair cut in a straight bob. She looked a bit how Angela should look if fate hadn't dealt her a cruel blow.

Saffron was lucky, if only she knew it. Apart from her mother, every other person on the planet wanted her in their lives.

Saffron

'Don't run,' Melanie said, holding her shiny nailed hands out to halt me. 'Not until you hear me out.'

More fat tears ran out of my eyes. I resorted to using the other gloved hand to wipe my nose, eventually, unwillingly, allowing the bird-patterned tissue to be tucked into my fingers. The shiny-nailed hands weren't the reason I didn't run. The reason I didn't run was because I couldn't. My disappointment was pulling everything I had out of me. I was nothing, except an empty space where all my hopes had been.

'Daniel told me everything last night,' she said.

'Little shit,' I said, wiping the tissue round my nose and across my top lip.

'He was worried about you. After he saw you on Thursday evening he couldn't keep it to himself.'

'*Traitorous* little shit, then. Perhaps you'd like to see something I have on my phone that will show you exactly what a little shit he can be?' I pushed the damp tissue up my sleeve and started to swipe angrily across my screen through my photos.

'I know about the grass burning thing, Saffy – we'll deal

with that separately. Daniel did a very selfless thing. He told me everything, knowing he'd get into serious trouble when you exposed him. He obviously feared for your safety more than he feared for himself.'

I wanted to throw her words back at her. To tell her Daniel was talking rubbish about my safety, that all week I'd known exactly what I was doing. I was seventeen! But the thought of my hold-all hidden in Mike's wardrobe as he plied me with alcohol and told me no one cared about me like he did, told me I was very wrong about that. I studied the ground beneath my feet, how the path dipped and bumped its way towards the grass edge of the green. Blue running shoes of a swishy-haired jogger went past. Heel, sole, toe. Heel, sole, toe. I allowed my mind to briefly rest in the silent space between us as my gaze followed them along the winding path, round to the left, round to the right. Heel, sole, toe. Out of sight. 'So, why you? Why didn't he tell my dad . . . my own parent?' I said, eventually.

'Because I just happened to be the first one Daniel came to and I made the decision not to tell your dad just yet. He can't seem to bring himself to tell you the detail so . . . I'm going to share it for him.'

I stole a moment to look her directly in the eyes – clear aquamarine, with an inner sunburst of gold, which sprayed itself like a halo round the black of her pupils. Carefully applied eyeliner and mascara accentuated them, perfect brows drew an arch above each one. Her hair hung in shiny perfection, while her jumper highlighted the hint of pink on her cheeks. Every time I looked at her I only ever saw the naked person who stole my mother's place in the bed and now here she was, about to tell me why she'd been in my family, clothed or otherwise, instead of the wild, auburn-haired butterfly who should have been there. I was very much all ears. My heart even gave its very own drum roll.

'I was not involved in your mum leaving. We did know each other, your dad and I, but only because we used to work in the same place together. That was all. You have my absolute word on that, Saffy. Your father loved your mum *very* much. She was everything to him. His *family* was everything to him. He was devastated when she left.'

I forced out a sharp and bitter snort. 'The wife he loved who *conveniently* disappeared. Puff!' I exploded my angry hands in her face as if she herself had turned my mother to dust.

'The day she disappeared . . . it turns out she'd already packed some of her clothes and taken them out of the house. She knew what she was doing. She'd taken some money and everything. She was always wandering off, seeking excitement, exploring, walking, looking for nature . . . leaving you kids at home alone. Only, one time she never came back . . . she wanted more.' She took a big breath. 'Your mum *planned* it.'

My jaw was stiff, my lips inflexible as I swallowed a ball of saliva. Did she think I was this gullible? 'My mother might have planned it, but she would not have left us for good. She would have found a house and come to get us . . . but you . . . *you* moved us away.'

'Saffy, your mother went to Australia . . . a one-way ticket. Very early on.'

The air sucked itself out of my lungs and came back to rush through my ears. The carefully made-up eyes at least had the decency to look bad about the lie she'd just told. 'I don't believe you,' I snarled. 'Dads do that kind of stunt. Not mums. Mums don't leave their children. They don't go to the other side of the world.'

'Sometimes they do.' She sighed quietly. 'Your mum was . . . impulsive. She always wanted excitement or the next adrenalin rush or thrill or whatever. She'd hire camper vans, weekends in tree houses or log cabins, boat trips or really expensive holidays abroad. She spent thousands of pounds. They argued about it . . . all the time. They were getting into debt, while she was always looking for something more . . .'

She was a butterfly looking for the next flower.

'She made one phone call to him, to tell him she couldn't be trapped any more and told him not to come looking for her because she was going travelling. She said she was a free spirit.'

'A butterfly jar . . .' I whispered. Her marriage, her house, her *children*, we were a jar she was trapped in.

We both simultaneously sank back onto the bench. She, trying to find words and me, trying to digest them.

'So the cards? In the briefcase?'

'He couldn't bring himself to tell you that she'd gone searching for more than she already had. He hoped and prayed she would change her mind. He told you she was ill, believing that one day she would come to her senses and return. But she didn't. When she eventually contacted him it was to tell him she'd joined some travelling commune in Australia and wanted a divorce. She said she knew she was flimsy as a wife and mother, but couldn't change . . . apparently "the wind knows her name".'

'The wind knows her name,' I echoed. 'But it can't be true. If she'd put us in debt how come we bought a bigger house?'

She held her palms out as if what she was about to say was simple. 'I sold my own house! We paid off the debts and started again. I loved him. I loved you all. I still love you all.'

A jagged silence followed, along with another bird-patterned tissue that made its way out of her bag again and was passed to me. 'He told you she had died because he wanted – needed – a family life, and he couldn't bring himself to tell his three beautiful children that their mother didn't want that kind of life any more. Especially you, Saffy . . . as the oldest . . . the one who remembers her. He loves you so very much but he still can't bring himself to look you in the eyes and tell you the truth, because the truth –'

'Is that she didn't love us enough to stay,' I interrupted, my voice barely audible.

The memory of my mother's hand cupping mine over the four shiny conkers, and her red lips telling me there would always be treasures to find if I looked hard enough played in my mind again. She had gone searching for treasures. Didn't she know that all along the treasure was right under her nose? That Dad and Daniel and Archie and me, we were her treasures?

Tom

Melanie: I've told her everything x

Me: How is she?

Melanie: She hasn't come home. She said she had stuff
to do. Please let me know if you hear anything xx

The message from Melanie came in hours ago but Saffron
hadn't contacted me, or answered my texts. I'd known the
minute I became involved last night that I'd be the last person
she'd want to see now. I'd packed her bag with all her things –
stripy socks complete with toes, the buttercup-yellow jumper
and, probably the one thing that knew her innermost thoughts,
an ancient teddy bear with dangling limbs, floppy head, missing
ears and one eye. The bedding and the towels were already
washed, her scent replaced by cotton-fresh detergent. She
didn't want me, and I had to let her go.

Saffron

Maggie snored gently while I sat, leaning against the cold wall of the bridge. William and Chuggy were nowhere to be seen and Ronnie's tent had been taken down, the grass flat and yellow where it had once been. The two veterans across the river now had another person with them, the three of them lit up by the orange glow of their fire.

I'd gathered all the cardboard left behind, and was sitting, exhausted, on a pile of it until all the light from the day eventually slipped into the night, the river now dark but flecked with silver from a full moon.

I'd walked for hours. Every road, alleyway, park and shopping centre in the city had been the backdrop for the stuff going on in my head. Everything was a turmoil of words and images, memories and new truths.

Melanie had called out as I left the bench: 'I love you, Saffy, like you're my own.' Those words now flung themselves around inside my skull on top of everything else in it. The photos of me on her Facebook account, my miraculously tidy bedroom, the homemade cake in my school bag, my favourite ice cream in the freezer. And the money poking out of her bag on Tuesday because she'd seen my hold-all and knew I was leaving.

Maggie stirred and coughed, then barely opening her eyes she reached for the bottle by her side. She drank and coughed intermittently for several minutes before the alcohol hit home and the lights came on, her once forget-me-not blue eyes, bloodshot and dull, focussed on me. Putting down the bottle, she reached over and picked up a pizza box, lifting the lid. 'Found it in a bin. Want some?'

'No thanks.'

'Did you see your mum?' The stuff in my head grew loud and more jumbled. *'Like you're my own . . .'*

'No,' I answered.

'Better left alone, hey?' she said, tearing a large bite out of one of the slices. I chose not to answer, but she'd already dropped the topic, picking a piece of pepperoni off the concrete and popping it into her mouth. 'Sometimes, Firecracker, God gives us pizza.' She held the box out to me. 'It's good, hardly touched.'

I held the palm of my hand up, declining her offer again. 'Do you even believe in God, Maggie?' I was wondering how anyone could believe in a God that would allow them to live out their lives like this, fishing out of bins, stinking of wee, running for ever from a tragedy too awful for her to live with.

'Of course!' she answered without hesitation. 'God is in my trolley.' Then she placed her half-eaten slice back in the box and hauled herself up again to root through the many bags wedged inside it.

I waited to see what on earth she was going to produce.

'Where are you?' Maggie muttered into the piles of rubbish heaped inside the trolley. 'He's here somewhere,' she called over her shoulder. Then, after ages, she suddenly yelled as if she had just seen a long-lost friend, 'Here is God.' Maggie smiled widely with her rotten teeth on display and pulled the bag out containing the bright red pashmina.

I was underwhelmed. 'It's just a big scarf, Maggie,' I said.

'It's not *just* any old scarf,' she replied. 'This one is extra special. I got it on a very cold day. So cold it could have frozen the tits off a witch.' She shivered, casting her mind back to some distant memory. 'I can still remember him all these years later. He was tall and flamboyant, with red boots that matched his scarf. He was walking past me, the same as everyone else, only he stopped and *actually* looked at me . . .'

Maggie closed her eyes, cradling her cheek in the cherry-red softness of her scarf, and I could see her grey chin hairs catching on the fine threads. 'Cashmere,' she said, her voice gentle as if the cashmere itself had made it soft. 'It was the worst winter we'd had for years. Heavy snow all over Christmas and the early part of the year. I'd paired up with another girl – Sally, she was called – we'd gone to sleep in the doorway of a department store but when I woke up in the morning she was dead! Right next to me. Stiff as an ice queen. I thought I might be going the same way, but later that same day, this man stopped, took his scarf off and gave it to me, right there in the street. It's so big I could wrap it round me twice. I reckon it saved my life. Now *that*, Firecracker, is God! God is a selfless act.'

Maggie carefully folded the scarf back up and gently placed it in the bag, slotting it back into the gap in her trolley from where it came. And as she finished the pizza and drank herself happy, and the moon slowly moved across the sky, I closed my eyes and turned back the clock. To my purple dressing gown and bunny rabbit slippers. To how I used to kiss Archie and Daniel goodnight, tiptoeing into their rooms. To how I'd stroked Archie's rosy apple cheeks and patted Daniel's soft red hair. To how I told them I loved them, as I did every night. To being warm and sleepy against Dad's chest. A teddy with floppy limbs and a droopy head in my arms. A tummy full of warm chocolatey milk. To how Dad kissed the top of my head as he did every night and told me he loved me. *'He couldn't bring himself to tell three little children that their mother was never coming back. That their mother didn't love them enough.'*

The engine of a motorbike on the road above my head startled me awake. The sky had changed from black to slate and a duck bobbed in the river, making a plopping sound in the water. Maggie had gone, leaving the empty bottle, the half-eaten pizza and a trail of dark urine where she'd been sitting. The dark stain on the concrete was heartbreakingly sad, marking a place where a strange old lady lived out her time in a polka-dot dress and a straw hat. It didn't take a rocket scientist to work out she was dying. Long, lonely years running from her nineteen-year-old self and finally Alexandra Margaret Barrington was near the finishing line.

On the other side of me was my hold-all. It had magically appeared in the night. On top of the hold-all, in a bag, neatly folded, was the red cashmere pashmina. I sat, perfectly still, studying these two items that spoke silent volumes until suddenly the jumble in my head found an order. The kaleidoscope made a final turn, having spent a long week showing me the shapes of people and lives, of misfortunes and struggles and generosity and evil and good. Its pieces now fell into a pattern that showed me how incredibly beautiful my life really was. Even Charlotte, the little honeysuckle weed who hugged me tight though I never hugged her back, found a place amongst all the shiny pieces. And somewhere deep inside me I realised that the cuckoo hadn't pushed me out of the nest, I had let myself fall.

As I placed the soft cashmere into my hold-all and then heaved it onto my shoulder, I knew that Maggie was so right. God was a selfless act.

Sunday:
Colours and Truths

Saffron

The ducks had long gone, quacking off for pieces of toast thrown from the windows of a boat further down. A boat where they didn't have to stare at a boy with chocolate-button eyes and a girl with mad ginger hair who were kissing . . . for a very long time.

The sky was now turning topaz blue from a climbing sun. The overnight mist that had lain like a veil on the river and the grassland around us was lifting as the day ahead began. 'I've already named this thing,' Tom said, referring to my earlier question, his arms still circled around me. 'Only, I've still got to perform the name-changing ceremony I told you about. We could do it now if you like.'

'OK,' I said, jumping up, ready to begin. 'What do we do?'

'Well, according to tradition . . . I need a virgin to urinate on the bow while asking Neptune's blessing to rename it.'

I screeched so loudly an exodus of birds flew out of a nearby tree. 'Are you serious?'

Dimples appeared on both sides. 'Yes, but I suppose we could go for the modern option and pour champagne on the bow and offer that to Neptune instead. Bit more expensive but much easier. Plus I've already got some.'

After we'd poured the champagne into the waters of the home port, poured some of it onto the bow, and offered a bit to Neptune, and Tom had said all the stuff about blessing his boat while I tried not to giggle, we drank the rest for breakfast.

'Little Annie,' I said, studying the beautifully painted sign in front of us, the yellow letters edged in red and decorated with colourful gypsy roses.

'Little Annie . . .' he repeated. 'A total wreck I fell in love with years ago but still needs a lot of work.'

'Thanks,' I said sarcastically, as he held my mad hair in his hands and looked into my eyes. Then he added, 'This particular wreck just needs reminding how beautiful and vibrant it is. And how maybe . . . it has room for two . . .'

We drained the dregs of our champagne, and walked hand in hand, slightly light headed, along the towpath, Tom pushing his bike with my hold-all once more over his shoulder. 'Thank you,' I said, my fingers tightening around his.

'What for?' he answered.

'For mending my family.'

His fingers tightened round mine in return. 'I'm coming with you. I need to make sure you and this ridiculously heavy bag make it back to them.'

So that's what we did. We went home together, to my family. My wonderful family with my brothers and my sister, my gran, and Melanie my almost-mother, and my father who loves us so much that once upon a time he hid the evidence of his love in the attic in an old briefcase whose fat buckled straps contained a truth.

Acknowledgements

A huge thank you to Liam for offering me his precious change at the ticket pay point of a car park in Cambridge when I didn't have enough to pay for my parking and who agreed to sit in a cafe and talk to me about his experience of life on the streets.

To the amazing Veterans for the Homeless UK, thank you so much for allowing me to join you in your sleep rough campaign in Chelmsford, Essex, to experience a tiny peek of what it feels like to sleep in the doorway of a high street on a cold night. Veterans for the Homeless UK, www.veteransforthehomelessuk. com, work tirelessly to highlight the plight of the many homeless on the streets of the UK, including the 7,000+ ex-service men and women, many of whom have PTSD and are now living rough. Your work is essential.

Thank you to the very helpful staff at Wintercomfort for the Homeless, Cambridge for agreeing to meet with me to impart your knowledge regarding support and available options for people living on the streets.

To everyone at Hot Key books for making this happen, and particular thanks to Emma, Jenny and Tina and for your support and enthusiasm.

ny thanks to Broo Doherty, my lovely agent, for your
derful, never-ending advice and support and for always
ing near the phone, a coffee or a glass of wine when I need
you.

To my amazing sister Pam for reading the draft of this book,
for having faith in the story and for believing in me. Your
ongoing support for my writing is invaluable. Thank you.

To Geraldine for always being on the end of the phone when
I need to unravel the thoughts and ideas going on in my head
so that I can write the next bit.

Endless gratitude to my wonderful husband, David, who
never minds that my idea of going to work involves a commute
to the sofa with coffee, a laptop, two dogs and a cat.

Thank you to Christina and Eric, my brilliant grown up
step-children, without whom I wouldn't know what it is to
be a step-mum.

Thank you to my friend Diarmuid Wilcox for showing me
your canal boat home all those years ago and planting in the
depths of my heart a secret desire to live on one.

To all my family and friends who are always so enthusiastic
about my books. You all make me feel so loved.

Phyllida Shrimpton

Phyllida Shrimpton is a full-time mother of a teenage daughter and currently lives in Essex with her husband, their rescued Newfoundland and small, badly behaved Jack Russell.

She achieved a postgraduate degree in Human Resource Management, but soon jumped ship to work with teenagers, including students with Asperger's syndrome, on an Essex-based agricultural college farm before eventually moving to live temporarily in the Netherlands. She is also an artist.

HOT
KEY
BOOKS

Thank you for choosing a Hot Key book.

If you want to know more about our authors
and what we publish, you can find us online.

You can start at our website

www.hotkeybooks.com

And you can also find us on:

We hope to see you soon!